FUTURE PERFECT
A Resurrection

My thanks to Susan, Katerina, Howard, Paul, Vivienne,
Nigel and Lady Lisa for their help and inspiration.
M.G.E.

Copyright © Martin G. Elster, 2018
Published by Elster Publications, London, 2018
ISBN: 978-0-9935300-2-9

Any resemblance to actual persons, living or dead,
is purely coincidental.

Typeset in Minion by Bopcap Book Production, Manchester.

FUTURE PERFECT
A Resurrection

by
Martin G. Elster

Timeframe: 2000

Our distant future destiny rules over us,
even when we as yet have no eye open for it.
Nietzsche

O God! Can I not save
One from the pitiless wave?
Is all that we see or seem
But a dream within a dream?
Edgar Allan Poe

The hatches are let down
And the night meets the day
The spirit comes to its own
The beast to its play.
W H Auden

I

Wednesday 21ˢᵗ June 2000, early in the evening. The plush lounge of a central London hotel.

IT SEEMED TO RALPH that she appeared from nowhere, like an exotic phantasm, even though he'd been expecting her for some time.

"Hello," she said softly. "I'm Abigail."

He turned in the thick armchair, tossed his newspaper onto the side-table, and quickly rose to his feet.

"Hello. I'm Ralph. Lovely to meet you!"

She smiled warmly and shook his hand, standing there before him like a rhapsody in gold: dark brown hair with chestnut highlights, flowing down in long waves from a central parting, a sultry honey-brown complexion, a short pale orange dress that revealed nearly all of her sun-tanned legs, and tasselled high-heeled rust-coloured sandals. She wore gold ear-rings and a small gold stud in her right nostril. Her face was exquisitely shaped and expertly made-up. Ralph looked into her eyes. They were an attractive tawny colour but seemed weary and oddly unfocused, like a pair of dead planets floating in space, bereft of gravity, and gave the impression of a deep and incurable melancholy. She clutched the strap of an expensive leather handbag, her upper arm squeezing against the heavy unsupported breasts flaunted by the plunging V-neck of her dress. He was glad that he was a few inches taller than her: it made him feel a little less intimidated. But nonetheless he felt short of breath.

"Please – sit down and make yourself comfortable," he said, motioning towards the armchair opposite his own. Her smile broadened and she sat down in the deep chair, for a moment revealing her bright yellow underwear before she crossed her bare legs. Ralph felt a surge of excitement. She was everything he could possibly hope for, exactly as his friend had said. And just the right age – roughly mid-thirties, he estimated. About twenty years younger than him.

"It's a warm evening. Can I get you a drink?" asked Ralph.

"Yes, thank you. A red wine would be lovely." She put down her handbag and adjusted the circle of amber beads around her neck.

Ralph waved towards the bar at one of the waiters, who nodded back. Then he reached over and awkwardly dragged a low circular cocktail table towards himself, before placing it in front of Abi's bronzed legs. She smiled appreciatively.

"Do you smoke, Abigail?" asked Ralph, sitting back and drawing a cigarette case from his jacket.

She shook her head. "No thank you, I don't. And just call me Abi. Everyone does."

"Okay, Abi it is. Seems a very short name for such an elegant lady. You look more like a Katerina or an Annabella, or something like that."

Her smile broadened, revealing immaculate white teeth under the full sensual lips. She was infinitely kissable, thought Ralph, as the waiter arrived. He ordered two glasses of wine and then put away his cigarette case. Not polite to make love to a lady with tobacco on your breath, if she doesn't smoke. And he was definitely going to make love to this one. He crossed his legs, rather too abruptly.

"Are you from London, Abi?"

"Yes, I've lived here most of my life, although my family comes from Surrey. We're very Home Counties."

Ralph nodded, uneasily. He knew it wasn't the done thing to enquire too much into the personal background of a working girl, who wouldn't tell you the truth anyway, so he changed the subject.

"I come to London a lot, on business, though I actually live in the East Midlands. It would be marvellous to explore London with you, Abi – you must know it so well – but I'm afraid I have to return home on the train tomorrow morning. Tonight is my last night here."

"Would you like to spend it with me?" asked Abi. Her calm directness was thrilling.

"Oh yes, I'd very much like to. Can you stay the whole night?"

"Of course. As per our telephone conversation this afternoon. I know that the beds in this hotel are big and comfortable." She smiled again. The waiter arrived with two glasses of red wine on a tray, and put them on the cocktail table.

Ralph laughed, to conceal his growing excitement. "Yes, yes, I imagine you've been in this place a few times!"

"Once or twice." She leaned forward to pick up one of the wine glasses. He felt a rush of desire as her breasts swayed under the orange dress.

"Do you do a lot of this work, Abi?" He swallowed hard, also picking up a wine glass.

"Only as much as I have to. With a select number of clients. With real gentlemen." This was the stock reply, but he liked it nonetheless. It might even be true. This woman was very sexy but far from being a common tart. She was classy and well-spoken, in an educated private-school way. She leaned over slightly to one side in the armchair as she slowly twirled her wine-glass. The sandal on the foot of her raised leg slipped down from her heel and dangled from her toes. The nails were impeccably painted. She was unperturbed, superbly relaxed, and looked straight at him. He couldn't wait any longer and downed most of his wine in a single gulp. Then he cleared his throat.

"Just to be discreet, you know… would you mind following me upstairs to my room, in about twenty minutes? I hope that doesn't offend you."

"No, not at all. I always follow the rules." She sipped at her wine.

"The rules?"

"Yes. Whatever the gentleman wants are the rules. That's the way I play the game." She smiled again, this time with a hint of mischief, no doubt aware of the effect she was having on him.

Ralph finished his wine and stood up, uncomfortably aware that he now had a semi-erection. He closed his jacket. The evening was getting even warmer.

"I'm in Room 424. Can you call on me at… exactly eight-thirty?"

Abi glanced at her watch, which glittered under the light of the big chandelier above them.

"Yes, fine, eight-thirty it is."

"I have a bottle of champagne waiting for us. Anything else you want, Abi, just say the word."

"You're very kind." Despite the charm of her smile, Ralph thought that her eyes still looked strangely unfocused, almost lifeless. It was something more than just the boredom of doing the same trick with the same men in the same place. But he was now so desperate to have her, he couldn't think about it any further. He had to get back and get ready. He winked at her and walked away. As he arrived at the lift door, out of sight, he swallowed a blue Viagra pill.

Abi straightened herself and uncrossed her legs. She sipped slowly at her wine and stared ahead into space, unaware of the people coming and going in the lounge, many of whom glanced at her, sometimes disapprovingly. She seemed oblivious to everything.

Ralph spat out the mouthwash and contemplated himself in the bathroom mirror. Not bad for fifty-five, he concluded. His thinning grey hair was brushed back to the nape of his neck to give a raffish man-of-the-world appearance, albeit in a somewhat old-fashioned style. His body was still presentable, despite the thickening midriff. He wished he'd spent a bit more time in the gym, but he'd always been too busy making money. The money that paid for his house, his wife, his children's education. And for women like Abi. He put on his bathrobe and checked that a condom was in the pocket, ready for action. He went back to the bedroom and hastily straightened the puffy pillows and the embroidered quilt. Yes, it was certainly a big comfortable bed, in a big comfortable hotel room. Definitely five-star quality. The clock above the dressing table clicked as it moved down to half-past eight. A second later there was a knock at the door. He hurried over to open it, and was thrilled to see Abi waiting there with a conspiratorial grin on her face.

"Perfect timing! And you look even more divine, if that's possible!" exclaimed Ralph.

She walked in, briefly looking around the brightly-lit room, and dropped her handbag on an armchair. She removed her beads and her watch and dropped them into the bag. Ralph gestured towards the coffee table, where a thick white envelope lay next to an ice bucket with a champagne bottle and two glasses.

"Do you want to check the envelope?" he asked.

"Of course not. I'll pick it up when I leave in the morning."

"Good. Some champagne?" he asked, a little anxiously.

"Maybe afterwards." She moved up close and looked him in the eye with that strange distant gaze. He could smell her sweet delicate perfume. The bow of her upper lip was a work of art and he was longing to kiss it. He took one of her hands in his and put the other around her back, drawing her close as if preparing to dance. She likewise held him, with her spare arm around his back. Her body was strong and firm, like an athlete's, and wonderfully warm, but the big breasts that now pressed against him were soft and yielding. Her arms were starting to thicken slightly, as appropriate for a mature woman. He kissed her cheek, inhaling more of her perfume, then moved to her enticing mouth, opening his own and planting a long kiss on her full lips. She immediately responded and their tongues met, mouths opening wider as they pressed their faces hard together. Her palpable generosity sent Ralph into a fever of desire, and his head began to swim. His pulse raced. He moved his hands down and reached under the short orange dress to feel the silky panties. A warm, full, sumptuously rounded bottom. He squeezed and in response she opened her legs a little. Ralph felt his cock surging into life, stiffening rapidly. The blue pill was working its usual miracle.

Abi drew back and looked into his eyes again. She placed her hands on his chest with the graceful solicitude of a courtesan from a bygone era. "What do you like?" she asked, smiling gently, speaking almost in a whisper.

Ralph breathed hard. "With you, love, I like absolutely *everything*!"

"I'm quite easy-going, but there's one thing I can't do," she said, still speaking quietly.

"Let me guess. No backdoor entry?"

She nodded.

"Why so? Are you afraid of catching something nasty? I have a good condom."

"No, it's simply too painful. An old war wound."

"No problem. I'm not too keen on that sort of thing anyway. Messy business."

She kissed him again. "You *are* a gentleman! Do you want me to

10

undress?"

"No, I want to strip you myself."

"There isn't much to strip!" she laughed, dropping her arms to her side. "But help yourself!"

She turned round and pointed to the zip at the back of her dress. Ralph took another deep breath and carefully tugged down the zip, all the way to her waist. He drew away the shoulder straps and the orange dress floated down to the carpet, leaving her naked apart from the flimsy yellow panties. But Ralph's attention was at once distracted by the tattoo between her shoulder-blades, precisely centred and elaborately drawn, just below the wispy ends of her dark hair. It was about three inches wide and looked like a black bird or demon of some sort.

"What an unusual tattoo," he remarked. "What's it supposed to be?"

"A winged dragon," replied Abi. "A friend gave it to me, quite recently. What do you think?"

"Very artistic, but a bit… well, sinister-looking, at least for my taste. You know, a bit gothic. I didn't reckon you as the tattoo type."

"It's the only one I've got," replied Abi. "There's nothing at the front. Look…"

She turned and showed him her big breasts, now hanging loose and heavy and free. Ralph moaned with joy and cupped them in his hands, fondling and lifting them to appreciate their smoothness and their weight. Then he noted that the thick nipple of her right breast was twisted out of shape, as if someone had deliberately mutilated it.

"What happened to this poor thing?" he asked, carefully touching the nipple.

She smiled, wryly. "A sex-game that went too far. Another war wound, I'm afraid. You could say it's an occupational hazard."

Ralph's curiosity was aroused. She was turning out to be a great deal more interesting than he'd expected. A most unusual woman, in fact.

"Sounds as if you've had some pretty wild customers. Any other wounds?"

"No. Aren't there enough for you already?"

Even more aroused, Ralph reached down and slipped off her yellow panties, which dropped to the carpet to join the dress. He stepped back a little to admire the carefully trimmed pubic hair, thick and dark, bordering the top of the shaved vulva. The scent of her crutch now rose to his nostrils and his penis quickly soared to a full erection and pushed its way out between the flaps of the bathrobe. With a knowing look Abi took it and slowly ran her hand up and down the stiff shaft as Ralph moved closer and delicately fingered her pussy. He was surprised by its wetness.

After a few moments he groaned. He couldn't bear the suspense any longer.

"Fuck! I've got to have you, Abi, right away! Lie back on the bed, love!"

Obediently she kicked off her sandals, moved to the bed and lay back on the shining quilt, spreading wide her sturdy legs and raising her knees with the proficiency of a trained gymnast going through her routine. She watched as Ralph pulled out his condom and hastily rolled it into place. Then he threw off his bathrobe and knelt down by the bed to adore Abi's fleshy vagina. She seemed proud to show it to him, easing the outer lips apart with both hands. To Ralph's astonishment, the aroused inner lips had opened out to form a perfect heart-shape. He exhaled heavily.

"Oh Jesus! That's the most beautiful thing I've ever seen!" He leaned forward and kissed the warm vagina full on the lips. The strong musky odour was intoxicating. Abi leaned her head back and let him eat her, which he did with eager licks and sucks, finally pushing his tongue all the way up inside her. Now moaning with pleasure, she grasped her knees and drew them all the way back, showing Ralph everything she had. The close-up view of her smooth-shaved dusky anus almost made him come. It was the supreme moment of intimacy, the full shameful confession of her magnificent physique. He got to his feet, put his knees against the edge of the bed, and at last sank his stiff sheathed cock into her pussy. It was like ploughing into a valley of oiled satin. The firmness of her passage made him tingle with delight, and told him that she'd never given birth to a child. His ardour growing, he leaned over her, supporting himself with his hands and then his elbows, and pushed in as far as he could, probing deeper inside her. She was utterly gorgeous, every last part of her…

Abi reached up and put her arms behind his back, drawing him down. "Oh God!" she moaned, looking up into his face with vacant eyes. "Do me! Do me hard!" Her muscles contracted and squeezed his cock. He continued to thrust, harder and faster, and felt his body slipping and sliding over hers as their sweat mingled. He started to pant. On a sudden impulse he put all the fingers of his right hand into her mouth… he just *had* to touch that mouth. She closed her eyes and sucked hard, as if the taste of her own sex on his fingers was the most delicious thing in the world. The sight of her blissful submission was so exhilarating that he abruptly felt himself coming and after a few more thrusts ejaculated, with a sharp grunt of surprise and disappointment. His heart pounded like crazy. It was a wonderful rush but all too quickly over… Somewhat embarrassed, he let out a long breath and leaned gently on top of her, still supporting himself with his elbows. He withdrew his fingers from her mouth as her feet rested on his back.

"I'm sorry, love!" he puffed. "You're just so bloody sexy, I couldn't stop myself. I haven't come that fast since I was eighteen!" He had in fact said this quite a number of times since he'd been eighteen.

She opened her eyes and shook her head, quickly recovering her composure.

"It's all right. I really don't mind. As long as you enjoyed it."

"I wanted *you* to enjoy it as well." He was still panting.

"Don't worry about me," said Abi. "If it helps, I'll let you into a little secret. I hardly ever come these days. If you'd kept going for an hour, it wouldn't have made any difference."

Ralph immediately felt better. He breathed deeply again.

"So what *does* make you come?"

She smiled weakly. "It's complicated. And a bit… hard to explain."

"I understand." Ralph withdrew his subdued penis from her body, rolled over onto his back to lie beside her, and relaxed. At least he had fucked her. That was the main thing. Relieved, he laid the back of his hand on his clammy brow.

"Do you still want me to stay the night?" asked Abi, closing her legs.

"Oh yes. For sure! Maybe we can try again… later on?"

"Of course. You can have me again, whenever you want. I'm here for you as long as I stay."

"Good girl!"

Feeling better, Ralph got to his feet and walked over to the coffee table. Discreetly he removed the used condom with a tissue. He took this into the bathroom for disposal and quickly washed his hands and his face. He returned to the bedroom and put his bathrobe back on. Abi was still lying on the bed, now on her side, her knees drawn up, facing away from him.

"Champagne?" he asked.

"No thanks. Not at the moment." Her voice sounded oddly distant.

"Fine. Let me know when."

Ralph expertly popped the cork and poured himself a full glass of bubbly. He swallowed it in one celebratory gulp, savouring its expensive fruitiness. Then he moved to the wardrobe to take the cigarette case from his jacket. He lit up a fag and inhaled the smoke deeply, walking up to the tall, lavishly curtained window to look out over Marble Arch for a while. Twilight had arrived, bringing with it a summer storm. On the horizon a heavy black cloud had appeared, blemishing the orange sunset as it rose like some alien monster above the distant rooftops of the city, silently discharging forks of lightning. Ralph looked down at the busy street in front of the hotel. The lights of the endless trail of passing cars always cheered him up. He still loved coming to London for business. And for pleasure. It was still a good life, and he was happy with it.

After a minute or two he turned to look at Abi and saw that she had curled herself up into a tight ball, her head and her feet tucked in, her arms wrapped closely around herself, every part of her body silent and motionless, as if she had withdrawn from this world and escaped to another, far away and beyond his reach.

II

Friday 23rd June, mid-afternoon. The office of hypnotherapist Dr Paula Masters, overlooking Regents Park, London.

As the intercom buzzer on her desk went off, Paula put out her cigarette. She pressed a button.

"Yes?"

"Abigail has just arrived, Doctor."

"Good. Ask her to wait for two minutes before sending her in."

"Will do."

"Thanks, Francine."

Paula closed the file marked "AMJ" and put it in a drawer. From here she pulled out a hand-mirror and examined her face carefully. She touched her short bobbed red hair into position, then took out a pair of large round spectacles and perched them carefully on her nose, constantly looking in the mirror to check her appearance. Unusually, she was wearing make-up. After a few moments she returned the mirror to the drawer and closed it. She got up and moved over to the large black leather couch that lay alongside one wall of her spacious office, which doubled as a consulting room, and puffed out a black leather pillow before placing it neatly at the head of the couch. Finally she carried a light aluminium chair to the front of her desk, to face her own seat. She paused to undo the top two buttons of her white blouse, exposing some of her pale if rather flat chest, and smoothed down her knee-length green-check pencil skirt. Then she returned to her seat behind the desk, swung her long slender legs underneath it, and placed both elbows on the desktop, pressing her palms together so that her fingertips touched her chin. On the middle finger of her left hand she wore a large black-stoned silver ring. She stared straight ahead. Now she was ready. She waited silently for the arrival of her patient.

A few seconds later there was a gentle knock at the door. "Come in," said Paula firmly.

A little diffidently, Abi stepped in, a friendly smile on her face. She wore a thin yellow shirt dress, held in by a brown leather belt to show off her trim figure. She carried a modest handbag, also made of brown leather, and was entirely without jewellery or make up, as per Paula's instructions. Her dark hair was tied up into a thick bun on top of her head.

"Good afternoon, Doctor Masters."

"Hello, Abi. So good to see you again. Please – take this chair."

Abi sat down and kept her legs tightly closed as she faced Paula across the table. Paula could see she was somewhat tense, as usual.

"You seem to have acquired a fine sun-tan," smiled Paula, nodding at the brown thighs.

"Yes, but I always get brown very quickly in the summer."

"Must be that Italian skin. I do envy you."

"White can be as beautiful as brown," replied Abi, hanging her handbag on the back of the chair.

"You think so? You're very kind. I can't imagine you as anything but brown. Does your tan reflect your health? How have you been, Abi, since we last met… what was it, over three weeks ago?" Paula reached for a pen and a notepad.

Abi sighed and put her hands on her lap. "Quite active, but I still get long periods of fatigue and some dizziness first thing in the morning."

"How's your appetite? Are you eating properly?"

"Slightly better. I'm just about maintaining my weight."

"Good. Are you taking the medication I gave you?"

"Yes, two tablets every day, without fail."

"Remind me – how long has it been since the car crash? Since you left hospital?"

"Last September. Nine months ago."

"Any recent checks?"

"Not since I last saw you."

"I think you'll find that your condition has stabilised. The aneurism from the head injury will always be there, but as you know it's quite small. It could stay in the same position for a long time, maybe several years. But do keep going back for check-ups."

"I hope one day they can operate on it. At the moment they say they can't – it's too risky."

Paula looked up over her round glasses.

"Still having the bad dreams?"

Abi nodded slowly. "Yes. Still very intense."

Paula began to write on the notepad. "Which ones lately?"

"Still the dream about the glass coffin. I'm lying trapped and paralysed and can see my own body lying there helpless. And the same bright lights shining down on me. Turning my body white. A strange shiny white. It feels like my body has become a hard shell, almost as if it's made of some sort of plastic. It's just so weird."

"It certainly is. Anything else?"

"Yes. Now there are lots of people wandering up to the coffin and staring at me. Some of them are licking their lips, some of them are laughing at my helplessness. Last night I dreamt there was a horrid old man in a smart suit, with narrow eyes and a thin beard and a big grin on his face, pulling out his penis and rubbing it over the glass, right by my head. Then the others started reaching for me but couldn't touch me because the glass was too strong. But I was worried they might break through and grab me. I'd be helpless, completely at their mercy."

"Does any of this arouse you? Turn you on?" Paula scribbled harder on her pad.

Abi paused and looked down at the floor. "Yes, it does. Even though I'm terrified, I still get excited when others look at me. When I woke up last night I was... quite wet."

Paula took a deep breath and shook her head. "There's no accounting for human sexuality, or human fantasy, especially when we start dreaming. But that's why it's so liberating, Abi. It's good to work through our fears and our emotions." She twirled her pen between her thumb and fingers. "Anything else you want to tell me?"

Abi looked at her. "Generally, I'm still feeling... empty and lost. I can remember all sorts of things, all kinds of memories, but they're like dreams, or odd fantasies. Like they're not really mine. I feel as if I don't know who I really am. I spend a lot of time just staring into space, as if I can't think for myself when I'm alone."

Paula frowned and nodded. "I'm afraid this is the post-traumatic stress we've talked about, Abi. And the damage to your brain resulting from the car crash. Thank goodness it wasn't any worse. It could have left you totally crippled."

"I know. I'm grateful to be alive. But I can't say I'm happy about my life. I just feel so… so lost." Suddenly she looked on the verge of tears.

Paula smiled encouragingly. "Let's see if we can help you find yourself. We definitely need another session, right away. Some foundation and reconstruction work. So you can tune into yourself a little better and feel stronger."

Abi nodded. "Of course. Whatever you say, Paula."

"Just make yourself comfortable, as usual, and lie down on the couch."

Abi stood up and kicked off her shoes. Paula watched intently over the rim of her glasses as her patient slowly removed her belt, then unbuttoned her yellow shirt dress and draped it over the back of the chair. She wore a plain white bra and knickers, routine underwear, which vividly highlighted her tanned skin. She walked over to the couch and gingerly sat on it as Paula picked up her own chair and brought it over.

"Make yourself comfortable, Abi. Relax."

As Abi lay back and straightened her body, resting her head on the black leather pillow, Paula sat on the chair beside the couch, facing Abi's head. She pulled her green skirt back a little so that Abi could see her knees and her thighs. She reached over and held her patient's hand. It was, as always, much warmer than her own.

"All right, Abi. Let's start with the basics. Close your eyes, relax, and – when you're ready – tell me your full name."

Abi took a deep breath and closed her eyes.

"My name is… Abigail Maria Janus."

Paula gently squeezed her hand.

"Good. How old are you?"

"Thirty-seven."

"Where were you born?"

"In Guildford, Surrey."

"Tell me about your parents."

"Dad was a lawyer. A successful lawyer."

"Was?"

"He died of a heart attack, when I was twenty."

"You still miss him?"

"Terribly. I adored him. I was always his Princess. I'll never get over losing him."

"And your mother?"

"Mum is…"

"Yes?"

"Paula, I'm a little hot. I need some fresh air. Can you open the window?"

"Of course." Paula walked over to the old sash window of the office and pulled down the upper section. There was a momentary hum of passing traffic, followed by the shrill caw-caw sounds of the exotic birds in the zoo across the road. She eased down the venetian blind, leaving the slats half-shut, to darken the room and subdue the atmosphere. Strips of sunlight played over Abi's recumbent body as a slight breeze caught the blind.

"You were saying about your mother…" went on Paula, returning to her chair.

"Mum is Italian… a very passionate woman."

"And?"

"She was originally a dancer."

"What kind of dancer?"

Abi sighed. "A striptease dancer. In Soho. Until she met dad."

"And dad rescued her from Soho?"

"Yes."

"And now?"

"Now she's an alcoholic, living on her own, not interested in me or anyone else."

"Any brothers or sisters?"

"An older sister. Annabel."

"What happened to her?"

"She drowned. When we were teenagers on holiday. She swam too far out to sea…" Abi's eyes closed harder and her brow furrowed. She looked as if she was about to cry again.

"All right," said Paula. "We'll put that memory aside for now. Tell me where you went to school. Your secondary school."

"St Margaret the Martyr."

"Where was it?"

"In Devon. Deep in the countryside. Near a big rambling wood."

"What kind of school was it?"

"A convent school. For Catholic girls. A boarding school. A very fine school…"

"And the Headmistress? Who was she?"

"Sister Helena Thomas. A strong Headmistress. Very strict."

"Indeed she was," smiled Paula. "A striking woman. Now no longer with us, alas."

"That's right. She died a couple of months ago. Of cancer."

"Yes. The school wrote to tell you."

Abi nodded, her eyes still shut.

"What did you feel when you received the letter?"

Abi sighed. "Mixed feelings. Sorrow… guilt… anger."

"Why so?"

"Because of what happened. At school."

"All right, Abi. This is obviously a big memory in your life. It's left a major psychic trauma that we need to look at if we're going to deal with your emotional problems."

Abi opened her eyes. "Haven't we gone through this memory before? Not so long ago?"

Paula took Abi's hand again. "Yes, we have, but I think we need to recreate what happened at school and explore it in more detail. Your feelings about Sister Helena are tangled up with your negative feelings about your mother, the primary female authority figure in your life, and they need to be brought out into the open so that you can understand them properly. That way we can reduce their effect on you."

Abi thought for a moment, then nodded. Paula let go her hand and moved the chair closer to her patient's head.

"All right, Abi. I'm going to put you under at this point. Are you ready?"

"Yes." Abi shut her eyes again.

"Good. Let's begin. I want you to take a deep breath and put your arms alongside your body."

Abi obeyed, and automatically stiffened her body, bringing her knees and her feet together, as if to bring herself to attention horizontally. Her arms pressed close to her side, and her hands touched her thighs. As she breathed in deeply her stomach sank and her ribs and her breasts rose, straining the white bra that held them in place. Paula leaned over and started gently rubbing Abi's brow with one of her long fingers, making a slow circular movement. Abi's head sank deeper into the black leather pillow.

"Now, Abi, I'm opening your Third Eye, as I've done many times before. Just relax and let the middle of your forehead open out, like a circular gateway… a gateway into the past."

As before, Abi found herself walking out of a dark cave, out into the sunlit day, somewhere by the sea.

"Move out of the cave and onto the cliff-side, Abi. Move right up to the ledge, overlooking the sea. Look down at the water below you. Deep transparent blue water, reflecting the sun. A beautiful, calm, sunny place."

"Yes," murmured Abi. "It's beautiful. So sunny…" As Paula continued to press down on her brow with the same circular movement, the scene opened up, wider and wider, like an expanding cinema screen.

"Look down at the water, Abi. Can you see? It's transparent and bottomless. It goes down forever, infinitely deep, going down, down, further down. An infinitely deep pool of sunny water…"

"Yes. It's beautiful. So deep… infinite."

"Now… when you're ready, Abi, dive into this deep cool water. Just like you're diving into a swimming pool. Falling, falling… falling down into the water."

Abi paused. Then she took a deep breath and gasped. She was now flinging herself off the ledge… in slow motion she floated down into the shimmering water, which parted soundlessly to allow her in, easily, painlessly, welcoming her into its cool, healing depths. As she continued to sink, she heard Paula's voice, as if from high above her in the sky.

"Now Abi, you're back at St Margaret's School. As a pupil, aged sixteen. The year is nineteen seventy-nine. In the month of March. Can you see the school clearly?"

Abi nodded.

"And you're going to one of your favourite places at the school. The Art Studio. Do you remember it?"

At once Abi found herself descending into the spacious Art Studio at the school, as if floating down through its roof. She recalled it in vivid detail: the large heavy old tables covered with big folders and vases with sheaves of paint-brushes sticking out of them, pencils and crayons sprawled everywhere, dried smears of paint over the furniture, dozens of garish paintings and drawings obliterating the walls, even hanging from pegs in the ceiling, odd experiments in pottery and sculpture piled up on top of the window-sills, the smell of turps, badly-mixed paint, and at the far wall, near the corner, the Stock Room, door ajar…

"You remember the Stock Room, don't you, Abi? Where all the paper and paint and so many other things were kept stored?"

Yes, she remembered. She walked up to the Stock Room and there, inside, was Mr Lawrence, the Art teacher, her handsome Andrew, apparently browsing through the paper stocks but in reality waiting for her to arrive. Waiting for Abi, his favourite pupil. Not a talented artist, but definitely a work of art, an object of beauty that he was always ready to appreciate.

"You remember Mr Lawrence, Abi? Your favourite teacher. What was his motto? Do you recall?"

Abi smiled. "Creation is Love," she intoned. "And Love is Creation."

"That's right. And you were the creation that he loved more than any other. You were his favourite girl, weren't you?" Paula withdrew her finger from Abi's brow and sat back in her chair.

On the couch, Abi sighed and nodded slowly. Now locked in her memory, like a dreamer unable to wake, she moved into the tiny narrow Stock Room, stacked high with shelves on both sides, and closed the door behind her. Without a word she and Andrew kissed and embraced, as they had many times before, and in a couple of moments her leg lifted up out of the grey skirt and her shoe rested on a shelf behind him as his hand slid up her brown thigh and eased into her crutch. Knowing what was coming, she wore neither petticoat nor tights so his hand pressed at once onto the hot cotton gusset of her knickers, and she grabbed his back and drew him closer to her with a schoolgirl desperation. He turned and pressed her against the shelves as her other leg lifted high and wide to let him come up against her body, which he held up with both hands under her buttocks. She raised her legs even higher. One of her shoes dropped to the floor. With one hand she hastily pulled aside the gusset of her knickers and at once his manly cock was inside her, like a thick burning rod that thrust all the way into her belly and gave her the only fulfilment that mattered…

Abi breathed heavily and moaned on the couch, her eyes firmly closed. Her body twisted to and fro and her hands eased over to the inside of her thighs. Her back arched a little.

"That's right," said Paula, smiling. "You remember the wonderful things he did to you. The pleasure that only a big strong man can give a passionate girl… you were so excited, weren't you? As his big hard cock pushed up inside you, deeper and deeper…"

Yes, deeper and deeper, over and over again. She held him close and hard, her mouth full of his tongue and her pussy full of his relentless pumping manhood. This was what she wanted, more than anything, this was what she lived for… giving herself to a big strong beautiful man… giving everything she had, everything she was… Oh God, he was so powerful, so desperate for her, so adoring, so hot, so hard… Oh God, yes… yes… I'm exploding, blowing apart… Oh fuck! Oh *fuck*!

Abi groaned on the black leather couch, turned slightly to one side and thrust her hand onto her crutch, squeezing herself hard as the orgasm arrived, buttocks twitching and legs pressed tight together. As she writhed, her knickers slid half-way down her buttocks. Paula looked on with bated breath and dry mouth, enthralled by the extremity of Abi's passion, its feral disregard for anything other than its own fulfilment.

After a few moments, Abi calmed down. She lay on her back again, her underwear in disarray. Paula cleared her throat and continued.

"What's your next memory, Abi? What happened afterwards?"

Abi sighed. "That last time... someone else came into the Art Studio, without our knowledge, because I must have left the main door open. And she heard what we were doing. After, when I left the Stock Room, I found my exercise book was missing... and later I discovered that Andrew's driving licence had been taken... as evidence. And that person went straight to Sister Helena and told her what she'd heard."

"She snitched on you."

"Yes. Straight away."

"Did you ever find out who it was?"

"No. I never knew."

"Carry on..."

"I was quickly summoned to Sister Helena's study... the same day, late in the afternoon. I immediately knew why. The missing items from the Art Studio had given me a warning."

"Were you frightened?"

"Yes. I was terrified. I had to rush to the toilet and empty myself before I could go to see Sister. Up to then I'd been one of her favourite pupils. Now I knew I was going to face her wrath. Many other girls who'd faced her had broken down under the pressure. She was such an overpowering person. So tall, with her long black dress and that big gold crucifix on her chest... "

"What happened in her study?"

"She was very calm and very quiet. She presented me with the evidence, and asked me to tell her the truth."

"And you confessed?"

"Yes. I confessed to everything. I had no choice. She was so firm, so persuasive and so sure of what we'd been doing. There seemed no point in denying it."

"And?" Paula leaned forward. "Tell me again, what happened next..."

Abi took a deep breath. "She told me that she was going to see the Chief Governor of the School that very evening and obtain his permission to sack Mr Lawrence without notice. He would have to pack his things and leave the premises the very next day. She would see to it that his teaching career was over. As for me, she offered me a choice of expulsion or corporal punishment. Although I'd sinned, grievously, she regarded me as the victim of the affair, as I was only sixteen and vulnerable to predatory men."

"And?" Paula adjusted her glasses.

"I chose to take the corporal punishment, there and then, in her office. She agreed that that was the right thing to do. Because I had to stay on at the school, to take my exams a few months later. And I didn't want my family to know what I'd been doing. They'd be so ashamed, and feel so let down."

"Carry on..."

"Then she called in Miss Davis, the Head of Science, who'd been waiting outside her study all this time, to witness the punishment. Sister Helena knew I'd choose the flogging. She took a thin sharp cane from a small cupboard by the window as Miss Davies walked in. I was so ashamed that I couldn't look at her, but I think she was embarrassed by the whole thing as well. I just stared at the old grandfather clock in the corner of the study as they talked quietly about what was going to happen. I was sweating with fear and shame… I was hot all over."

Paula adjusted her position on the chair. She gripped her white knees with both hands, while her notepad rested on her lap. "Now, Abi, tell me what you remember about the punishment. In detail…"

Abi moaned and turned over to one side, facing away from Paula, and put her hands on her knees. Her body bent as she drew them up. Her eyes were still firmly shut. The memory came back with hallucinatory vividness, as it always did… just like a recurring dream…

At Sister Helena's command, Abi shuffled off her shoes and then unzipped and dropped the grey skirt, before draping it over a nearby chair. She had no half-slip or tights, as it was now after lesson-time, and below the waist wore only her white socks and white knickers. To her relief, she was not required to remove anything more, and Sister Helena pointed to the large mahogany Headmistress's desk, gesturing to her to bend over it. As if in a trance, she did as she was told and Sister then instructed her to spread her legs, feet as far apart as possible. This pushed her belly and her chest down onto the polished desk and pushed her bottom further out. As both Sister Helena and Miss Davies moved closer to her, she was seized with an anxiety that they would smell the odour of her backside and her unshod socks. She heard Miss Davies cough and felt her face grow hot with shame. She listened as Sister Helena told her that she was now going to receive twelve strokes of the cane, as punishment for the sin of lust. She shut her eyes tight. Her heart pounded. She listened to the heavy ticking of the grandfather clock. After what seemed a long pause, she felt the tip of the cane gently tap her bottom before moving away again. There promptly followed a fast swishing sound and a sharp crack as the stick cut into her buttocks, like a line of burning acid suddenly thrown over her rump. She groaned. It was much, much more painful than she had imagined. She let out a long gasp…

Abi writhed on Paula's couch and grasped her buttocks with both hands, moaning with pain. The black leather squeaked under the pressure of her body. Paula folded her arms tightly.

Abi shut her eyes harder, and she uttered deep groans as the second and then the third cane-stroke lashed into her. The sound of her buttocks being struck echoed around the study. When the fourth crashed down on her, there was a sharp slashing pain, as if her flesh had been viciously cut with a knife. She let out a long "ohhh!" and shuddered. The pressure of the beating had made her raise her feet so that she was now up on her toes, tensed, bracing herself for more blows. She felt Sister Helena's hand firmly pushing down into the small of her back, to reposition her body. She let her chest and her belly sink down onto the desk and placed her feet flat on the floor again, although she couldn't stop her buttocks twitching. The caning resumed, and was every bit as painful as before. After the fifth and the sixth strokes, she began to tremble and exhale in short uncontrollable bursts. There was a pause, the silence punctuated only by her staccato gasps. Again she heard the ticking of the grandfather clock. Then the stick moved down and gently tapped her upper thighs, as Sister again took aim. A moment later there was another swish and the cane tore into the back of her legs, much more painful than before, and at once she cried out. The second bit into her thigh even harder and she let out a shrill "aahh!" before suddenly starting to sob. It was too much. She couldn't control herself any longer and let herself cry, quietly but intensely, her head grinding down on the desk as the tears oozed through her eyelids and spilled over her face. She felt her shoulders and her legs trembling. Her body had taken on a life of its own and she was like a helpless rider on a runaway horse…

Paula watched enthralled as her patient, deep in trance, repeatedly twitched and rolled and jack-knifed her body, grasping and slapping her upper thighs, sobbing and moaning. Then Abi yelled out and started to cry. Paula squirmed in her chair, now feeling herself becoming wet. She resisted the urge to reach under her tight skirt and touch herself. She continued to grasp her knees and cover her lap with her notepad, as if to conceal her arousal.

Abi felt her tears falling onto the mahogany desk as the cane reverted to her buttocks, coming down hard each time. But mentally she kept the count: nine, ten, eleven... then a pause. She was crying uncontrollably, but not too loudly. Finally, two more lashes ripped into her bottom, in quick succession, and it was over. Not twelve, but *thirteen* strokes! Why had Sister Helena cheated her and added an extra stroke? The cruel injustice of this error, this unwarranted excess, finally made her cry out loud, with rage and resentment as much as pain, and then she was puling like a thrashed infant, finally submitting to the brutal humiliation her Headmistress had dealt out to her. Her body was trembling and shaking all over. Through her sobbing, she heard Sister Helena take a deep breath and walk back to the cupboard, to which she calmly returned the cane. She heard Miss Davies noisily clear her throat. It was over...

It was over, and Abi was crying like a child, still twisting and rolling on Paula's black couch, her legs tight together, her body shaking, her hands having now dragged the knickers entirely off her twitching buttocks, which she continued to grasp with both hands. Paula ignored the hot tingling sensation in her crutch and decided it was time to bring the session to an end.

"All right, Abi. The punishment is over now. Relax. You're in Sister Helena's study... stand up... compose yourself... wipe your eyes – with that tissue that Miss Davies has given you – and put your skirt back on. That's right. Zip it up... and then put your shoes back on. You've paid the price of your sin. It's over now..."

At once Abi relaxed and stopped shaking. Within a few seconds her breathing had returned to normal. The couch was still and silent.

"You're now back in your dormitory. With your friends – Mitzi, Penny, Trudi and the others. Remember?"

Abi nodded. "Yes. I remember."

"So tell me what's happening," said Paula.

"I'm lying on my bed, face down," replied Abi. She rolled onto her belly and lay there. Her face pressed into the black leather pillow.

"How do you feel?"

"Dreadful. My bottom feels numb and swollen all over. Likewise the back of my legs."

"What happens now?"

"My best friend – Trudi – is rubbing oil over my bare bottom, over my thighs, to relieve the stinging pain. She feels sorry for me…"

Paula put her notepad on the floor and leaned forward. Gently she pulled Abi's knickers down as far as the knees. Then she started to rub and caress the buttocks. Abi moaned with relief. Paula closed her eyes.

"It's so nice…" went on Abi. "Such a relief… after what's just happened to me. But I can see that the other girls are standing back, shaking their heads, looking shocked and horrified. And one or two of them are laughing at me… laughing at the big red stripes over my bottom. Laughing because I'm no longer the Form Captain, just another silly girl who's been caught and punished… and one of them will now be taking over from me as Captain."

"How do you feel about that?" Paula continued to rub the fleshy tanned buttocks, hardly daring to breathe.

"Ashamed… humiliated… I've been demoted. Turned into a laughing-stock. A butt for jokes. I'll never be the same person again." Briefly she sobbed.

Paula leaned further forward. Her voice deepened as she spoke into the back of Abi's head. "Do you think, Abi, that maybe you weren't really the stuff that Form Captains are made of? That maybe you were deluded about your true self, your real character? That you were in fact a lesser person than you imagined?"

Reluctantly, Abi nodded. "Yes, I *was* deluded. I wasn't fit to be Form Captain. I understand that now." Her sobs turned into a sustained infantile grizzle, partly muffled by the leather pillow, as if she couldn't bear to acknowledge this downgraded estimate of her worth. Paula listened for a while, a sardonic smile on her face. Eventually she decided that the point had been satisfactorily made and she should now calm her patient down.

"It's all right, Abi. Just relax. Forget the pain and humiliation. Let it go. You're with your true best friend now. The one who cares about you most." She stopped rubbing and carefully pulled up the cotton knickers, returning them more or less to their proper position, and moved back to sit up in her chair once again. As instructed, Abi calmed down and was silent.

"Turn over onto your back and make yourself comfortable," said Paula.

Abi obeyed. She was now fully relaxed, as if nothing at all had happened. A small tuft of dark pubic hair peeped out above the elasticated waistline of her underwear.

"Now let's fast forward to the exams, in the summer of that year: nineteen seventy-nine. What happened?"

"I failed the exams. I should have passed, easily, but I couldn't concentrate, either before or during the exams."

"Why?"

"Because by the time I took them, I knew I was pregnant. By Andrew, of course. That ruined everything. I flunked the exams completely. "

"So…?"

"So I couldn't get into sixth-form college, as I'd planned. Or go to university afterwards."

"And?"

"And I went to live with Andrew, who eventually found another job, in a small private school to the south of London… and I had his baby."

"Why? Why did you go back to him? And why have his baby?"

Abi pondered for a while, then smiled a little.

"Because… Creation is Love, and Love is Creation."

"I see." Paula paused for a few moments before continuing. "Tell me about the baby. Your Love-child."

"It was a girl. Her name was Dolores. She was pale, like Andrew, with his red hair, and slender, but otherwise she looked very much like me. People said she was very beautiful, but sad. So we called her Dolores. Or Dolly, for short."

"Remind me what happened."

"Andrew was poorly paid and struggled to make ends meet. I couldn't get a proper job, so eventually I turned to what my mother had done. Exotic dancing. In big towns… then in London. In the end I couldn't resist the offers to have sex for money – lots of money – and ended up as a working girl."

"A prostitute."

"Yes. I became a prostitute." Abi's eyes closed tighter.

"And when Andrew found out?"

"He was furious. He felt betrayed, though I loved him just the same as before. He divorced me and gained custody of Dolly. He had sole access to our little girl…" A thin tear rolled out over her cheek.

"And then…?"

Abi sighed. "And then, some years later, Andrew couldn't cope anymore. He had other relationships with women but none of them lasted. Dolly was a difficult child. He couldn't find enough money to support the two of them. He became very depressed. His relatives started looking after her. Finally he took an overdose…"

"Do you forgive him for what he did? At school, and then later on?"

"Yes, I forgive him. He did everything out of love. Whatever went wrong was as much my fault as his."

"Even though you were only sixteen when he seduced you?"

"I seduced him as well. We both wanted each other, so badly… it was love at first sight. True love. When that happens between two people, right and wrong doesn't count for much."

"And Dolly?"

"She was taken into care…"

"How old was she?"

"Eleven."

"Did you ever see her again?"

Abi shook her head.

"Do you want to see her again?"

"Oh yes, yes – more than anything in the world. I only hope I live long enough…"

Abi began to sob. A larger tear rolled over her cheek, then another, which reached the edge of her mouth. An expression of despair crept over her features. Paula decided that her patient had had enough. She leaned forward and pressed her finger onto the centre of Abi's brow, again making a slow circular movement.

"Now, Abi, I'm closing your Third Eye. Just relax and let the middle of your forehead become a gateway… a gateway back to the present time… the here and now."

Abi felt herself being drawn into the dark cave of her inner self, as the images of the school and her past life faded into the distance. Suddenly there was a bright light, shining through a gap in the roof of the cave, and she opened her eyes and found herself looking up at Paula. She blinked rapidly, re-orientating herself to the bars of sunshine from the window and the sound of the birds from the zoo.

"How do you feel, Abi?"

"Drained. Exhausted."

"It's been a tiring session. But you've acted out and reaffirmed a number of important things from your past. Especially about Sister Helena. What do you feel about her now? Do you still feel any anger towards her?"

"No, I don't. She did everything she could to let me survive at the school. She had to cane me to avoid expelling me. It was my fault that everything went wrong. And Andrew's fault. But he paid the price, many years ago. And now Sister Helena is dead as well. There's no point in dwelling any further on what happened."

"Good. That's very positive. Anything else? About your mother, perhaps?"

Abi reflected for a few moments. "My mother is a hopeless alcoholic. I know that she's wanted nothing to do with me, ever since she found out about my... profession. God, what a hypocrite! She denounces me for being the same as her! But I'd like to see her again... before she dies as well."

"Yes, I think you should see her. But give it a few weeks before you do. After we've had another session here."

"All right."

Abi was still a little dazed. Paula took her hand and helped her to sit up on the couch. Then she walked over to a jug of water on a side table and poured a glass for her patient. Abi took the water and gratefully began to drink. She realised that she'd been sweating heavily throughout the session. And her eyes were damp.

"I think I've been crying," she said.

"Yes, you have. But that's good. Crying is therapeutic. It means you're making progress."

Abi nodded. She drank the rest of the water and returned the glass. She repositioned the bun of her hair, which had worked loose on the couch. She wanted to talk about something else.

"How are things with you, Paula?"

"Pretty good, thank you. Business is so-so, but I still love therapy work. It's so satisfying. There's nothing else I'd rather do for a living." She stood by Abi, smiling down at her.

"And Lola? How is she doing? Still at art college?"

"Yes, she's now starting to enjoy it. I knew she would, once she realised the extent of her creative talents. Some of the teachers there have made a big impression on her, and it shows in her work. You know what teenagers are like. Always eager to emulate someone who can help them develop their potential. And help them crystallise their personalities. Lola's at a very delicate age. Just turned nineteen."

Awkwardly Abi got to her feet. She readjusted her underwear. "How's that troublesome boyfriend of hers?"

"Sebastian? Oh, he comes and goes. She needs to find someone more suitable. Someone her own age, who shares her outlook on life. He isn't good for Lola."

"And the drugs?"

Paula shrugged. "She still needs her 'gear', but it's under some sort of control. She's been off the heroin for over a month now. She's getting by with cannabis, which worries me a lot less."

Abi stretched out her arms and slowly swivelled her hips, to loosen her muscles. She still felt rather stiff. "Good. It would be awful if she ended up being just another junkie."

"Yes, that would be a real tragedy for me, after being her adoptive mother for so many years. I've tried hard to bring her up properly.

We're all doing our best for her, I can promise you. I'm glad that *you've* never had a problem with drugs, Abi."

Abi smiled. "I'm happy enough with the pills you give me."

"Oh yes, of course, that reminds me – I must let you have another month's supply." Paula reached into a drawer of her desk and took out a labelled cardboard packet, which she handed over to her patient. "Same dose as before. Twice a day."

"Thanks."

"You look rather hot, Abi. Do you want to take a shower next door?"

Abi frowned and thought hard for a few moments. Then she shook her head.

"No thanks. What I need right now is some fresh air. I think I'll take a walk around the green at Primrose Hill to lift my spirits. Then I'll go home."

"Good idea." Paula removed Abi's yellow shirt dress and leather belt from the back of the aluminium chair and handed them to her. As her patient put the dress back on, she pressed a button on her desk intercom.

"*Yes?*"

"Francine, Abigail is ready to leave. Could you see her out, please?"

"*Of course, doctor.*"

As Abi finished dressing and retrieved her handbag, Francine came into the office. She was a buxom middle-aged woman, still attractive if rather vulgar in her short white nurse's tunic, long blonde hair and heavy make-up. Her lacy nurse's hat verged on the burlesque.

Abi kissed Paula on the cheek. "Thank you for everything, Paula. I think it's really helped, getting those negative memories out into the open. I feel much better now."

Paula beamed. Her big blue eyes were bright. "That's what I'm here for, darling." She returned Abi's kiss, at the same time carefully and deliberately squeezing the latter's left hand in her own. For a few moments she fixed her eyes on Abi's. "See you in three weeks' time, Abi! Make sure you stay in touch! Make sure..."

"Yes," said Abi slowly, returning the gaze, her expression suddenly vacant. "I'll make sure... I'll stay in touch."

"Brava!"

Francine saw Abi out of the office and Paula sat down at her desk. She removed her glasses. She reached into one of the drawers and pulled out a clear plastic bag containing fluffy white powder, some of which she spilled carefully onto the desktop and arranged into a thin six-inch line. She took a large banknote, rolled it into a short tube, and leaned forward to inhale the powder through one nostril, snorting the whole of the line in a couple of seconds. She sat up straight and gasped out loud, as if in relief. For a while she closed her eyes. Then she reached into the largest drawer of the desk and took from it some neatly folded clothing: a sky-blue blouse, grey skirt, long white socks, a half-slip petticoat, a pair of tan-coloured nylon tights, a white bra, and finally a pair of well-used white knickers, all of which she laid out with loving care over the desktop. She picked up the blouse and smelled the underarm. She pressed the garment against her face and caressed it with her nose and her cheeks, sniffing it and exhaling noisily. She moaned with satisfaction. With one hand she pulled back her tight green-check skirt and opened wide her long muscular thighs, exposing her silky black panties. The gusset was thoroughly soaked. She began to rub her genitals, through the wet panties, and with her other hand continued to press the blouse against her face, rubbing it with her nose and her cheeks, repeatedly sniffing the fabric and exhaling noisily. What bliss! She had in her hands the very Cloths of Heaven...

At length she heard a sound and turned sideways. Francine was standing at the office door, staring hard at her, a frown of disapproval on her face. There was a long silence. Paula put down the blouse. But she kept her hand on her crutch.

"You have to understand," she said in a hoarse voice. "She's my Masterpiece."

Slowly the women smiled at one another, their eyes twinkling.

III

Monday 26th June, eight o'clock in the evening. Abigail's flat in Notting Hill, London.

Abi opened the lid of the slow cooker again. It was almost nine hours since she'd started on the lamb casserole. Her guest had rung an hour ago to say that she'd be there in a few minutes, but hadn't turned up yet. Pretty soon the lamb would be too soft and mushy to enjoy. But the aroma was still superb, with undertones of garlic, rosemary and red wine. She closed the lid and turned to the vegetables, still lying raw in their pans, and shook them around to keep them firm and loose.

She tightened the string of her blue-striped cotton apron, which was the only garment she was wearing, and walked into the lounge to check that the wine and glasses were ready on the tiled coffee table. Then she remembered that she'd checked only ten minutes ago. She rubbed her forehead. Her memory was still playing tricks on her. It was better than it had been immediately after the car crash, but nothing like as reliable as before. She still couldn't remember the crash itself, and would have been unable to recall anything of her life previous to it without Paula's help over the last few months… She suddenly felt weary again, and a little giddy, and decided to lie down for a while in the large bedroom. She switched off the jazz music playing softly on her hi-fi stack. Above it, on a wall-mounted shelf, was an antique bronze statuette of a Greek dragon that Paula had recently given her as a gift. It seemed to glare down at her, its eyes bulging and its teeth bared.

At that moment her entry-phone buzzer sounded. Abi hastened to the panel.

"Yes?"

"Hi, it's me. I'm here now. Sorry I'm so late."

Abi was relieved. "That's all right. Come on up." She rapidly untied the pony tail at the back of her head and shook her hair loose. Then she moved back to the coffee table and poured two glasses of red wine. Still standing, she began drinking from one of them.

In a few moments the bell of her front door rang and Abi hurried forward to open it. Before her stood Lola Masters, a petite slender pale-skinned girl known to her teenage art-college peers as the Goth-Dolly. Her long mane of red hair was highlighted with broad sweeps of scarlet, and she wore a short black-leather basque with a tangle of lacing at the front that tapered down no further than her navel. Below this was an impudent display of bare belly, then a tiny pleated red-check skirt, very low-slung, held up by a thick leather belt just above the level of the pubic hair. Black fishnet tights and matching boots completed the outfit. Hanging from a chain around her neck was a silver death's head pendant. She looked weary and frazzled and somewhat shaky on her legs as she stared at Abi with swollen eyes.

"I'm sorry I'm late, Mama," she said, pouting girlishly. She moved hesitantly towards Abi, who was standing in the tiny hallway, and closed the door behind her. Shaking her head, frowning, Abi opened her arms to take her and Lola slid into them with a sigh of relief, putting her arms around Abi's naked back. She turned her face up and the two kissed passionately for the best part of a minute, their lips sucking and squeezing, each moaning with delight to be back in the other's embrace again. As always, Lola licked the gold stud in Abi's right nostril, and Abi reciprocated by licking the identical stud in Lola's left nostril. Then they pressed their dainty upturned noses together and shut their eyes. It was their ritual love-greeting.

"Do you want to eat?" asked Abi softly.

"You mean something other than you?" replied Lola, her eyes widening in jest.

"Yes. I've made you a lamb casserole that's been on the slow cooker all day. It's even tastier than me. And I've got you the best wine I could find." She ran her finger over the freckles on the bridge of Lola's nose.

Lola closed her eyes, as if slightly in pain. She shook her head. "I'm sorry, Abi. I can't eat at the moment. I haven't got any appetite. I feel a bit… hung over. Had a heavy weekend. Overdid it again…"

"So who were you with over the weekend?" asked Abi, suspicion growing in her voice. The grey shadows under Lola's eyes and their dull glazed look were ringing familiar alarm bells.

Lola sighed. "An old friend."

"Let me guess. Sebastian?"

Lola paused. She didn't want to reply. She looked away and pulled at one of her big red plastic ear-rings.

"Just be honest, Baby," continued Abi. "Please don't lie to me."

"All right, Mama. Yes, I spent the weekend with Sebastian. At his swish place in Islington. I don't know how he gets all his money…"

"Yes you do. He sells drugs. And he's a gangster."

"He can be really nice, you know…"

"Until he whips your bottom. And worse…"

"Actually, I quite like it. You know what a kinky bitch I am."

"He's bad for you, Lola. He's taking advantage of you."

Lola paused again. "I need him."

"You mean you need his drugs."

"And his big black cock." She smirked mischievously.

"I don't care about his cock. Did he give you heroin again? Tell me the truth…"

Lola looked down at the floor and nodded.

Abi groaned. "No wonder you don't have an appetite! And no wonder you look as white as a ghost! And here I am, silly old Abigail, spending my whole day cooking for you and looking forward to feeding you."

"I'm sorry," whispered Lola, still looking at the carpet. She was as shamefaced as a naughty child, and plainly unhappy. Letting down her lover had become another bad habit.

Moved by her contrition, Abi held her tighter. "You're as big a fool as I am, Miss Masters. And they don't come any bigger than me!"

Gently Lola undid the apron string behind Abi's back. "You must be a fool to stay with me, Miss Janus…"

Abi lifted the collar off her neck and dropped the apron to the carpet. "What choice do I have? I love you so I have to stay."

Faced with her lover's naked body, and her naked affirmation of love, tears suddenly welled in Lola's eyes. Narcotic exhaustion always made her over-emotional.

"I love you too, Abi. Please look after me. Don't stop feeding me." She laid her head on Abi's shoulder.

"Come on Baby," said Abi wearily. "Let's sit down and relax." She led the girl into the lounge and over to the settee. With a sigh of relief Lola sank back into the comfortable cushions and watched as Abi knelt at her feet and set about undressing her: first the hefty black boots, then the fishnet tights, which Abi slid off with practised skill, ensuring that none of the netting was broken. Lola gazed adoringly at Abi's jiggling breasts as she worked.

"I see you're still going commando," said Abi, a note of reproach in her voice.

"Yep. I like to tease the boys by giving them a peep of my ginger bush." She demonstrated by lifting the front of the short tartan skirt.

Abi shook her head and knelt up straight. She began to untie the complicated lacing at the front of the basque corset. "Don't you tire of wearing this goth-punk gear?"

"It's good for my art-cred," replied Lola.

"Art-cred?"

"My artistic credibility. If you're not a great artist, then at least you can turn yourself into a work of art. That way you become part of the creative process, and then whatever you do eventually turns into art as well. Anyway, that's what Miriam says."

"Miriam?" Abi was now half-way down the lacing, revealing Lola's white chest.

"Yes, Miriam Hirst. The principal lecturer on our Photography Module. She's brilliant. And a great photographer. You must have seen her stuff in the magazines. Sometimes the big-selling papers as well. She's quite famous, you know. She's even written a couple of books!"

"She sounds like an interesting woman. I'm glad you have such fine lecturers at the college. But I don't read very much, I'm afraid. These days reading gives me headache. I prefer to listen to music. Almost there…" Abi gave a final tug and the lacing was undone. She pulled the basque apart. Lola's small breasts were now fully exposed.

"I hate my tits," said Lola glumly. She slipped the basque off her shoulders and threw the garment to one side.

"Why?"

"They're so small and puny. Like a pubescent girl's. Even the nipples are tiny."

"They're charming tits," smiled Abi. "I like them."

"Why?"

"Because they're *your* tits, darling. That's all that matters to me."

"I wish I had big ones, like yours. Big Mama boobies!"

"My boobs are getting rather *too* big," replied Abi. "They're becoming a nuisance."

Lola giggled. "Yes. They look like the tits on a Spanish peasant woman who's had too many kids. But I'd still love to have a pair like that."

"Why? You can help yourself to mine whenever you want."

"Mmm… that's true." Lola smacked her lips lasciviously and grinned. She undid her belt and twisted herself over to one side to allow Abi access to the back of her tartan skirt. Abi tugged at the zip and then yanked the skirt off in one swift movement. She held it up and marvelled at how tiny it was. Lola leaned further back into the cushions and spread her slender legs wide, deliberately showing Abi all of her pubic hair and her pink moist pussy.

"Do I smell nice?" said Lola archly.

"Yes. Very sweet. Just like a teenage girl should." Abi ran her finger up and down the vaginal lips, gently separating them as they swelled. Lola sighed, as if in pain.

"Please do me, Abi. I need it, right now. Please, *please* bring me off…" She gazed longingly at her lover as she fingered her pendant, now the only thing she was wearing.

As always, Abi responded to the girl's desperate neediness, and after a brief pause leaned down and licked the peach-pink pussy, brushing and sweeping the ginger pubic hair with her tongue. Lola moaned loudly. Within seconds she was flooded; Abi could see the sex-fluid oozing out and running down between the taut buttocks before dripping onto the settee. She pushed her tongue deep into the girl's silky passage and moved it around with firm heavy flicks and lunges. Lola's moans grew louder and she spread her thighs wider. She raised her knees with her hands. Her body began to quiver. Her buttocks clenched. Abi now moved her thumb to the stiff clitoris right by her face and began to rub it.

"Ooh… that's lovely!" gasped Lola. "Oh fuck-fuck-*fuck*…"

Abi continued to rub, fast and hard, but now withdrew her head from Lola's crutch and knelt up to look at the girl's face as a smile of crazed delight crept over her features. Lola's eyes stared wide at the ceiling… then she shifted her head and looked straight at Abi, barely recognising her. She was now approaching orgasm and was completely lost: "fuck-fazed" as she called it. Her expression of joyful astonishment, goggle-eyed and open-mouthed, was what Abi loved to watch more than anything else. It reflected back her own desire for death… a desire that she knew Lola shared, for the most part unconsciously, since she wasn't mature or experienced enough to understand what it really meant. Abi knew that this longing for death was what held the two of them together. Each sensed her impending disintegration in the other. The Angel of Death was close to them both, at any moment ready to spread its tenebrous wings and sweep them into oblivion. If they could die together, in each other's arms, it would be the ultimate ecstatic union! And yet she loved Lola with all her heart, as if she were truly her own long-lost daughter, and wanted her to live on after she, Abi, was gone. But she knew that the heroin-addicted Goth-Dolly yearned for death as well…

"Aaaahh!"

As Lola came, fully fuck-fazed, she grasped the cushions with her trembling hands while her shoulders and her head moved up almost to Abi's, and she stared her lover directly in the face to display her orgasmic destruction as close up as possible. It was the moment of supreme surrender. She opened her mouth and gasped, blowing her breath into Abi's face. Then her eyes turned up into her head, her head and her shoulders leaned back, and she slowly fell back into the cushions, arms and legs wide apart. The joyful demented smile was still etched on her face as she carried on twisting and groaning. Abi continued to rub the clitoris and Lola continued to twitch her legs and buttocks as she gave herself up to one jerking paroxysm after another. Sex-fluid continued to ooze out of her pussy, now leaving a large heavy damp patch on the settee cover. Finally Abi took a deep breath and stopped. She was now thoroughly wet between the legs as well. But she would bide her time…

At length Lola rolled over onto her side, moaning and breathing heavily. Her eyes were closed. Ecstasy was quickly giving way to exhaustion. She let out a short rasping fart.

Abi smiled and rose to her feet. She stroked Lola's brow. "Baby, I'm going to the kitchen for a moment. Why don't you go to the bedroom and rest?" Lola nodded weakly. Abi took her glass of wine with her and moved to the kitchen. The slow cooker was still hissing away. She switched it off, finally giving up on the casserole. She took one of the pills from the packet that Paula had recently given her and gulped it down with the wine. As she finished the drink an idea came to her. She reached up to one of the wall-cupboards and extracted a jar of orange honey. She picked up a tea towel. She walked back into the lounge and saw that Lola had indeed moved to the bedroom, leaving her clothes strewn over the carpet and the settee, which of course needed cleaning. Abi sighed, but with pleasure. In truth she loved clearing up after her Baby.

In the bedroom Lola had flung herself on top of the quilt and lay on her front, breathing heavily. Abi put the honey and towel on the bedside table, dimmed the small lamp, and sat down beside the girl. She began stroking and massaging the lean pale body and Lola whimpered with pleasure.

"Ohh… you're so good at this!"

"I do have some professional experience," replied Abi, smiling.

"I bet you have! So how many clients did you fuck this weekend?"

Abi pressed harder, making Lola groan. "I think the idea is that they fuck *me*, darling."

"All right. So how many people fucked you? Be honest. Just like me."

Abi paused. "About a dozen, all through the weekend."

"Fucking hell! You really are a whore!"

Abi spanked one of Lola's buttocks, loudly and only half-jokingly.

"Ow! You're good at spanking too, Mama!"

"You deserve it, cheeky brat."

"I know. Do it some more. I love it when you smack me."

"That's why I *won't* do it, darling. You'll just turn it into another bad habit. I can see that Sebastian has left a few marks on your bottom. What did he use?"

"Nothing much. Just his big leather belt. It did sting, though. Do you get whacked by your clients?"

"No. I don't allow them to flog me. If I did want a beating, it would have to be for a good reason. Because I had really done something to deserve it. And it would have to be done by someone I genuinely respected. And someone I liked." Briefly she recalled her caning at the hands of Sister Helena. Then she resumed the massage, pressing her thumbs into the winged dragon tattoo that was the twin of her own, in the centre of Lola's back.

"So you don't like your clients?" continued Lola.

"No, not really. Some of my regulars are likeable guys, pretty decent, but I can't say I feel much for them. I don't want any emotional attachment with clients."

"Do you ever come when they fuck you?"

"No, never."

As always, Lola was pleased by this answer. "So you do it just for the money?"

"Yes, just for the money. It's the only thing I can do that pays for a nice place like this."

"Well, it's a lovely place. I like this part of London. It's so… classy. Not like where I live."

"Are you still at the squat?" asked Abi. "In Hackney?"

"Yep. Still hanging on there… until they throw us out."

"Sounds depressing."

"No, I like it there, with the other guys. They're all art students, so it's very bohemian."

"Good for your art-cred?"

Lola scoffed. "I suppose so. Good for lots of hash, anyway."

"You'd never go back to live with Paula?"

"No thanks! She'd drive me crazy in half an hour. She's a total control freak. I've had enough of her bossing me about. Now I've tasted freedom, I'll never go back. Even if I have to sleep on the streets."

"You'll never have to sleep on the streets. You know you can always stay here."

"You never bring your clients back here?"

"No. I only do outcalls. My bed is reserved for me and my lovers."

Lola smiled contentedly. "Well, it's nice to know I have a second home whenever I need one. And a second Mama to look after me."

"When did you last see Paula?"

"I don't know. I haven't seen her for weeks."

"Don't you think she worries about you?"

"Huh! The only thing that bitch worries about is herself."

"She told me she was worried about you going back on heroin."

"Bullshit," muttered Lola. "She's taken plenty of gear herself over the years. She still does a line of coke now and then."

"Really? She always seems very sober when I see her."

"She's very professional. She doesn't let it interfere with her work."

"What would she say if she knew we were together... doing what we're doing?"

Lola laughed. "I don't know what she'd do to you. I suppose she'd strike you off her patient list. As for me, she'd probably take a cane to my arse... just like she used to when I was younger."

"Did she really cane you?"

"Yep. She sure did. But not all the time. Only when I deserved it, I guess. I was a wild brat all right, when she first adopted me."

"You're still a wild brat, Lola."

"Uh-huh. That's why you like me, isn't it?"

"Partly." Abi caressed the girl's thighs. They were wide enough apart to display the russet pubic hair. Tenderly she ran her finger over a couple of small red pimples, close to the cleft of Lola's shapely buttocks, just above one of her thighs. She adored any sign of vulnerability in her Baby, however slight. "And maybe I like you because you remind me of my daughter. Or make me think of what she'd be like now..."

Lola turned and looked up quizzically. "You wouldn't fuck your own daughter, would you?"

"No, of course I wouldn't. But it's part of the reason why I feel about you the way I do – because you're nearly the same age as her. I must admit... I also want you because you look a bit like me when I was younger... in your face... in your expressions."

"I'm not as good-looking as you," laughed Lola. "I don't know anyone who is."

"And I don't know anyone as pretty as you," replied Abi.

Lola looked pleased. "Do you really love me?" she asked quietly.

"You know I do."

"More than anyone else?"

"More than everyone else, all put together."

"Oh Abi…" Lola squeezed Abi's hand. She twisted her body and they both lay down on their sides, facing one another. They held hands and looked intently into each other's eyes. It was a moment of complete contentment, each silently acknowledging her fulfilment in the other. They kissed, slowly and softly, to prolong the moment.

Finally Lola smiled. "You're like the mother I wish I'd always had," she said. "My gorgeous Big Mama. With the big peasant woman's tits! Maybe I can make up for lost time with you. I'm still a kid, you know. A wild and wayward brat. I still need plenty of motherly love."

On hearing this, Abi was suddenly overcome with sadness. She took a deep breath and looked away into the distance, now with a weary detached expression on her face. "My Baby, I don't know how much mothering I can give you. I don't think I'm going to be here for much longer. I don't have a lot of time left…"

Lola was alarmed. Her eyes widened. "Why? Are you sick? Is it that blood clot on your brain?"

"Maybe. But it's more of a feeling that… things are coming to a head. Big things that I don't understand. I don't think I can go on much longer as I am, Lola. I feel like a machine that's starting to run down."

Lola bit her lower lip with anxiety. She tried to lift Abi's mood, running her finger up her tanned athletic arm.

"Abi, you need to go out more. I mean, apart from meeting all those clients."

"I guess so." Abi still sounded flat and dejected.

"Listen. There's a Summer Party at the art college next week, to celebrate the end of the academic year. Will you come with me? Please?"

"You really want me to come? Why?"

"Because I want you to meet my lecturer, Miriam."

"The famous photographer?"

"Yes. She went to a convent school, just like you did, but I think it was a bigger one, and very old-fashioned and devout. Somewhere in Ireland, where she grew up, long ago. She's now in her late fifties. But she's so young at heart."

"I'm not too keen to be reminded about convent school. Or about the Catholic Faith. I've sinned beyond any hope of redemption…"

"But Miriam isn't really religious, like a true Believer would be. She says she's a lapsed Catholic, who's lost her Faith – but she's fascinated by the emotional power of religion. She says she likes to use it to help her make photos. She wants to capture the love of God, and the sacrifice of Christ, and turn them into art. She says Love and Art are one and the same thing."

Abi rested her head on the pillow and smiled softly. She looked far into the distance again and sighed. "Love is Creation, and Creation is Love." She squeezed Lola's hand.

"Yes. That kind of thing."

"All right, darling. Miriam does sound like an interesting lady. I'll go to the party and meet her. If you really want me to."

Lola was animated. Her green eyes widened. "Oh yes, I'd *love* you to meet her. You and her are my favourite two people, in the whole world. It would be brilliant if you got to know each other!"

"How much have you told her about me?"

"Only that you went to a convent school. I told her that you weren't a Believer any more. I told her that you were half-Italian, and had a private income. And I showed her a photo of you. One I took when we were outside Westminster Cathedral last month. She loved that long white dress you were wearing… you know, the frock with the fancy shoulder straps. She said she'd really like to meet you."

Abi could see that this was something Lola wanted dearly. She knew she couldn't refuse.

"All right, my darling. It's a date."

"Oh, *great!*" Lola lay back on the bed, sank her head into a pillow, and stretched out her arms contentedly. There was a big smile on her face, her fatigue suddenly forgotten.

Abi reached for the honey jar on the side-table. "And now, it's *my* turn."

"Your turn?"

"To enjoy myself."

"How?"

"By giving you a little treat. Just lie still…" Abi sat up and swung one of her legs over Lola, then turned herself so that she knelt astride the girl's midriff. Smiling mischievously, she unscrewed the lid of the jar.

"Oh Mama, you look fantastic from this angle. Especially your tits."

"Baby, I've always wanted to give you my milk. Straight from my breasts. But I don't have any to give. I wanted to feed you with a tasty meal tonight, but I couldn't. I'm so frustrated. So now I'm going to try *this*…" She put her finger in the honey-jar and extracted a thick blob of golden-orange honey, before proceeding to daub it all over and around one of her big nipples, which became erect almost at once. Lola looked up astonished, her mouth hanging open. Then Abi daubed the other nipple, again spreading honey generously over and around it. She screwed back the lid and put the jar to one side.

Lola sighed. Her eyes shone. "Abi… that's *so* fucking horny!"

Abi leaned down over her. "So which one do you want first?"

"Oh, the mangled one. It's the one I love most."

"I know," replied Abi. "Here it is… take it." She eased her nipple down into Lola's mouth, which closed firmly but gently around the disfigured teat. Lola sucked, softly at first, then rapidly increased the pressure. She moaned with delight at the sweetness of the honey, and at the sweetness of the moment.

Abi closed her eyes and her mouth slowly opened wide. She gasped each time Lola increased the pressure on her nipple. Instinctively the girl moved her hand to the top of Abi's muscular thigh until it reached the shaved crutch. She moaned again when she realised how wet Abi was.

"Go on, Baby," breathed Abi. "Do it now. All the way in!"

Lola complied and pushed two fingers high into Abi's vagina.

"Aaahh…"

Abi's head dropped and her face now hovered only a few inches above Lola's. Her dark hair fell over part of the girl's face, spilling onto the pillow. Lola continued to suck the nipple, harder and harder, her shining eyes looking up into Abi's with a tigerish intensity, as if she was ready to bite off the teat at any moment. Excited by the delirious expression on her lover's face, Lola worked her fingers faster and deeper into Abi's cervix, pleasuring her more and more with each twist and thrust. Now it was the older woman's turn to surrender… to give Lola the satisfaction of watching *her* in intimate close up as she collapsed into blissful orgasm. There was no stopping now. She wouldn't let her Baby down. She never did.

IV

Friday 30th June, at Midnight. The night of the New Moon. The office of hypnotherapist Dr Paula Masters.

Clad in a long black dress, a solemn expression on her face, Paula sat at her desk. The only light came from the desk-lamp. An upright joss stick burned on a side-table near the closed window, emitting a sickly-sweet odour. She opened the ornate wooden box in front of her and extracted her deck of Tarot cards. She placed the deck on the sky-blue schoolgirl blouse, normally kept in her drawer, which had now been opened and spread out to be used as a tablecloth.

As soon as her electronic desk clock flashed four zeros, to indicate the arrival of midnight, Paula pronounced the customary invocation in a slow, vibrating monotone.

> *To Arxegono Fidi*
> *To Megalo Drako*
> *O Opoios eitan kai*
> *O Opoios enai*
> *O Aionas ton Aionon*
> *Einai me ton pneuma sou!*

She took the cards and started to shuffle them, her eyes firmly shut, repeatedly muttering "To Megalo Drako". At one minute past midnight she stopped and put the deck face down on the tablecloth. She opened her eyes and took the top card from the pile. She turned it and laid it down slightly to the left of the centre of the cloth. It signified the Past.

The Blasted Tower. The destruction of an edifice. Paula smiled with satisfaction.

She took the second card, again from the top of the pile, and laid it to the right of the first one, in the dead centre of the tablecloth. It signified the Present.

Queen of Cups. An emotional woman bearing an artistic Gift. Paula frowned. This made little sense.

She took the third card and laid it to the right of the other two. It signified the Future.

The Hanged Man. A self-sacrifice, martyrdom. Exactly what Paula wanted to see. She felt a thrill of excitement.

A final card was required. She moved her hand roughly halfway down the pile and carefully cut the deck. From the re-arranged stack she took the top card. This was the Supernal, the Overriding Power which determined the rest of the reading. She placed it above the line of three cards she had previously drawn and turned it over.

The Judgement. The final Reckoning; Resurrection. Paula took a deep breath. The conclusion of her Masterpiece was now close at hand, whether she wanted it to be or not. The precipice was approaching fast.

She lit a cigarette and moved to the window, looking out at the darkened zoo across the road. She raised the lower section of the sash window and, as usual, took pleasure in listening to the nocturnal moans and wails of the animals. Suddenly there was a rumble of thunder in the middle distance, only a mile or two away, and a gust of wind sighed into the room like an invisible demon, bending the joss stick and dispersing the plume of incense-smoke across the office. Paula smiled. It was a good omen. The Dragon had answered her call.

V

Saturday 1ˢᵗ July, the early hours of the morning. The bedroom of Abigail's flat in Notting Hill, London.

Abi wanted to turn over but couldn't. Her body was rigid. In her dream she was once again back in the bright neon-lit gallery, lying naked on a large table, or perhaps an altar-top, completely paralysed. She couldn't move a muscle. Her eyes were fixed, staring up at the high ceiling, but nonetheless she could perceive everything going on around her. She was flat on her back, her arms stretched out perpendicular at both sides and her legs raised at the knees and open very wide, bringing her heels almost back to her buttocks. Her body was a hard shining white, like porcelain, as if it had been meticulously crafted and painted. Every last dark-brown hair had been shaved off – from her head, her crutch, her armpits, her eye-brows, even the fine faint down from her lower back.

Unlike in the previous dreams, the glass cabinet which had protected her was no longer present. For the first time, she was fully exposed. Suddenly she was surrounded by half a dozen figures dressed in full-length black robes with hoods. The figure by her right shoulder dropped his hood, and she saw it was once again the grey-haired elderly man with narrow eyes and thin beard and malicious grin who had previously rubbed his penis over the protective glass. Now he had unlimited access to her. She was powerless to stop him. She was seized with terror but still couldn't move. He extended a hairy, thickly veined arm and his hand slowly squeezed her breast. His grin widened. At her left shoulder, a black man's muscular forearm leaned forward and his big strong hand began squeezing her other breast. Now other hands were on her thighs, running up and down them, and yet another began pressing the flesh on her belly. She felt more hands on her buttocks, eagerly rubbing and kneading them, and finally she was being rubbed and squeezed absolutely everywhere. Helpless, overwhelmed, she gave up and submitted, letting the multitude of invading hands take the whole of her body in any way they wished. As they took her, the robed figures were moaning and muttering in a strange foreign tongue.

At the foot of the altar, directly facing her open crutch, stood the leader of the group, the High Priestess. Abi tried to discern her face but couldn't. The head was bald and white, just like her own, and the Priestess held up a black phallic-shaped dildo, about a foot long, which looked like some sort of wand. On one of her long bony hands was a large black-stoned ring. She began intoning in the same foreign tongue as the rest of the group, but much louder and more distinct. The others fell silent to listen to her, and abruptly removed their hands from Abi's body. The Priestess took a deep breath and brought the wand down to the level of the altar-top. Abi knew what was coming. The Priestess leaned forward and Abi caught sight of her big blue eyes as she felt the bulbous head of the dildo press into her vagina. A pause, then a forceful thrust, and the thick wand was surging up inside her, filling her up to the navel. Abi couldn't even move her vaginal muscles to respond. As the wand sank all the way into her, there was a collective groan of satisfaction from the assembled group.

For a while the wand lay inert and motionless inside her, creating a cold, numbing sensation; and before long Abi realised that it was drawing the remaining life from her, like some demonic magnet, relentlessly sucking her thoughts and her energy into itself, reducing her to a state of non-existence... nullifying every part of her being. Finally the Priestess withdrew the wand in a single sweep and there was a shout of exultation from the group. At this moment Abi knew that her life-force had been extracted by the wand, that it had stolen her mind and her soul and left her lying on the altar as nothing but a corpse, a lump of frozen matter. She was like a butterfly pinned to a board. Time stood still. Everything ceased but her consciousness of her own cessation. *This* was her ultimate fate, her final defeat... the eternal awareness of her own death, the endless time of not-being, of never coming back to life... knowing nothing but her own extinction in the present moment, forever... Her final act was to emit a long rasping death-rattle from her throat and she woke to find herself gasping loudly on her quilt, on which she had fallen asleep, naked, a little while earlier. She rolled over to one side, drew up her knees and took several deep breaths. She could scarcely believe that she was still alive.

After a while she realised that the bedroom door was ajar and the light from her lounge was shining in. Still dazed and groggy, trembling from the memory of her horrific dream, she got to her feet and staggered out into the lounge. She was surprised to see that the main ceiling light was on. A wine-glass lay on its side on the coffee table, over which a pool of red wine had been spilled. The bronze statuette of the winged Greek dragon sat on top of the hi-fi stack, instead of its usual place on the wall-shelf above. Even more disconcerting was the open door at the opposite end of the lounge, leading to the small entrance hallway. She walked over to this area and found, to her consternation, that the heavy front door of her flat was also wide open. Beyond this the communal lobby light was on, indicating that within the last few minutes someone had used the time-delay switch as they exited her flat and left the building. She could hear the rain falling and the wind gusting in the street outside. With shaking hands Abi closed the front door and sank to her knees, sobbing in despair as she folded her arms around herself. She realised that her life was no longer her own, and might never be again. She had to see Paula, as soon as possible. There was no-one else who could help her.

VI

Wednesday 5th July, in the evening. Shoreditch Art College, London.

Abi and Lola, sitting in the rear of the taxi-cab, held hands as the vehicle slowly approached the Art College, situated a little way off Old Street. As usual the London traffic was heavy, even as late as nine in the evening.

"I'm going to tell everyone you're my older sister," declared Lola with a note of triumph. "Do you mind?"

"No, not at all," replied Abi. "But do you think they'll believe you?"

"Oh yes, I'm sure they will. We look slightly similar, even though I'm a pale-skinned red-head. Well, maybe I'll say I'm your half-sister." She paused. "Didn't you tell me once you had a sister who died when you were younger?"

"Yes, I did have a sister, a long time ago," sighed Abi. "She was a year older than me."

"What was her name?"

"Annabel. She was only sixteen when she died. She drowned swimming out at sea, when we were on holiday." She looked ahead, far into the distance.

"Oh, how horrible!" exclaimed Lola. "Where did it happen?"

"Somewhere in Greece… on one of the islands. For some reason she was dragged down into the water and couldn't make it back to the surface. They found her body later."

"That's so tragic. It must have been really hard for you. Were you close to her?"

"Yes, very close. She was the most wonderful girl you could imagine. It was like having… Wonder Woman as your best friend. She was always there for me, always looking after me. And she was so beautiful…"

"Just like you?"

"She looked like me… but she was more attractive."

"Wow! If only I could have met her!"

"If only…" Abi closed her eyes as she remembered the sight of Annabel's naked corpse lying supine on the marble slab in the morgue. Above all she recalled the expression on Annabel's face: tawny eyes staring into space, mouth open and features contorted as if she were about to start crying like a pathetic child. It was the very picture of despair, an acknowledgement of ultimate defeat that Abi still struggled to associate with her confident vivacious sister. It was a grotesque negation of everything she had been in life. That distorted face had haunted Abi ever since… as if it was a premonition of her own fate.

The taxi pulled up in front of the entrance to the College. It was a large rectangular 1960s block, five storeys high, featuring plenty of glass and concrete. Lights blazed everywhere in the building. Abi paid the fare and the two of them got out. A group of half a dozen scruffily dressed male students, roughly Lola's age, were clustered on the short stairwell leading up to the entrance, conspicuously drinking beer and smoking cannabis. Their conversation dropped away as Abi and Lola walked up to them, still holding hands. Abi wore a diaphanous white full-length frock with slender shoulder straps and an elaborate drawstring around the waist, giving her an elegant Pre-Raphaelite look, even though her breasts and her white panties were slightly visible under the semi-transparent gauzy material. Lola wore a red latex mini-dress with thin straps and a large heart-shaped cut-away at the rear, leaving most of her pale back exposed. Her face was heavily painted with black mascara. The boys stared at them, grinning sardonically at Lola, with whom they were obviously familiar.

"Okay, dick-heads," said Lola. "Are you going to let us through?"

"Whatever the Goth-Dolly wants," said one of the boys, bowing and stepping to one side. He held up his joint. "Fancy a drag, darling?"

"No thanks," replied Lola haughtily. "I've got better things to do tonight."

A couple of the boys scoffed, while the others stared at Abi.

"Are you one of our new teachers, Miss?" said one of them to her, impertinently.

Abi flashed a smile at him. "Maybe. If you're up to being one of my students."

"Come on, Sis, just ignore them," said Lola, drawing Abi to the top of the steps. They moved through the entrance doors while the boys looked pointedly at one another, raising their eyebrows and whistling silently. The one who had spoken to Abi grabbed at his groin and hungrily licked his lips.

The bright foyer was manned by an elderly security guard, who gave Lola a friendly nod, and then they were into the main gallery, the large rectangular hall in which the party was being held. Here the lights had been turned down and the walls covered in black drapery to highlight a flashing ultraviolet beam from high up on the rear wall. About fifty students and a few members of staff were milling about in the semi-darkness against a background of pre-recorded rock music. This was merely an appetiser for the main event, which was to be a session by a band of musicians dressed as demonic aliens – complete with rubber masks – who were busily preparing the electrical equipment for their concert on a stage at the front of the hall.

"Who's the band?" asked Abi. "They look rather menacing."

"They're college students who've formed their own heavy metal band. They call themselves Koronzon."

"Those speakers look very big," said Abi. "Sorry to be a killjoy, but I think the music is going to be too loud for me. Heavy noise always gives me headache."

"It's all right," replied Lola. "We can go next door to a smaller room when the band starts." She looked down at Abi's hips. "Ha-ha! The ultraviolet is really showing up your knickers! You look so-o-o slutty!"

Abi was unperturbed. "I don't care. I'm happy to give the boys a cheap thrill."

Lola laughed. "It won't be just the boys getting a thrill. Oh look – there's Miriam, over there, by the bar. Let's get some drinks." Still holding hands, they wandered over to the makeshift bar in a rear corner of the hall. The semi-darkness and the flashing light made it difficult for Abi to see Miriam properly, but she could discern a medium-height older woman with short grey hair holding forth to a group of students who were hanging on her every word. Abi and Lola arrived at the bar and the latter ordered two wines. They clinked their glasses and drank the cheap plonk. It was another hot evening. More and more people were streaming into the hall to join the party.

After a few moments Lola abruptly turned and waved. Miriam, now free of her students, was approaching them, a firm smile on her face. She and Lola kissed each other on the cheek; then Miriam held her hand out to Abi, who warmly shook it. She was at once impressed by Miriam's sharp features: high cheek-bones, aquiline nose, and intelligent dark eyes which immediately held the attention. Her face was enhanced by her white ruffled shirt, so lacy as to be positively gothic, and tight black leather trousers tapering down to a pair of buckled boots. Her figure was a little full but she managed to carry off her clothes with panache. Her dark grey hair was close-cropped, with a severe short back and sides that made her look decidedly masculine. She wore small silver ear-rings shaped in the symbol of Venus.

"Hello, Miriam," said Abi. "So pleased to meet you."

"And I'm delighted to meet you, Abi. You look as lovely in the flesh as you do in Lola's photograph. Thank you for wearing that gorgeous white dress!"

"It's turned out to be a bit more revealing than I'd expected."

"Oh, why not show off a beautiful figure if you have one? I wish I did!" There was a trace of Irish lilt in her voice which Abi found attractive.

"I like your lacy shirt," said Abi. "I've never seen one so finely embroidered."

Miriam beamed, as did Lola, relieved to see that her two favourite women were hitting it off so well. "I fear both of us are too elegantly dressed for the occasion," said Miriam. "Have you been to any student parties before?"

"Only as an outsider. I'm afraid I never made it to college."

"Never mind. It's overrated. Creativity is much more important than higher education. Don't you agree, Lola?"

"Oh yes, absolutely!" enthused Lola.

"My ex-husband would have agreed," said Abi. "He was an art teacher. He always believed that creativity and love were one and the same thing."

Miriam was impressed. "He was right. They come from exactly the same source. The heart, the soul, call it what you will. Creativity and love are the only things that give life meaning. Otherwise we might as well just go around producing offspring, banal replicas of ourselves. Do you have any children, Abi?"

"I had a daughter, when I was very young, but… I lost touch with her, many years ago. What about you?"

Miriam shook her head. "No, I've never had children, or been married. I've devoted my life to my work, my creativity – and to passing on whatever I can to these unruly devils."

"Lola has told me about your photographic work," replied Abi. "And all the places where your pictures have appeared. She says you've photographed some famous people."

"A few. Singers, writers, movie stars. I love doing portraits of glamorous actresses."

"Sounds like a wonderful way to make a living," said Abi. "I wish I'd studied photography, or art of some kind. Sadly it never happened."

"Despite your ex-husband being an art teacher?"

"I wasn't a good enough pupil."

"Oh, I'm sure you could…"

At that moment a few high-pitched chords of an electric guitar screeched from the stage, so sharply that a number of people in the hall flinched. Abi held her forefingers to her ears. The screeching quickly ceased.

"Oh dear," said Miriam. "The band are tuning up. I can't say I'd recommend listening to them. If you want to talk further, Abi, we can adjourn to my room upstairs. I have a nice bottle of wine up there, locked in my desk, and some of my photographs to look at, if you're interested."

"Oh yes, I'd love to see them."

"Do come and join us, Lola," said Miriam.

Lola was looking back towards the entrance to the hall. "I'll join you soon, Miriam. But I have to see someone first."

Abi turned and saw a burly black man, in his late thirties, staring at Lola and slowly nodding at her. His appearance was odd for two reasons: his hair was bleached blond, almost peroxide, and he wore a sharp expensive-looking suit, quite out of keeping with the appearance of everyone else in the hall. His gaudy shirt was wide open at the neck.

"Let me guess," said Abi to Lola. "Sebastian?"

"Yes," replied Lola. "I'm sorry, I have to speak to him, just for a minute. Excuse me." She promptly left and walked away towards him, rather hastily.

Abi shook her head. "I don't think that man is good for her."

"Is he her boyfriend?" asked Miriam.

"Yes, I suppose he is," said Abi, a little dejected.

"Well," said Miriam, "you can't do much to influence the love-lives of teenagers these days. In fact all of us have to learn about relationships the hard way. That's certainly been my experience."

Abi turned and saw that Miriam was looking at her intently. She nodded. "Yes, that's been my experience as well."

There were a few more noisy chords from the guitar on the stage. A machine had started to spread stage smoke around the hall, absorbing and dispersing the ultraviolet light.

"I want you to tell me all about your relationships," said Miriam, touching Abi's bare arm. "Before Koronzon turn our brains to mincemeat." She led Abi off to a door at the side of the hall, and they entered the comparative silence of a corridor. "My room is on the second floor. Here's the lift."

The door slid open and they got into the small brightly-lit lift. The two women stood close and looked hard at one another, each leaning back against opposite side-walls of the compartment. Now that she could see Miriam clearly, Abi was struck by the focus and the intensity of her black eyes, which exerted an almost hypnotic effect on her. She found it relaxing, even pleasurable. She felt that she could trust the older woman implicitly. But then, she had too readily trusted people in the past and had too often paid the price...

"Do you know much about Sebastian?" asked Miriam.

"I shouldn't say this, but… I think he supplies Lola with drugs," replied Abi.

"Really? Then it isn't just Lola. In the last few months I've seen him around the college quite a bit, talking to some of the other students. And sometimes in a nearby pub."

"Doesn't that concern you?"

"Yes, it does, if he is dealing drugs. But I don't feel I can moralise to the students about drug-taking, or about what they do with their personal lives. I've used various… pharmaceuticals myself in the past, as have many artists."

"For artistic inspiration?"

"Yes. For enhancing visualisation. Drugs can be beneficial if you don't become addicted."

"I'm afraid Lola is becoming addicted."

"Then you must do your best to help her," said Miriam. The lift door opened. "Here we are: second floor." They walked along another corridor and finally arrived at a door with a sign stating "Miriam Hirst: Principal Photography Lecturer". Miriam unlocked the door and switched on the light as they entered.

The large room looked more like a school classroom than Abi had expected: big wooden tables grouped in fours, dozens of photographs covering the walls, a slide projector at the rear pointing towards a white screen at the front, a well-stocked bookshelf and a display of antique cameras. Abi wandered over to one of the side walls to inspect the photos.

"Are these your pictures?"

"No," replied Miriam. "They're all by my students." She unlocked a cabinet in her desk and extracted a bottle of red wine.

"Including Lola?"

"Yes, one or two are by her. She has the makings of a decent photographer, if she can think more carefully about composition."

"There seems to be a lot of black and white – not much colour."

"Yes, that reflects my current aesthetic view. I've been trying to develop a contrast between a monochrome background and the foregrounded human figure, which is rendered in colour." She picked up a large folder from her desktop.

"Why?"

"Because my view of the world these days is pessimistic. A degraded, polluted environment, a soulless society obsessed with materialism, increasingly authoritarian politics. Set against this is the only repository of true life, the individual human being. That's why the only colour in the pictures is in the human figure, which is portrayed as strongly and vividly as possible."

"Your students share your views?"

"Many of them do, artistically if not politically. Art students tend to be radical anyway. But I also encourage them to express their own views. Some of them, like those here, are helping me with my current project." Miriam moved to the centre of the room and perched on one of the tables, putting her boots on one of the hard wooden chairs. Her leather trousers squeaked as she made herself comfortable. She ignored a twinge of arthritic pain from her knee. "Some red wine?"

"Oh yes, thank you."

"It's a decent Shiraz. Much better than the ghastly stuff they're serving downstairs." She unscrewed the top. "Unfortunately I don't have any glasses. Do you mind drinking straight from the bottle?"

"No, not at all." Abi joined her in the middle of the room, sitting down on the desk opposite her, and likewise put her white sandals on a chair. They faced each other, about a metre apart. Miriam took a swig of the wine, then handed the bottle to Abi, who also swigged some down. Miriam smiled as she opened the folder on her lap. She was pleased to see that Abi hadn't wiped the top of the bottle before drinking.

"I see that you like your red wine, Abi."

"Yes, if it's as good as this."

"Carry on – take as much as you want."

On the ground floor the band finally started up in earnest, with a shrill jangle of guitars and a thumping bass that seemed to vibrate through the entire building. The two women smiled and shook their heads. Abi downed more of the wine as Miriam put on a pair of round spectacles. For a few moments she sifted through the papers in the folder.

"This is some of my recent work, reduced in size to fit into this folder. The final photographs, when they go to exhibition, will be much larger."

"Oh, you have an exhibition coming up? Where?"

"In the Black Sun Gallery in Whitechapel. Have you heard of it?"

"Yes, it rings a bell. I think I may even have been there once… a long time ago. What are you calling the exhibition?"

"It's going to be called 'Divine Woman.'"

"Sounds inspiring."

"It opens next month. You must come and see it, Abi."

"I'll make sure I do."

Miriam handed Abi a number of the papers, which were roughly the standard A3 size, and Abi passed the bottle back to her.

"Oh my goodness!" exclaimed Abi, leafing through the papers. "These are extraordinary…" The photos were depictions of the successive stages of the Crucifixion, featuring various nude, voluptuous young women as Christ, their bodies vividly coloured in pink, light orange, bright yellow or strong flesh tones as they struggled to carry a jet-black cross. The pictures showed Christ kneeling, crouching, down on all fours, even crawling as the big heavy cross almost crushed the Redeemer with its weight. In the background were greyish mono-chrome figures dressed in modern clothing, laughing, shouting, jeering at Christ's obvious pain and degradation. To her astonishment, Abi felt a thrill running through her crutch as she looked at the female Christ's facial expressions and at the mockery on the faces of the onlookers, and she was suddenly aware of the weight of her buttocks on the table. She kept her legs firmly closed.

"The Christs were modelled by some of my students," said Miriam. "Do you like them?" She swigged at the wine again. Her cheeks were growing a little red, partly from the alcohol and partly because she could see that Abi was aroused by the pictures.

"Yes, they're beautiful," replied Abi, still examining the photos. She took a deep breath. "And... if it doesn't sound too blasphemous... they're very sexy as well."

Miriam smiled, delighted by Abi's reply. "Yes, they're intended to be sexy, though I'd prefer to use the word erotic. A woman's love – in my opinion anyway – is always more physical and earthy than a man's, more immediately *real*, and I don't see why the Divine Love of Christ shouldn't be conveyed in such a way, through a woman. Now that we're moving into a New Millennium, Christianity has got to change – or it will wither and die, and the forces of Darkness and Evil will triumph over the forces of Love."

Abi looked up at her. "Lola told me you were a lapsed Catholic. A convent school girl."

"Yes, I am. And she told me that *you* were, as well."

Abi smiled, wryly, as Miriam handed the bottle back to her. "I'm more lapsed than you can probably imagine," she sighed. "I'm a fallen woman, all right."

"Maybe lapsed, maybe fallen, but hardly a sinner."

"Oh yes, a big sinner. You wouldn't believe how big, Miriam!"

Miriam looked at her intently. "Try me," she said.

The alcohol had emboldened Abi. "Has Lola told you what I do for a living?"

"No, not at all, but I think I can guess."

Abi took another gulp of the wine and laughed. "Go on then!"

"Are you in the sex industry?"

Abi nodded, and raised an eyebrow. "How did you guess?"

"You have the looks, the glamour, that provocative way of carrying yourself and looking at people… as if you're calmly assessing how much they desire you."

"Oh my God, is it that obvious?"

"No, it isn't obvious. But I have an artistic interest in the way women express themselves sexually…"

"Don't you mean erotically?" said Abi, teasing her.

Miriam laughed. "I mean both. The erotic usually leads to the sexual."

"It does indeed," replied Abi, handing the bottle back.

There was a knock at the door.

Miriam turned and called out. "Yes?"

The door opened and one of Miriam's goth-girl students peered round it. "Sorry to interrupt, Miss Hirst."

"That's all right. What is it?"

"Lola asked me to tell you that she had to leave the party. She says sorry but she has to go somewhere. She doesn't know when she'll be back. If she doesn't come back, she said that Abi should return home whenever she wants, without her. She'll ring in the morning."

"All right, Donna. Thanks for letting us know." The girl smiled awkwardly and left, closing the door.

Abi sighed. "I know exactly where she's going, and why. Sebastian."

"Obviously. To get drugs."

"And sex, very likely. Lola prefers them both at the same time."

"A very difficult girl. I believe she's an orphan."

"Yes. In recent years, she's been adopted. By a professional psychotherapist, here in London. Doctor Paula Masters. Have you heard of her?"

Miriam shook her head. "No, I haven't. I do my best to stay away from shrinks. They always end up fucking your mind. And charging you a fortune for the privilege."

"You'd think having a therapist as an adoptive mother would help her," continued Abi, "but I can't see that it has." She refrained from mentioning her own involvement with Paula, in case it made Miriam think less of her.

Miriam sipped at the bottle, which was now only half-full. "Sometimes a girl can't be helped. Even when she has a friend who loves her as much as you do."

"I love her as if she was my own daughter. I do everything I can for her."

"Abi… I shouldn't say this, but you're too good for her. Even if you are a sex worker!"

Abi snorted. "A whore, you mean."

"No, that's just what men call you." She handed the bottle back to Abi.

"It's also what the Roman Church would call me," said Abi. She put the bottle down beside her, realising that she had drunk enough for the time being. Downstairs in the hall the band had suddenly stopped.

Miriam smiled. "You *were* a devout Catholic, weren't you? As a child, at convent school. A true Believer."

Abi nodded. "Yes. Probably as devout as you were. But I wasn't up to being one for real."

"On the contrary," said Miriam. "You're still a real Believer. And you're still a true Catholic. Not in the theological sense, but in the emotional sense. In the spiritual sense."

Abi was surprised. "You think so? Despite being a whore?"

"No, *because* you're a whore. Because you're a fallen woman. You still seek redemption. You still seek Divine Love. As I do myself. I can assure you, the Church would regard *me* as a fallen woman as well, although for slightly different reasons. To do with sex, of course. You and I are very similar, Abi. The difference is that I'm an artist and you… you're a work of art. A thing of great beauty."

Abi felt herself growing hot. She smiled awkwardly. "You're too kind, Miriam."

"No, I'm being quite objective." Miriam paused for a moment. "Abi… as an artist, as a professional photographer, I'd like to ask you to do something for me." She took off her glasses.

"I'm listening."

"Would you model for me? For some photographs like the ones you're holding?"

Abi was taken aback. "But why me? Why not use these models here?"

Miriam shook her head. "They simply won't do. I can't find anyone who's suitable for the ultimate image, the Crucifixion itself. Christ nailed to the cross. The orgasmic moment of death. The eternal Divine Moment!"

Abi raised both eyebrows. "You want to nail me to the cross?"

"Oh no, not for real. The nails would be airbrushed in, afterwards. You'd be tied to the cross with straps and cords. You'd have a foot-rest to take most of your weight. It wouldn't be painful. Well, it might strain your upper body just a little, but you wouldn't need to be up on the cross for very long."

Abi looked again at the pictures in her lap, at Christ's suffering face. Suddenly her mind was made up.

"Yes, I'll do it. I'd love to model for you. Whenever you want."

Miriam beamed. Her dark eyes shone. "That's marvellous! You don't mind being featured in my Black Sun exhibition? Being on public show, naked?"

"No, I don't mind. I want to leave something of myself for posterity. Something beautiful."

"The pictures *will* be beautiful, I promise you."

"Where will you take the photos?" asked Abi.

"In my studio. In Bethnal Green."

"Do you actually have a cross there?"

"Yes, a full-length wooden cross, specially made for me by a handyman student. I can hoist it up with a winch, after tying you down while it's horizontal."

Abi ran her finger over her lips. She tried not to show her growing excitement.

"I would of course pay you for your time," said Miriam.

Abi shook her head, emphatically. "No, Miriam, no payment. I want to do this for free. It really excites me."

"Oh, you wonderful creature," sighed Miriam. Her cheeks were now vividly flushed. Her neck above the lacy white shirt was also red.

"Although…" said Abi, smiling archly, "I suspect that posing nude as Christ on the cross would complete my Fall from Grace. I'd surely end up in Hell!"

Miriam laughed. "My darling Abi, if anyone is destined for Heaven, it's you. Let the Church go to Hell!"

Abi laughed too. "I'll drink to that!" A little tipsy, she reached for the bottle and knocked it over with her wrist, so that the bottle disgorged the remainder of the wine behind her back.

"Oh no! Look what I've done! I'm so *clumsy*!" Abi hastily lifted up the bottle behind her, but almost all the wine had run out and pooled over the table, some of it already dripping onto the parqueted floor. "I'm *so* sorry, Miriam!"

"It's all right," replied Miriam, "I'll deal with it. Just stay where you are…" She quickly clambered down from the table and returned to her desk, from which she took a box of tissues and a small bottle of mineral water. She hurried back to where Abi sat.

"At least I didn't get any of it over your pictures," said Abi, still mortified.

"That doesn't matter – they're only computer print-outs anyway," replied Miriam. "But you've got some over that lovely dress. Here, by your bottom…" She handed Abi some tissues and proceeded to wipe away the wine on the table with several circular sweeps of the absorbent paper. She could now smell Abi's perfume, mingled with the scent of her warm body. She could see the small beads of perspiration on her chest.

Abi leaned to one side and dabbed the tissues over her raised haunch, to little effect. The wine had seeped through to her underwear. "Oh dear. This dress will have to go to the dry cleaner."

"I hope they can get the red stain out," said Miriam. "It might not be easy, with that fine white material. Let me see… do you mind if I try?"

"No, not at all."

Still standing, Miriam soaked a succession of fresh tissues with mineral water and dabbed them over Abi's upper thigh and the side of her buttock. This brought her face to within a couple of inches of Abi's. Suddenly she stopped dabbing and Abi straightened her posture. The two women looked hard into one another's eyes. They made the same decision at exactly the same moment and kissed each other, gently, slowly, on the lips. They made no other movement.

After a few moments Miriam drew back a little, catching her breath. She stared intently at Abi. "You are so *utterly* beautiful," she whispered. Hesitantly she touched Abi's thigh.

Abi put her forefinger up to the older woman's lips. "Not yet," she said softly. "When the time is right. Only then." She withdrew her finger.

Miriam nodded. "When the time is right."

"And then, yes," said Abi. "With no limits."

"No limits whatsoever," replied Miriam. "My darling, I'm going all the way to Heaven with you."

"You may end up in Hell," smiled Abi. "That's where I'm destined to go."

"It doesn't matter," said Miriam with a quaver in her voice. "Wherever *you* are, Abi, that's Heaven. The rest means nothing."

Downstairs the band started up again, even louder than before.

"Now that's *my* idea of Hell!" laughed Miriam.

VII

Wednesday 5th July, approaching midnight. Sebastian's flat in Islington

The red Porsche coupé slid to a halt in the car park at the rear of the small block of flats. Sebastian turned off the engine and the CD player. He squeezed Lola's bare white thigh.

"Okay, Lolly. Let's go up."

Lola turned to him. "So who's this friend of yours that's so keen to meet me?"

"Actually, you've met him once before."

"Oh? Who is he then?"

"Marcus."

"Marcus? You mean the bent copper?"

"Yeah." Sebastian avoided her gaze. He scratched his blond hair.

"Oh *shit*, Sebastian! You bring me all the way here and *now* you tell me! I can't stand that creep! He's a total sadist!"

"I know, darlin', but he's got a very nice present to give you, like I said earlier."

"Fifty grams?"

Sebastian nodded. "And some free Charlie as well."

Lola sighed, loudly. She was angry. "I guess he's passing me whatever gear he took from the last dealer he busted."

"I guess he is. But it's always top-grade stuff, I promise you."

"He's an arsehole. A real pervert. He totally gives me the creeps."

"Lolly, you can't afford to turn down a big freebie like this. Not when you owe the Boss so much money already."

"No, I suppose not…"

"And for fuck's sake, don't let on that you know Marcus is a cop. Or you'll end up floatin' in the Thames with a slashed-open throat. Got it?"

"All right," replied Lola glumly. "Got it."

They exited the car and walked into the rear of the flats, Sebastian's arm around her waist. A carpeted mirrored lift took them smoothly to the top floor, where his flat was located. In the expensively-furnished lounge the bright lights were full on and some cool acid-jazz was playing. On the black sofa sat Marcus, dressed in a Hawaiian holiday shirt and knee-length shorts, grinning at them as they entered. He was a large fat white man in his early forties, his short dark hair receding fast at the front. He had a thick heavy nose, greasy skin, and still carried the acne scars of his youth on both cheeks. Lola felt her stomach turn as soon as she saw him.

"Hi, Lola," said Marcus. "Nice to see you again, darling. Love the sexy dress!" He gestured towards the armchair opposite him but didn't bother getting up. Sebastian threw off his jacket and sat down beside him as Lola took the big chair. She smiled reluctantly at Marcus, who was already examining her legs.

"I've asked Charlie along to keep us company," said Marcus, pointing to several lines of white powder laid out on the glass coffee table. "I've already said hello to him. Hope you don't mind." He handed Sebastian a curled up banknote.

"Don't mind one bit, buddy," said Sebastian, leaning forward. He formed the banknote into a hollow tube and proceeded to snort the white line nearest to him. Satisfied, he nodded and returned the note to Marcus.

"Come on Lola," said Marcus. "Your turn."

Despite her unease, Lola took the tube and leaned forward. She knew it was the only way she could cope with what was coming. She took a long deep snort of the powder and then sat back in the armchair, gasping, her eyes widening. She looked up at the ceiling and moaned. It was certainly top-grade stuff. Her head was already charging away, leaving her body somewhere behind her.

"Good stuff?" asked Marcus.

"Uh-huh," replied Lola. "Fucking excellent." She spotted a thick black leather belt hanging over the sofa's arm, by his side.

"There's plenty more where that came from," smiled Marcus.

"And some smack?" asked Lola.

Marcus nodded. "Yes, plenty of smack. Enough to keep you going flat out for a whole week, darling! Are you interested?"

"Yep, definitely," nodded Lola. "Is it a gift from you?"

"Sure. A free gift. In return for a little… performance from you, tonight. You know, like last time. It was a few months ago, but I'm sure you remember."

Lola nodded. "I remember all right." Both Marcus and Sebastian were staring at her. "Can I have another line first? To get me into the mood?"

"Oh sure!" exclaimed Marcus. "There are three lines left. Take your pick, darling."

Lola got down on her knees and slowly snorted another line from the coffee table, longer than the first, and seemingly even stronger. Her head was now galloping fast, and a delicious numbness swept all over her.

Suddenly Marcus leaned forward and grabbed her red hair. He lifted her head.

"I think you're ready now, baby! Yes?"

Lola closed her eyes and nodded. She was resigned to her fate.

"Come on, Lolly," said Sebastian, getting to his feet. "Over here, on the rug."

Marcus let go of her hair and she got up, a little unsteady. Sebastian took her by the arm and stood her on a thick white circular rug in the centre of the lounge. Marcus walked towards them, the belt in his hand and a glint in his eye.

Sebastian stood at Lola's side. "Shoes," he said.

Lola shuffled off her black velvet shoes. Sebastian kicked them away, then reached for the clasp at the back of her red latex dress, at the top of the heart-shaped cut-away. The dress fell to her feet and Sebastian stooped to pick it up as she stepped out of it, now completely naked. Marcus had a big grin on his face and swung the belt from side to side as he stared at her body.

"Position," said Sebastian.

Lola spread her legs wide, her feet well over a metre apart, and placed her hands on her head. Her ribcage protruded starkly.

"Knees," said Sebastian.

Lola bent her knees a little, which pushed out her arse. This instantly aroused her. She was now eager to submit.

Sebastian smiled at Marcus. "She's ready for you, buddy!"

Breathing heavily, Marcus walked up to Lola. He squeezed one of her small nipples until she winced. Then he reached down to her crutch and felt her pussy.

"Is she wet?" asked Sebastian.

"Yes, nice and wet," replied Marcus, staring into Lola's glazed green eyes. She moaned sharply as he pushed a fat finger a couple of inches up inside her. "Lovely!"

"Charlie always has that effect on her."

"Which is why Charlie likes *her* so much," said Marcus. He stepped back and swung his belt in front of her. "Now, little girl, you're going to get what you've got coming to you. You know that, don't you?"

"Yes," replied Lola, growing excited. "I know I've got it coming to me."

"Kiss the belt, slut!" snarled Marcus, holding it up to her face.

Lola did as commanded, planting a long kiss on the belt. It was stiff and new and had a strong odour of leather, which always turned her on.

"Ask me to hit you, hard."

"Hit me hard, Marcus. Fucking hard." She started to breathe heavily as well. But she avoided his eyes.

"Say 'please'…" he said, his breath now so heavy it was hissing.

"Please, Marcus. Hit me really hard. I deserve it. I've been a bad little girl."

Abruptly Marcus swung the belt and lashed Lola on the thigh.
"Ooh!"

"You like that, bad little girl?"

"Yes, I like it. Hit me some more… please."

Marcus proceeded to hit her in a long sequence of snappy lashes, over her belly, her thighs, her breasts, her arms. She yelled out in response, as she was required to do, but really felt the pain… and genuinely felt the pleasure as well, courtesy of the cocaine. She shut her eyes hard, repeatedly crying out after each lash: "Ow!... Ow!... *Ooh*! Oh God, *fuck*! Ow… ow… *oww*!" But she doggedly held her submissive position, as if out of pride.

As Sebastian stood aside to watch, Marcus moved behind her and laid into her shapely buttocks and the back of her thighs. Lola's cries grew louder and sharper and her knees bent and twisted more and more under the non-stop pressure of the beating.

"Take it, you bitch! Take it!" shouted Marcus. Finally he tired of the effort and paused, breathing hard. He returned to her front.

Lola opened her eyes and her body began to tremble and shake. She sobbed. A solitary tear rolled down her cheek. Marcus caught it with his finger and licked it.

"Mmm… you're getting there, darling." Abruptly he grabbed her red hair and yanked her down to the floor, so that she was now on her hands and knees. He hung the belt down over her face.

"Want some more, you bad little girl?"

"Yes," said Lola, gulping. "I want some more." She caught the leather belt in her mouth and sucked on it, gorging on the taste of the leather. Tonight she was going all the way.

"You kinky bitch!" Marcus pulled the belt from her mouth and started lashing her again. Sebastian stood away from the action, smirking, and lit a cigarette. As the blows rained down on her back and her buttocks and legs, Lola lay flat on her belly and adopted a broken, twitching crawl, interrupted by each fresh blow. After a minute or so, Marcus paused. He walked up to her side and with his foot half-rolled, half-kicked her over onto her back. Her eyes were now wide and slightly crazed, staring up at him. Lola raised one arm, as if to plead for mercy, and he immediately lashed her hand, hard. She cried out but continued to hold her arm aloft while Marcus walloped it continually, up and down the forearm, until she couldn't stand it any longer and dropped the arm, squealing with pain. There was a broad crazy-girl smile on her face, as if she was trying to conceal her pain by pretending it was all a big joke. Provoked by this, Marcus leaned down and went to work on her belly and breasts, ruthlessly swinging away while she twisted and jack-knifed her body on the rug, again crying out and yelling. She lay first on one side, then on the other as the belt rained down on her without mercy. Then she folded herself up into a ball, wrapping her arms around herself, and began howling and trembling. Still the belt lashed down on her buttocks and thighs, which were now covered in vivid red welts and starting to bleed in a few places, the blood spotting the surface of the skin.

"Hey man, ease up," said Sebastian. "The kid's had enough. We don't want her ending up in hospital."

This snapped Marcus out of his frenzy, and he stood up, short of breath, wheezing. Lola lay twitching and whimpering on the floor like a beaten dog.

"All right," gasped Marcus. "Let's ease up." He pulled out a handkerchief and wiped the sweat from his brow. He belched. "Okay. Now it's time for *your* trick, my friend." He returned to the sofa to take a rest.

Sebastian went into the kitchen, opened the fridge and returned with a syringe, which had been prepared some time ago. He crouched down by Lola. His voice was soft and comforting.

"Okay, Lolly, it's all over now. Seb is here to take the pain away. This is your favourite hit, sweetheart." Lola offered no resistance as Sebastian found a vein in her forearm and injected the needle, carefully avoiding the red marks left by the belt. He was obviously well-practised. Marcus watched intently, fascinated by a ritual he knew nothing about. As the heroin flowed into her, Lola sighed with relief and pleasure. Her twitching stopped in a few seconds and she rolled flat onto the floor, down on her belly, now completely tranquillised. No more pain, no more worry... no more anything. A look of blissful acquiescence stole over her face as she stared glassy-eyed into the fluffy weave of the rug. She stretched out her arms and legs, exulting in the extremity of her capitulation.

Sebastian stood up and put the syringe back into its container.

"Nice work, my friend," said Marcus. "Thanks for knocking the bitch out."

"My pleasure."

"Are you leaving now? As we agreed?"

"Yeah. I have another rendezvous. Over in Hackney. To shift some of your gear."

"Good-oh. Will you be long?"

"As long as you want. I'll be back in the morning, if that suits you."

"Suits me fine, my friend," grinned Marcus.

Looking a little uneasy, Sebastian put on his jacket. "Hey, buddy, you make sure she's still in one piece when I get back, huh?"

"Oh yes," said Marcus. "In one piece, for sure. But it might not be a very pretty piece."

"Just take it easy, yeah?" said Sebastian. "Remember, we don't want no trouble." He turned away and walked calmly out of the flat.

Marcus spent some time gloating over Lola's inert body. Then he stood up and undressed, tossing his clothes over the sofa. Naked, he walked over to the virtually comatose girl. He knelt down behind her and rubbed her heavily marked buttocks. She was covered in welts, all over. A lovely job. All his very own handiwork… The profusion of lurid red marks and the girl's total helplessness quickly brought him to a full erection. He pulled Lola's slender legs wide apart, until the ginger pubic hair and the vagina were exposed. Noisily he cleared his throat to gather a mass of saliva in his mouth, then spat it out into the crevice between her buttocks, holding them apart with both hands to ensure that the bulk of his spittle fell onto her smooth pink anus.

Lola stirred, sensing that something unusual was happening.

"Sebastian? Is that you?" she moaned, drowsily.

"No darling, Sebastian has gone out for a while. It's just you and me now." Marcus took a deep breath and pushed his middle finger into her sphincter, squeezing as much of the spittle into it as he could.

Lola's eyes opened, expressing alarm. "Fuck… what are you doing?"

"I'm finishing the job, baby. The punishment this bad little girl deserves."

Marcus leaned down over her, supporting himself on one elbow, and slid his stiff cock along the crevice between her buttocks, moving it up and down, transferring some of the saliva onto his lengthy member. Finally Lola realised what was happening.

"Oh no… don't do that… *please…*"

"Oh *yes*. You're getting it, bitch, good and proper. Right now…" With the aid of one hand, Marcus eased his cock into her anus, which slowly opened out to accommodate him. Although the pain was muted by the heroin, the shock of being forcibly entered made Lola gasp. But she was too weak to make any movement. She couldn't fight back. Nonetheless Marcus grabbed the back of her neck with one of his big meaty hands and pressed her face into the rug.

Lola winced. "Oh you barst… you fucky *bastard…*" she gasped. Then she groaned loudly as Marcus pushed down hard onto her, thrusting himself all the way into her rectum. She felt as if her abdomen was being cut in half by a fiery truncheon. Wave after wave of grinding pain surged up into her bowels. Her fingers clawed desperately at the rug and she shut her eyes. Her voice became guttural. "*Ohh…*you pig! You fucking corrupt *pig!*"

"What did you say, you little goth-slut?" snarled Marcus as he ploughed his cock in and out of her rear. "Corrupt? Who are you calling corrupt? Huh?" Briskly he slapped one side of her face with his thick hand.

Lola whimpered and shook her head. "Nobody," she murmured. "Nobody… *ahh!*" She bit into the rug and began to cry. "Oh Abi," she whispered through her sobs. "I'm sorry… I'm so sorry…"

VIII

Tuesday 11ᵗʰ July, in the early afternoon. Miriam's studio in Bethnal Green, east London.

Miriam's studio-workshop was a unit in a busy and somewhat run-down industrial estate just off Cambridge Heath Road. Abi arrived there via taxi-cab shortly after lunch, although she hadn't had anything to eat, consuming only coffee and fruit juice since breakfast. She thought it advisable to keep her stomach empty for the session that lay ahead. She was tired after another night of disturbing dreams, in which she was once again displayed for all to see in a full body-length glass case under the merciless neon lights of a public gallery. This time Sebastian, complete with blond hair, had been one of the crowd of people gazing lecherously at her paralysed white body. With an effort, she banished the dream from her mind. Her lack of sleep was now beginning to catch up with her, but she was determined not to let Miriam down. She was dressed casually in a white T-shirt, denim shorts and gym shoes, with a large handbag for her personal items. Her dark hair was tied back into a long ponytail. She wore no make-up or jewellery, as per Miriam's instructions.

The entrance door was marked "Shoreditch College Photography Unit". She pressed the button in a panel by the side and heard Miriam's voice on the intercom.

"Hello, Abi. So pleased you could make it. Come right in, darling."

As soon as she entered the unit, Abi relaxed. The reception was a small white-painted area with a desk, behind which Miriam was waiting for her, smiling warmly. She was also dressed casually, in a grey track suit that matched her hair. Once again she wore her round glasses and the Venus ear-rings. The women kissed one another on the cheek, and Miriam led her into the main studio. Abi was relieved to see that it was nothing like the gallery in her nightmares, being a very spacious but drab workshop constructed of bare breeze-block walls, a concrete floor and a high timber-framed ceiling. The side walls were covered with hardboard display panels, to which a multitude of photographs and other illustrations had been attached. There were lights mounted on stands, waiting to be switched on, and a camera on a tripod. Cupboards and old wooden cabinets lined one wall.

"It's a bit darker in here than I expected," said Abi. "I can hardly make out the end of the room."

"Yes, I use minimal light in here until I actually start working," replied Miriam. "That way I reduce the power bills, which keeps the College happy. It pays all the rent for the workshop, so I can't complain. Fancy a cup of coffee?"

"No thanks, I've just had some. I must confess, Miriam, I'm a little tired. I had a bad night's sleep, as I so often do these days. But I don't think it should affect what we're doing. Perhaps a cup of tea?"

"Of course." Miriam went over to a small corner table on which were several mugs, a kettle and various packaged drinks and food. Abi followed her.

"Would you like a biscuit? Or some cake?"

"No thanks," replied Abi. "I like to work on an empty stomach."

"How very professional you are!" said Miriam. She glanced at Abi's T-shirt and noted that she wasn't wearing a bra. As she put the kettle on and prepared the cups, she looked pointedly at her guest.

"Thank you for your letter, Abi. I understand everything so much better now. About your car crash, and your subsequent health problems. Do you remember the accident?"

"No, I'm happy to say I can't remember a thing. I know that my car was a complete write-off. Somebody rammed into me at high speed and forced me off the road into a ditch. I'm lucky to be alive. I haven't been able to drive since then."

"It certainly explains your chronic fatigue. If you want, I can give you something to perk you up this afternoon. I use it frequently myself."

"That would be helpful."

"And thank you for explaining your relationship with Lola. I had suspected that you were... involved with her."

"Oh. Why?"

"Those identical nose studs. Classic same-sex fusion-wear. Always a giveaway!" Miriam laughed and poured the hot water into the cups.

"Yes, I suppose it is," smiled Abi, touching her stud. "Anyway, it's better to be honest with you, in case you find out from someone else."

"The way Lola speaks of you is also a giveaway. She adores you,

Abi. No doubt at all about that."

"Yes. I know how she feels about me. I adore her too. I just wish I could keep her away from… the wrong sort of people."

"I fear she'll always be drawn to the wrong sort of people. I think she uses them as a means of self-harming. Unconsciously, of course. So what happened to her after the college party?"

Abi frowned as she took the cup of tea from Miriam. "I haven't seen her since then. She rang me a couple of days ago to apologise and told me she wasn't feeling too well. Obviously she's been overdoing the drugs again. She also told me she's leaving Sebastian, who must have upset her for some reason. She sounded quite angry."

"She's leaving him? That sounds encouraging!" said Miriam, sipping at her tea.

"Yes, but she's left him at least half a dozen times before. She always goes back to him, and always for the same reason."

"Oh dear. It's a familiar tale. All too often with a tragic end." For a few moments they sombrely pondered Lola's future. Then Miriam reached into a little drawer at the top of the small table and took out a pill-box.

"Abi, I have something for you. To perk you up, and put you in the right frame of mind for our work this afternoon."

"What is it?"

"Some private medication. I use it myself from time to time, to give me a lift. Will you trust me and take it? I guarantee you'll enjoy the afternoon far more."

"All right," smiled Abi. "I trust you, Miriam. Otherwise I wouldn't be here in the first place."

Miriam smiled back and extracted a large gold-coloured pill, about a centimetre wide, and handed it to Abi. "Just swallow it, in one go. I assure you, darling, you won't regret it."

Abi immediately did as requested and washed the pill down with a gulp of the tea. Today she was in the mood to be reckless and do something completely different... something radical and rebellious. "So when do you want to start?" she said.

"Whenever you're ready," replied Miriam, quickly finishing her tea. She paused awkwardly. "First can I ask... did you do as I requested in our phone conversation yesterday?"

"You mean shave off my pubes?"

"Uh... yes. I hope that's all right."

"Oh yes," laughed Abi. "That's no problem. I'm always happy to do that for special clients. I'm now as smooth as a baby."

"And your underarms?"

To Miriam's astonishment, Abi abruptly raised her white T-shirt above her head and took it off, thereby revealing her immaculately shaved armpits, as well as her entire chest and belly. Miriam's attention was quickly diverted to the large pendulous breasts. She noted that one of the thick nipples was twisted and disfigured, but decided to say nothing. In fact the sight of Abi's body had momentarily left her unable to speak.

"Is that okay?" asked Abi.

"Uh, yes... absolutely fine," said Miriam, clearing her throat.

"Do you want me to shower before we start?"

"No, unless you particularly want to. I'm happy with your natural body-smell," said Miriam, recovering her composure.

"Good. So am I."

"Do you need to go to the toilet?"

"No, I'm fine. Can I put my clothes over this chair?"

"Of course."

Abi promptly dropped her denim shorts and then the blue cotton panties beneath them. She kicked off her gym shoes and stood there entirely naked. It was obvious to Miriam that she had no inhibitions whatsoever about exposing her body. After all, she did it almost every day to earn her living. And it was indeed a superb body… Miriam quickly turned her attention to the job in hand.

"Do you mind if I take a few preliminary shots of you, before we start? Just some simple face and body photos?"

"No, not at all."

Miriam switched on a couple of the lights above them, which hung from chains attached to the ceiling. The bulbs were shielded by metallic shades which had the effect of increasing the light. She walked over to her camera, a large, heavy-looking device, which had already been set up on a tripod. She disconnected it and beckoned Abi towards a spot beneath the brightest of the lights. Abi stood a metre in front of her, on a rug which protected her feet from the hard floor.

"All right, darling, I want to begin with a few close-up face shots."

"Do you want me to smile?"

"No. Just look thoughtful. Think about what you can do to help Lola…" Miriam started snapping, taking close-up frontal and profile pictures. After the first few shots, she paused. "You know, you remind me a little of Hedy Lamarr, the famous Hollywood actress, from way back in the nineteen-forties. Have you heard of her?"

"Yes. Wasn't she considered to be very beautiful?"

"Indeed she was. She had an exquisite face. Superbly sculpted, much like yours. Although in profile your nose isn't quite as *retroussé* as hers…"

Abi was amused. "Is that bad?"

"No, it's good. It gives your face more character, more strength." Miriam started snapping the camera again. "And your body, darling, is like Ava Gardner's! But with more muscle. Quite magnificent! Did you do a lot of sport when you were younger?"

"Yes, I did. Lots of hockey and tennis. And swimming. None of which I can do anymore."

"Well, you've certainly kept your figure very well." Miriam took a couple of steps back and took some shots of Abi's nude body. The pubic hair was completely shaved off, as requested, which exposed the upper folds of her genitals. Miriam's heart began to race as she snapped the camera. She barely resisted the temptation to zoom in…

"If I've kept my figure it's because I don't eat too well. Not since the accident."

"In that case, carry on not eating too well!"

"Lola says my breasts are too big and heavy".

"Nonsense. They're just right for a mature woman. A real woman has to have real breasts. Who wants little girlie-boobs? Now – can you turn round for me?"

Abi complied and Miriam took some shots of her back and her derrière.

"Interesting tattoo you have there, Abi. Between your shoulder-blades." Miriam zoomed in and took a close-up of the tattoo.

"Yes. Lola arranged to have it done for me."

"At the same place, I presume, where she got *hers* done. Lola's tattoo is identical to yours. I spotted it some time ago, when she modelled for some of my female Christ photos."

"That's right. You're very observant. They're exactly the same design."

Miriam adjusted her glasses. "It looks like a winged dragon of some sort. Quite demonic. A bit nasty, if you ask me. What does it signify?"

Abi paused.

"A supernatural connection. I can't explain it properly, and neither can Lola, but it creates a bond between us that transcends life and death. It's some kind of black magic, according to Lola. You know what a far-out goth-girl she is."

"How intriguing." Miriam was mystified, not only by the tattoo but by the nature of the connection between Abi and Lola, which was obviously stronger than she had assumed. She instinctively felt there was something unhealthy at the root of it. Perhaps Abi *was* destined for Hell after all – destined to be dragged there by Lola.

"Does my bottom pass the screen test?" asked Abi, trying to change the subject.

"Oh yes, it certainly does. With flying colours. For a woman of thirty-seven, Abi, you look quite wonderful. And your skin is the colour of fresh honey – all over! I'm so envious! Tell me, how tall are you? Without footwear."

"Five feet seven. Do you want to measure me?" Abi looked back over her shoulder and smiled mischievously.

Miriam stopped shooting. "I'll take your word for it, darling. I'd better not get too close. Not if we want to finish the job on time."

"There's no hurry. I'm here for you all day, if you want me," said Abi, still smiling. Miriam realised that the gold pill was beginning to take effect.

Abi continued. "Why do you want to know how tall I am?"

"I need your height for the cross," replied Miriam. "To get the foot-rest set up properly. I'd guessed five-eight, which is my height, so the setting I've made should be right."

Abi turned to face her. "Oh yes, the cross! I'd forgotten all about that. I haven't seen it yet. Where is it?"

Miriam moved over to the side wall and threw a couple of light switches, illuminating the far end of the workshop. She pointed towards a huge brooding horizontal object, pitch-black, suspended about a foot above the concrete floor. As soon as Abi saw the structure lying there she walked over to it, barefoot, oblivious of the rough cold concrete. The top of the cross, lying nearest to the far wall, held a thick wire cable which ran all the way up to a steel pulley in the ceiling; from here the lengthy cable ran down to an electrically powered winching mechanism bolted to the floor, some six metres in front of the cross. The whole thing could be raised or lowered simply by pressing a control switch one way or the other on the top of the machine. The base of the cross was connected to a hefty steel hinge, also bolted to the floor.

"This contraption is amazing!" exclaimed Abi. "It's so *big*! Can I sit on it?"

"Of course," said Miriam. "It'll easily take your weight. There's a support under the top of it anyway."

"It must be at least ten feet long!" exclaimed Abi.

"Actually it's nine feet," smiled Miriam. "And the transverse beam is six feet long. You can see the straps at either end which hold the wrists up."

Gingerly Abi sat down on the crossing point of the jet-black crucifix and opened her legs to plant her feet on the hard floor, on either side of the central beam. The feel of the glossy painted wood under her buttocks was thrilling. She closed her eyes and took a deep breath.

"What do you think?" said Miriam, now standing beside her.

Abi looked up. Her eyes were bright with excitement. "I can't *wait* to be tied onto this thing and hoisted all the way up. I've been thinking about this all the time since our talk at the college party, wondering what it looked like."

Miriam was taken aback. "Really? Since last week?"

"Yes. But in all honesty, for much longer than that!" laughed Abi. She paused. "Miriam, I have a terrible confession to make. When I was at convent school I used to fantasise about being crucified, naked, in front of a crowd of people. All of them respectable types: teachers, priests, parents."

"Oh, how sexy! Why in front of those respectable people, do you think?"

Abi opened her legs wider. "Because they reinforced my shame. And it was the shame that turned me on. Isn't that hopelessly sinful?"

"No, not at all. Strange sexual fantasies are natural, especially in childhood. How old were you?"

"The fantasies started when I was twelve. Well, almost thirteen."

"Where did you have these fantasies?"

"At first in the School Chapel, while I was on my knees praying and looking up at the figure of Christ on a big brass statuette of the Crucifixion. For some reason the sight of his suffering began to excite me. Then I'd imagine myself in his place, nailed to the cross, minus his loincloth, displaying my fanny to all and sundry. Later, I'd have the fantasies in bed, while the lights were out in the dormitory."

"Did you masturbate to the fantasies?"

Abi nodded. "Oh yes, for years. Lots of the girls masturbated. At first we were terribly ashamed and did it quietly. Later on, when we got older, we'd swap our fantasies… we'd whisper them to each other while we... while we were busy doing it under the sheets. The dorm became quite a noisy place, I can tell you! What about your school in Ireland?"

"Yes, a lot went on there, including seduction and sex. I lost my virginity to another girl when I was fifteen."

"I lost mine to my art teacher when I was sixteen. It was mainly my doing – I was the one who seduced *him*. I got him the sack and earned myself a five-star caning."

"Was this the same art teacher who became your husband?"

"Yes. And the father of my daughter. Conceived in the Art Studio at school!"

"Oh, *Abigail!* You've clearly been a bad girl from the outset! Maybe you *are* a hopeless sinner after all!"

"I'm afraid so."

"Let's talk about our schoolgirl sex lives later on. We don't have the time right now."

But Abi was enthralled, her mind still back at St Margaret's. "Now I think of it... some of our fantasies were pretty strong stuff, you know. I thought I'd forgotten all about them, but now... everything is coming back, so vividly!"

"I think the pill you took is helping as well, Abi. It's relaxing you and stimulating your memory, or your imagination, which is much the same thing. Do you feel good?"

"Oh yes, *yes,*" she sighed. "Better than I've felt for *ages.*"

"I'm so pleased. Let's start."

"Do you want me to loosen my hair?"

"No, keep the pony-tail intact. Can you make the band any tighter? I'd like the hair over your head to be pressed down as much as possible."

Abi started to adjust her hair as requested. "Have you used this... device before?" she asked.

"Yes, a few times. For taking pictures. In fact I've decided to keep it here permanently, like a big wild beast that you keep in the shed at the end of your garden."

"To impress your visitors?"

"That kind of thing," smiled Miriam. She moved away to gather her equipment: camera and tripod, a tall main light, a reflector, a short aluminium folding step-ladder, and couple of plastic bottles. The far wall was already covered with a grey velvet backdrop.

"This is about as tight as I can get my hair," said Abi. "Will it do?"

"It looks just fine. All right, darling – lie back on the cross..."

Abi took a deep breath. She moved her bottom down the cross

before lying back on the cold shiny wood. This was something of a balancing act, since the width of the beam was little more than six inches. The outside of her buttocks were squeezed and hung over either side of the timber in a very unflattering way. She placed her feet on the foot-rest, which was a diagonally cut block of wood, slotted into one of several holes, then spread her arms out along the transverse beam. Her head lay back on the hard flat wood, fractionally above the crossing-point. It all felt uncomfortable, slightly precarious, and far from sexy.

"How does it feel?" asked Miriam, looking down at her.

"Rather awkward…"

"Don't worry, you'll be fine when it's hoisted up. Now I'll strap down your wrists and your ankles." Miriam started with the wrists, securing them with padded black leather straps which were threaded through gaps in the wood and tightened from behind it. As her wrists were pressed down, Abi opened the palms of her hands. Suddenly she felt a thrill of excitement, like nothing else she had felt before.

"That's right," said Miriam. "Open out your palms as much as you can. When I have the pictures I'm going to airbrush some large thick nails into the middle of them."

"Wasn't Christ nailed through the wrists?"

"Yes, he was, but nailing the hands looks much more… meaningful. They're so much more erotic than the wrists!" Miriam proceeded to strap the ankles, again with padded black straps, so that Abi's feet were securely tied down and touching the foot-rest. The insides of her ankle-bones rubbed against one another. She squirmed with excitement.

"Can you open your knees comfortably?"

"Yes" replied Abi. "About a foot or so." As she opened her knees to test her posture, Abi's heart began to race.

"Are you feeling better now?" asked Miriam.

"Oh yes. In fact… I'm getting quite excited." She laughed nervously.

Miriam smiled. "I thought you would. It's a wonderful sensation, isn't it, being tied down and helpless? It's inexplicable, like all the most powerful experiences in life."

Abi sighed and nodded. Miriam knelt down by the cross and ran her hand over Abi's belly. The latter moaned with pleasure. Then Miriam gently fingered the deformed nipple.

"Did someone do this to you deliberately?" she asked, quietly.

"Yes. Someone drugged me and went too far with a set of needles. I'm sorry if it spoils your picture. Can you airbrush it out?"

"I could, but I don't want to. I'm going to keep it in, somehow – I'm not sure how, but I *will* include it in the picture. Oh Abi, it makes you even more beautiful. A sacrificial wound! On such a sensitive spot! I just *adore* it!" Miriam leaned over and gently kissed the wrenched nipple. Abi groaned with delight. Miriam took off her glasses and moved her face up close to Abi's. She looked intently at her beautiful captive. "Abi, I want you to enjoy this experience as much as you possibly can. With no inhibitions. Let yourself go and take as much pleasure from it as you can. All I ask is that you strike the poses and make the expressions I need…"

Abi smiled. There was now a soft dreamy submissive look in her eyes. "I'm completely in your hands, Miriam. There's nowhere else I'd rather be. I'll do whatever you want."

"Oh my sweet darling…" Miriam gave her a long and tender kiss on the mouth, to which Abi eagerly responded. For a few moments their tongues slid and rubbed together. Then Miriam stopped. She knelt up and put her glasses back on. After playfully pressing her finger on Abi's lips, she stood up and walked over to the winching machine.

"Are you ready?" she called out.

"I'm ready!" replied Abi.

"Here goes!" Miriam pressed the switch and the machine whirred noisily into life. There was a jerk on the cable and the gigantic black cross shuddered into life. Abi was shocked by how much movement and play there was as the crucifix slowly lifted her up and forwards. The pressure rapidly mounted on her wrists and ankles as the weight of her body pulled against the leather straps. The whirring continued relentlessly. Her buttocks began to slide down and she pressed hard onto the foot-rest, bringing her knees stiffly together. She started to breathe heavily, taking the strain that now seized her body everywhere. The contraption continued to shudder, adding to her anxiety.

"Aaaahh…!"

Miriam paused and took her finger off the switch. The whirring ceased. The cross now lay at an angle of forty-five degrees, hoisted half-way up.

"Are you all right, Abi?"

Abi crooked her head to look at Miriam, her chin pressed down onto her chest. "Miriam… it's a lot more stressful than I thought it would be!" she gasped.

"I think I need to adjust that foot-rest," said Miriam. "Hold on." She hurried forward and quickly undid the metal peg holding the foot-rest from behind. With one hand she lifted Abi's feet and with the other she pulled the wooden block out of its socket, then transferred it to another socket a couple of inches higher up. As soon as Abi's feet rested here, she let out a long sigh of relief. The pressure eased. Miriam resecured the foot-rest with the metal peg and adjusted the ankle straps. She stepped back.

"Better?"

"Oh yes, much better!" replied Abi. Now she was able to put more weight on the foot-rest and even open her knees.

"Good. Let's carry on."

Miriam returned to the winching machine and pressed the switch. The whirring noise resumed and the cross shook back into life. As it slowly, uneasily attained its maximum vertical position, the pressure on Abi's shoulders increased, especially in her armpits, and her ribcage pushed forward and felt as if it was opening out. Her breasts lifted high and eased apart. As the crucifix finally came rumbling to a halt, fully erect, her entire body jutted forwards, leaning away from the upright beam. Her buttocks were at least six inches away from the wood. She gasped and moaned again, but this time more with pleasure than with pain. She opened then closed her knees, and realised that her crutch was wet. She looked up and, to her astonishment, saw that the ceiling had disappeared, leaving only the vast expanse of the summer night sky, transparent and clean, filled with thousands of stars. Beyond that she felt there was a benevolent Presence gazing down at her. Something or someone that loved her…

Miriam released the switch and walked up to the cross. Her head was roughly at the level of Abi's genitals. "Oh my," she smiled. "*What a spectacle!* How do you feel now, Abi?"

Abi looked down at her. "Oh Miriam… it's so strange, but … I feel as if someone else is up there above me, in the night sky… looking down on me from above the stars…"

"Night sky? But it's only three in the afternoon!" A little concerned, she squeezed Abi's foot. "Are you sure you're okay, darling?"

Abi looked up again. Miriam's touch had banished the vision, and the workshop ceiling had returned. She shook her head. "Don't worry. I feel fine… it feels just incredible up here, spread out like this… I'm just so *free.* Like I'm embracing the whole world. I can't describe it… I feel as if I'm rising up…" She began writhing, slowly, from side to side.

"All right, Abi. I'm going to start taking some photos. Just relax." Hurriedly Miriam pulled the tripod into place and crouched down behind the camera, a few metres in front of Abi. She began clicking at once, first taking pictures of the spread-eagled body before zooming in to capture the expression of astonished joy on Abi's face.

"Abi… can you look down at me for a moment?"

Abi did as instructed.

"How do you feel now?" asked Miriam. She was concerned that the pill she had given Abi might be causing her to hallucinate.

"Spaced out…" replied Abi, as if in a trance. "Just totally spaced out… like I'm being drawn upwards into the sky… drawn out of my body… It's a wonderful feeling… so strange…" She continued to writhe, now backwards and forwards as well as sideways.

Miriam glanced down at one of the plastic bottles on the floor, by the tripod. It was full of amber-coloured body oil. She picked it up, along with the aluminium step-ladder, and walked over to the foot of the cross.

"Abi, I'm going to massage you, to calm you down. And to make your body shine. Just relax, darling." Miriam promptly poured a generous quantity of the oil onto her palms and crouched down to rub Abi's feet.

As soon as she felt the sensation of the oil being spread over her feet, Abi's attention was drawn downwards, back to her body. She looked down and to her astonishment saw that where Miriam had rubbed the oil, her natural flesh-tone had disappeared and she was turning into gold. Not just the skin, but the whole of her body was becoming gold, as if Miriam were King Midas, changing her into gold with every touch. Now she was moving up the calves and the shins, which were doing the same… then the knees… then the firm thighs, front and back, transforming into liquid gold, which followed exactly the contours of her body... then her hips, her backside, and her crutch... Miriam's hands moved smoothly over her genitals and up between her buttocks... then around to her lower back, up around the midriff... the shining gold streamed unstoppably up like molten lava, but without pain or discomfort... in fact it felt wonderfully warm as it flowed over, as it *became* her... it was exhilarating...

Miriam quickly brought the step ladder up to the cross and ascended it. Now her head was almost up to the level of Abi's. She poured more of the amber oil from her bottle and continued with the massage, seeing the tranquillising effect that her action was having on Abi.

Abi was now calm and steady and still as she emitted a series of long deep groans. Miriam's hands softly caressed her belly, which seemed to fill with molten gold-lava... then her breasts, cupping them lovingly in her hands to replicate their shape... it felt as if Abi's chest and lungs were now filling with gold as well, and her breathing seemed to stop... there was no longer any need for her to breathe, as her body was completely self-sufficient... the hands ran up her back, then behind, above and under the shoulders, over the smooth hollows of the armpits... then they stretched out in both directions to caress the arms... the wrists and the open hands, even each finger, streaming with liquid gold... then Miriam's hands ran tenderly around the neck, the ears, the back of the head, over the delicate features of the face... the chin, lips, cheekbones, nose, eyes, brow... all now shimmering with light, like a golden mask... finally they ran over the top of Abi's head... and she was at last all gold, every single part of her... gleaming with the self-generating, divine luminescence of gold... like the luminescence of the stars themselves, which she sensed, without having to open her eyes, had reappeared above her... and she was totally still, timeless, fixed in an ecstatic cruciform posture, her face now lifted to the heavens... a state of total perfection... she could no longer feel Miriam's hands... she was all alone, frozen in bliss, transfigured...

Suddenly Abi felt once again the Presence from above... from beyond the ocean of stars in the night sky... coming down to touch her... she felt long slender hands slowly, gently descending on her from above, reaching down to caress the back of her head. As soon as the hands touched her, she knew that the Presence was Annabel, her long-lost sister... rays of light flowed through the hands into Abi, as if coming down from the stars themselves... and she opened her mouth and sighed with joy, as if she was now saved, delivered from all the pains and burdens of her existence. The divine hands moved down her back and Abi felt the whole of Annabel's luminous Being standing behind her, in place of the wooden cross. Her sister was taller and stronger than her, as Abi had always recalled; full of vitality and confidence and devotion, always there for her... like her very own queen. Without the slightest hesitation, Abi let go and allowed her older sister to enter her and take over her body, her feelings, her thoughts, even her soul... she willingly abandoned herself and became one with Annabel, who flowed into her and filled her like a giant wave of shining love...

Annabel woke, with a smile of radiant joy on her face, and looked down from the Cross.

Miriam had clambered down from the steps and was now snapping away on her camera, determined to capture the expression of bliss on Abi's face, and capture the lustre of her body, its natural honey-brown tone splendidly enhanced by the amber oil. As Abi smiled down at her, Miriam stopped. She left the camera on the tripod and came closer. Abi's tawny eyes were shining with an unnatural brilliance that Miriam had never seen before. As if they had turned to gold...

"Yes," said Abi in a strange distant voice. She stared vacantly at Miriam, as if looking through her at someone else. Her face was ecstatic, as if she was about to weep with joy. Her knees parted, twisting her ankles. "Yes... *yes...*"

Miriam knew that the moment she had been waiting for had arrived. Hurriedly she removed her glasses and kicked off her plimsolls. Then she stripped off her grey tracksuit top and bottom, and finally her black knickers. Her entire body felt aglow with excitement, liberated from all constraints. She undid the straps holding Abi's ankles and removed the peg from behind the foot-rest. She held Abi's legs up high, grasping them with one arm around both calves, while she moved the foot-rest up by several notches, to a position almost two feet higher on the beam, before resecuring it with the peg as before. As Abi once more rested her feet, her knees, now raised to the height of her hips, opened out. Miriam carefully pushed them wider apart, until they were stretched out at almost the same angle as her arms. Abi's shaved vulva was fully exposed. Her sex was wet and swollen, and obviously in a high state of arousal; its inner labia had opened out to form a perfect heart-shape, and fluid from it had run down the inside of both thighs. Using her hands to keep Abi's legs spread wide, Miriam leaned forward and lovingly kissed the vagina. Abi let out a loud groan and the smile on her face broadened. For a few moments Miriam gently licked the stiff engorged clitoris. Then she plunged her tongue deep into the Holy Grail itself...

Annabel leaned back against the cross and gazed up at the starry sky. As Miriam started to lick her in earnest, hands caressing the inside of the spread-eagled thighs, the stars began to fall from the sky, one by one; and as each star fell, Annabel's golden body began to vibrate. She was in complete rapture, and pushed her groin into Miriam's face as the older woman's tongue lunged and twisted into her with ever-increasing urgency. Now Miriam too was moaning with pleasure; her face and even some of her grey hair was soaked in vaginal fluid. The musky odour filled her head like a narcotic. Eager for more, she began to rub her thumb rapidly over the distended clitoris.

Annabel lost all track of time. She was delirious. Her glowing body oscillated more and more quickly. Her thighs jerked and flailed uncontrollably and her buttocks slapped harder and faster against the wooden cross. Her wrists and her ribs were almost breaking under the pressure on them, but nothing was going to stop her now. The stars fell faster and faster, in greater numbers, many at a time, and soon they began to thin out, leaving larger and larger patches of inky-black sky. As they vanished, her body became ever more unstable, trembling and shaking more and more violently. Annabel knew that she was heading for destruction, but yearned for it without the slightest concern or hesitation. This was her fate... her deepest desire, the purpose and meaning of her existence. Finally the last few stars disappeared and the darkness of the void beckoned, as if the entire universe had become nothing but a vacuum of blackness, demanding to be filled... At this moment Annabel felt an eruption starting between her legs, an intense fiery explosion... and as if in slow motion, her golden body exploded, disintegrating in all directions at once, as if a bomb inside her had gone off... she was opening out like the supernova of a massive sun, bursting out into tiny gaseous fragments everywhere... her abdomen, chest and head erupted, her limbs flew apart, and even the smallest parts of her, her hands, her feet, her fingers and toes, dispersed into a multitude of tiny atoms, each glowing and burning with gold... It was the final ecstasy, the supreme moment of annihilation... yet she retained an awareness of herself spreading out everywhere and filling the entire cosmos... As the golden atoms moved farther away, to the very edge of her comprehension, they began to slow down...

they gradually coalesced into concentrations of golden gas, of various shapes and sizes… like clumps of solid matter… some massive, some tiny, some of them grouping together, some falling a greater distance from one another… and they began to form into spinning balls, like planets, rotating at different speeds on their own axes and circling in regular orbits around her. Annabel realised that these spheres of gold were her children, taking their life from her death… their creation from her destruction… living in a universe beyond her, yet forever part of her… eternally *her*. She had become divine.

IX

Monday 17ᵗʰ July, late in the afternoon. The office of hypnotherapist Dr Paula Masters.

"It was the most incredible, humungous, mind-blowing orgasm I've ever had," declared Abi, once more lying on the black leather couch in her white underwear, eyes closed. As usual Paula sat beside her on a chair, primly dressed in blouse and pencil-tight checked skirt, writing notes on a pad on her lap. Sunbeams streamed through the window blinds.

"It sounds truly awesome," replied Paula, somewhat perturbed. She removed her glasses. "Do you recall what happened next?"

"When I came round I was lying on the cross, which had been lowered back to its horizontal position. I was still strapped down. Miriam was all over me, making love to me."

"How long did that go on for?"

"I'm not sure. I'd lost all track of time. We ended up doing the *soixante-neuf* for absolutely ages. Luckily my feet *weren't* tied down and my legs were free. I lost count of how many times I came. Miriam came too, several times, on top of me."

"Double cunnilingus on the cross? How divinely blasphemous!"

"It was totally divine, I can promise you."

"It must have got rather messy after a while – all those humungous orgasms."

"Yes, it did get messy. Luckily Miriam's studio has bathroom facilities, so we spent a long time in the shower afterwards."

"And after that?"

"She drove me to her house in Camden Town and cooked us a lovely meal. Then I spent the night there, and the next morning. We carried on making love. It was very emotional, very passionate. Like nothing I've ever experienced before."

Paula scowled, but her voice was unchanged. "I must admit, this woman has some style. It's one hell of a way to seduce somebody – crucify them!"

"She wanted to photograph me, for her upcoming exhibition."

"She wanted to fuck you." Paula put her glasses back on.

"Lots of people want to fuck me. That's how I make my living."

"So this is different?"

"Yes, very different. I feel safe with Miriam. She really cares for me. She understands me. I've never felt so close to anyone since I was a child. I think she's in love with me."

"Are you in love with her?" Paula sounded concerned.

"I don't know. But I know I love being with her. I love the way she looks after me."

"Looks after you? My goodness, Abi, it was *very* irresponsible of her to give you that pill. It was obviously a powerful drug. It could have done untold damage to you." Paula scribbled on her notepad.

Abi opened her eyes. "What do you think it was?"

"From your description, it sounds like Ecstasy, or some variant of MDMA. Not the sort of thing you should be taking, given your condition. Does Miriam know about your health issues?"

"I've told her a little. About the car crash and my problems since then. But not everything."

"Have you told her about the treatment you're receiving from me?"

"No. I don't want her to think I'm... flaky or unstable."

"Very sensible. I don't think you should tell her anything. If you do, she might become jealous and try to undermine the work that we're doing."

"I don't think she's that type. She's very broadminded and liberal."

"Believe me, darling, nobody is broadminded or liberal when it comes to being in love."

"Yes... you're probably right. I won't mention it to her."

"So how have you felt since... that mind-blowing experience?"

Abi closed her eyes.

"Physically, I'm okay now. I had nervous tingles and rushes for a day or two afterwards, but then they stopped. The real problem is that... I keep feeling that Annabel is with me."

Paula stopped writing and took off her glasses. She stared hard at Abi. There was the slightest hint of a quaver in her voice.

"Annabel is with you? Your older sister, you mean?"

"Yes."

Hastily Paula resumed writing. "Exactly when did this feeling begin?"

"When Miriam was rubbing my body with oil. While I was upright on the cross, hanging from my wrists. I felt as if Annabel was above me, up there in the sky... and then she flowed down into me as I became more and more excited. When I had the first, really massive orgasm, I felt that it was happening in *my* body but Annabel was the person who was experiencing it. She had taken over my body…"

"Did this worry you? Or frighten you?"

"No. Because I loved her and trusted her, I was overjoyed to surrender to her. In a way I can't explain, we had the orgasm together. That's why it was so powerful. The two of us melted into one another, as if we'd become the same person. It was just wonderful. Totally ecstatic."

Paula closed her eyes and took a deep breath. "And since then?"

"Since then, I've been aware of her being with me… like a Presence who walks with me and talks to me. I keep hearing her voice."

"Is she there all of the time?"

"No, only some of the time. She comes and goes."

"Do you think that this Presence is actually Annabel? Her spirit or her ghost… contacting you from beyond the grave? Or is she some kind of hallucination?"

"It feels as if it actually is her. But she's not a ghost, in the normal sense. I don't see her like a phantom standing there beside me… I just feel her inside me."

Paula continued to scribble furiously. "Is she still sixteen? The age at which she died?"

"No. It's odd, but she's the same age as me. Well, a year older than me, as she always was."

"How intriguing. So what does Annabel say… when she's talking to you?"

"She tells me I should quit doing the work I'm doing. That it's immoral and destructive, and takes advantage of other people."

Paula snorted. "Easy enough to say. But you've been a sex worker for years, Abi. And it's given you a comfortable life, with plenty of money and as much free time as you want. A beautiful flat in London. What else could you possibly do that pays so well?"

Abi sighed. "Nothing. You're right, I know. I'm stuck with this work… unless I deal drugs instead. Which I couldn't do…"

"Of course not. Drug dealers harm others. They make money out of other people's misery. *You* make money out of their pleasure. It's altogether different."

"Yes. Maybe what I do isn't so immoral after all."

"It's not immoral, I assure you. You have to carry on with it, Abi. What else does Annabel say to you?"

"That I'm in danger, and mustn't trust any of the people around me, except for Miriam."

Paula sighed. "Yes, I fully expected her to say something like that."

Abi opened her eyes. "Why?"

"Because, my dear, Annabel is a classic schizoid projection – a projection which your mind has created to express your paranoid anxiety. An anxiety that's fully understandable, given your recent history and your medical condition. Your confusion since the crash."

"You mean that she *is* a hallucination?"

"Essentially, yes. She's a fragment of your subconscious mind which has broken away and taken on a psychic existence of its own. It's all there in the writings of Jung, you know. The danger is that Annabel could end up possessing you, so that you lose your mind completely."

"You mean I'm going mad?"

"No, not necessarily. Your brain has been traumatised by the drug that Miriam so recklessly gave you, obviously with the intention of stimulating you for her own selfish advantage. Abi, two people can't *actually* exist in the same person. But they can *appear* to exist, if the mind becomes sufficiently deranged. Multiple personality is a sign of severe paranoia, and suggests the possibility of serious mental illness. It requires urgent treatment."

For a while Abi contemplated the implications of what Paula had said. She looked deflated, but also felt a little relieved.

"Can you treat this paranoia? Or do I need to see somebody else?"

"I can certainly try to treat your problem, Abi. I've come across cases of paranoid delusion a number of times before, and the right type of hypnotherapy often works wonders."

"What do you suggest we do?"

"Give me a day or two to consult my records and think about suitable therapeutic treatment. In the meantime, take a double dose of the pills you've been taking for the last few months. I'll give you another packet today. And darling – make sure you stay away from *all* illegal drugs! Remember – they're illegal for a reason!"

Abi nodded. She laid her head back on the cushion. Uneasily, Paula stroked her chin and tapped her notepad with her pen. As she looked at Abi, who was staring vacantly up at the ceiling, an idea came to her.

"Abi, to help you deal with this problem, I'm going to put you under for a little while. To take you back to somewhere we've been before. Are you ready?"

"Yes." Slowly Abi shut her eyes again.

"Good. Let's begin. I want you to take a deep breath and put your arms alongside your body."

Abi obeyed and stiffened her body, bringing her knees and her feet together. Her arms pressed close to her side, and her hands touched her thighs. She breathed in deeply; her stomach sank and her ribs and her breasts rose, straining the white bra. Paula leaned over and started gently rubbing Abi's brow with her forefinger, making a slow circular movement. Abi's head relaxed into the black leather pillow.

"Now, Abi, I'm opening your Third Eye, as I always do. Just relax and let the middle of your forehead open out, like a circular gateway… a gateway into the past."

Once again Abi found herself walking out of a dark cave, out into a sunlit day, by the sea.

"Move out of the cave and onto the sandy beach, Abi. Look out to sea at the transparent blue water, reflecting the sun. A beautiful, tranquil, sunny place... looking out to sea."

"Yes," murmured Abi. "A beautiful place..."

"It's a Greek island. There are high slopes on the coast around you, covered all over with lush green trees and bushes that reach all the way down to the blue water. You're fifteen years old and you're on holiday here with your family. Do you remember?"

""Yes... I remember..."

"You're looking out to sea, wondering where Annabel has gone. You were swimming in the sea with her, but when you turned back she refused to come with you. For some reason she carried on swimming, and went further out... until you couldn't see her anymore."

Abi shook her head. "I don't know where she is... she should be back now, on her way back, but I can't see her anywhere in the water."

"Finally you ran back and told your parents that she was missing. But none of you could see her. You all called out for her, shouting out at the sea... calling her name..."

"Yes. We ran up and down the beach and called for her... but there was no reply... Finally dad ran to get help... and I knelt down at the edge of the water and realised that I wasn't going to see her again... I just *knew* that she'd gone."

"The next time you saw Annabel she was in the morgue, the following day, after the police had recovered her body."

"Oh God, yes... in the morgue." Abi's face began to contract with grief. Her mouth turned down.

"Tell me what you saw... this time in more detail. Describe the morgue."

"It was a small room... brightly lit, by big neon lights in the ceiling.

White tiled walls… a narrow window with rusted iron bars… a cracked cement floor… the smell of disinfectant. It was a nasty, horrid place."

"And Annabel?"

"Annabel was lying there naked, on a grey marble slab in the middle of the room. That's how they found her, washed up on the beach, without her bikini. Her body was twisted and covered with scratches and scars… covered with wounds… Her shoulder was broken and stuck out at an odd angle. Her palms were turned up… She looked so helpless – as if she was imploring someone to save her. But nobody did…"

"And her face?"

Tears began to run down Abi's cheek as she recalled the scene. "Her face was… horrible. Her features were twisted. Her eyes were open wide and staring up at the ceiling… her mouth was gaping, as if she was screaming in terror at the moment she died. Screaming like a terrified child calling for help… she looked as if she had died in despair… in total horror…"

"It was grotesque, wasn't it – to see Annabel looking like that?"

Abi nodded. She started to cry, softly.

"Abi, you should know that Annabel didn't drown by accident. She was a strong swimmer… the champion swimmer of St Margaret's School." Abi's brow creased. She was puzzled. Paula continued. "When Annabel was out at sea, she sensed that something uncanny was present beneath her, deep under the water. That's why she swam so far away. Finally she saw something huge and dark and powerful… something monstrous, moving about in the thick swirling weeds down there on the sea bed. It looked like an exotic sea-dragon. For some reason, she was drawn to this creature and swam down towards it… she dived down beneath the surface of the water."

"Oh God… why?"

"Who can say? Only Annabel could explain why. It was probably something… erotic that suddenly woke in her, which she couldn't control. She was excited and fascinated by this powerful monster and couldn't resist it… in some strange way it attracted her, hypnotised her, drew her down to itself… drew her down to her doom. Because as soon as she swam down close to it, the dragon reached out its tentacles and pulled her into its embrace… and it slowly crushed her to death. That's why her body was covered with wounds, and why her ribs and her arms were so badly broken. Do you remember now?"

Abi groaned. "Yes, yes, I remember now. Oh God, how awful. No wonder she looked so broken. So horrified by what she'd seen…" She began to perspire.

Paula nodded. "That's right… she died in a state of sheer horror, in terrible agony, drowning in despair. Do you know why? Because that vile monster sucked out her life, sucked out her soul, while she was drowning. That was the *true* horror… Annabel's very soul was devoured by this dragon from the deep. It was a beast that came up from Hell itself. To take Annabel back down to Hell with it! In other words, Abi, Annabel no longer exists, in this life or the afterlife."

Abi shook her head from side to side, sobbing. She was now sweating with anguish. Paula touched her wrist. "It's all right, Abi. There's nothing you can do about it. What happened all those years ago wasn't your fault. You were the sensible one. It was Annabel who was reckless, who was perversely drawn to danger and threw away her life… and even lost her immortal soul. But she was damned from the beginning. There was something corrupt deep inside Annabel, which none of you could see. She let you all down, Abi. Especially *you*, her younger sister, who relied on her so much, who thought she was noble and trustworthy and worshipped her like a hero. That's why everything went wrong at school, Abi, the following year. Because you reacted by behaving recklessly, just as Annabel did… *you* were drawn to a powerful beast that took you into its embrace. A beast that ravished you – in his own classroom! That's why your school career was ruined, and why you've ended up where you are today… it was all Annabel's fault!"

Abi moaned. "Oh Annabel… why?"

"If you see Annabel again, Abi, that's the question you must ask her. Will you ask her?"

"Yes… I will. I'll ask her why…"

"You'll find she won't be able to answer your question. Because Annabel doesn't exist anymore, Abi, except in your own imagination. If you bear that in mind, at all times, you won't be troubled by her again. Do you understand?

"Yes… I understand."

"Very good. Now, darling, you need to relax. Withdraw back into that cool dark cave and lie down. Just rest… relax for a while. Sleep… sleep…"

Abi immediately calmed down and fell asleep. Paula got up and moved to her desk. On it lay a number of hefty old psychiatric and pharmaceutical textbooks. She put down her glasses and casually leafed through one of the books, without paying any attention to its contents. She glanced at the aluminium chair on which Abi had deposited her yellow shirt dress and her large handbag. Paula noted that a long pink envelope was sticking out of the top of the bag. Curious, she extracted it. The envelope was addressed to Abi and had been delivered to her that very morning. It had already been opened. With her back to Abi, who was sleeping soundly, Paula quietly pulled the card from the envelope. On the front was a painting of a gorgeous red rose. Paula opened the card to look at the inscription within, a quotation from a poem, which was written in tall, elegant handwriting.

Beloved, let your eyes half close, and your heart beat
Over my heart, and your hair fall over my breast,
Drowning love's lonely hour in deep twilight of rest.
              Miriam

Paula frowned. She returned the card to its envelope and put it back in the bag, in exactly the same position. She adjusted her short bobbed red hair and returned to the chair next to Abi.

"All right, Abi. You've had a good rest. It's time to wake up now." She leaned forward and pressed her finger onto the centre of Abi's brow, again making a slow circular movement. "Now, Abi, I'm closing your Third Eye. Just relax and let the middle of your forehead become a gateway... a gateway back to the present time... the here and now. And slowly, slowly... open your eyes." The tawny eyes opened as commanded.

"How do you feel?"

"Calmer than before. But confused... about my sister."

"You need to forget her, darling." Gently Paula touched her patient's wrist. "Just remember, if she does come back – ask her to explain why she did what she did. She'll disappear, I promise you."

Abi nodded.

"And I'd suggest that you stay away from Miriam if possible."

"Why?"

"Because she'll probably remind you of Annabel, after what happened in her studio. And that's not good for you."

"Well, I won't be returning to her studio. That was a one-off experience. At the moment she's gone to New York, to give some lectures and discuss a future exhibition there. I won't be seeing her for a couple of weeks."

"All right. When you do see her, don't accept any more pills from her. Doctor's orders!"

Abi nodded again. "I think I should get up now."

Paula held Abi's upper arm to help her sit up. Abi's body was hot and clammy, as was customary at the end of these therapy sessions. As she rose, Paula could see her sweat stains glistening on the black leather couch. She suppressed a sudden thrill of excitement. "Better?" she asked.

Abi nodded. Paula moved away and stood by her desk, smiling, as Abi put on her shirt dress.

"How's Lola doing?" asked Abi.

"She's not been too well lately. Too many late nights again, I suppose. But she tells me she's left Sebastian."

"Good. About time!" said Abi, as if this was news to her. She slipped on her shoes and picked up her handbag. Paula handed her another packet of the medication.

"Remember – double dose! Two tablets twice a day!"

"Yes."

Paula summoned Francine via her desktop intercom. She kissed Abi on each cheek, and Abi reciprocated, while Paula deliberately squeezed her left hand in her own. She fixed her eyes on Abi's. "I'll ring you in a few days, darling. Make sure you stay in touch! Make sure…"

"Yes," said Abi, returning the gaze, her expression momentarily vacant. "I'll make sure… I'll stay in touch."

"Brava!"

Francine came in, dressed as usual in her short white nurse's tunic, and saw Abi out. Paula took a deep breath and extracted a cigarette from a case in her desk. She lit up and went to the window. The sun had disappeared behind some dull grey clouds, and Paula pulled up the blinds while she inhaled the smoke. She was pensive and uneasy.

Now she understood the meaning of the Queen of Cups in her Tarot spread. It was Miriam.

Francine returned to the office. "Anything wrong? You look a wee bit… concerned." She removed her kitsch nurse's hat and dropped it onto the desk.

Paula spun round. "You bet I'm concerned! That fucking photographer has thrown a king-sized spanner in the works. She could derail the whole project. The last thing we want is Annabel coming back from the dead!"

"Can't we do something about the photographer? Scare her off?"

Paula shook her head. "She's too well known. Lola has told me all about how famous she is. She has influential friends and contacts all over the place. That means it would be too risky to make any move against her." She drew hard on her cigarette and walked to the desk.

"You can't make Abi break off the relationship?"

"No. The affair has just kicked off. Her emotions are running high. Nothing I can say will persuade her to drop Miriam. Even with hypnosis, you have to go with the flow, not fight against it."

"Then you'd better talk to the Boss," said Francine. "After all, it's his money that's paying for all this."

Paula nodded. "I'll ring him tonight. I need some time to think about what we ought to do next." Glumly she put the cigarette out in an ashtray. Francine smiled and moved up to her. She touched Paula's long thin arm.

"I think you need to relax, sweetheart. Even someone as brilliant as Doctor Masters has to have some… refreshment from time to time."

Paula grinned. "Oh yes? And what does my dutiful nurse have in mind?"

Francine moved up close and squeezed Paula's trim backside with both hands. She stood some six inches below Paula, and looked up at her slyly. "How about some… horizontal refreshment?"

Paula reached down behind Francine and lifted up her short tunic. She squeezed her plump buttocks. "Why, you wicked old tart – you're wearing your lacy thong. Most unprofessional!"

Francine ran her tongue around her heavily rouged lips. "Tell me, doctor. Is that big beast of a strap-on still in your desk?"

"Funny you should ask… yes, that big beast *is* in my desk."

Francine brought her face up even closer to Paula's. "In that case… why don't you strap it on and give me a good hard fuck on the couch? While it still smells of Abi…"

Paula licked her thin lips. "That's what I like about you, Frannie. You always make me offers I can't refuse!"

The two women pressed their faces together and hungrily plunged their tongues into each other's mouths.

X

Monday 17th July, late in the evening. Abigail's flat in Notting Hill, London.

The sun was so bright and so hot that the white sand beneath Abi's feet almost burned her. Alone, with no-one else in sight, she walked slowly along the beach, wearing a yellow bikini. The sky was an intense azure, almost dark blue, and dazzled the surface of the clean, calm, transparent sea. There was no movement on the water, not a single wave. It looked more like an enormous swimming pool than the sea, but the horizon stretched out into infinity, as if it were indeed a vast ocean. Around her, curving on both sides like a pair of giant horns, was a bay formed of steep sloping hills, which were covered in a dense forest of dark green trees and bushes that ran all the way down to the water. She felt as if the forest was full of strange and sinister presences which were staring at her, watching her every move. There was no sound, either from the forest or the sea.

She turned away from the water and looked at the high sloping hill behind her, which was also covered with dark vegetation. There was a narrow gap in which a long flight of white marble steps had been cut, constructed with perfect precision, running straight up to the very top of the hill. It was the only way out of the deathly calm bay, so Abi walked up to it and started to ascend the steps. With surprising rapidity she reached the top. Here the ground was flat, paved with perfectly engineered white flagstones, and contained a small white marble temple, with a Greek pediment above the columned entrance, facing her and obviously inviting her to enter. She walked straight in and her eyes were dazzled by the bright neon lights in the ceiling. In the centre of the temple was a massive glass cabinet, irregular in shape, placed on a granite plinth; and at its head, at the far end of the cabinet, stood Paula, patiently waiting for her. Paula's vivid red hair fell in a long flame-coloured cascade down to her waist, and she wore a full length black gown with a large gold crucifix on her chest. She looked like a High Priestess awaiting her celebrants. She smiled, and with her left hand beckoned Abi to approach the cabinet. On the middle finger she wore her customary black-stoned silver ring.

As Abi moved up to the glass structure, which lay on the plinth at waist height, she realised that it was shaped like a six-sided coffin, broadening out widely at the shoulders. To Abi's surprise it contained a life-sized crucified figure, lying horizontally. The huge cross appeared to be made of gleaming black onyx, and on it lay a nude woman's body, made from what seemed to be beautifully sculpted white marble.

Abi moved closer and at once realised that this was Annabel. Her sister was completely shaved, with no hair anywhere, and lay with her arms outstretched and knees raised, opened wide and sharply bent, bringing the feet up high on the black cross so that they were almost touching the buttocks. It looked as if Annabel were about to give birth. Her hands and her twisted feet were cruelly pinned down with large thick black nails. As Abi moved right up to the glass and touched it, she saw that Annabel's face was disturbingly contorted, her mouth gaping wide open and her eyes – their pupils painted black – rolled up into her head. It was impossible to say whether she was expressing terror or ecstasy or despair, or a grotesque and indecent combination of all of them at once.

"Annabel brought this on herself," said Paula, looking at Abi. Her voice echoed strangely around the temple.

"Oh my God. Is she dead?"

"Yes."

"How did it happen?"

"It was the sea monster. The Dragon of the Deep. He devoured her because she swam out too far. She swam down to him at the bottom of the sea because she wanted to die."

"Why does she look so horrible? Why is she in such pain?"

"Because she's a sinner and she's lost her soul," replied Paula. She looked down at the white figure.

Abi was aghast. "Where is her soul?"

"In Hell. Eternally damned."

Abi looked at her sister's face and began to cry. "Annabel... oh Annabel! Please come back! Don't leave me! I need you so much!" She climbed on top of the glass cabinet and lay on her belly, hugging the coffin with her arms and her legs, getting as close to Annabel as she could. But the glass was impenetrable, too strong to break, and as much as Abi pressed against it and tried to open it, the cabinet held firm.

She looked up and saw that Paula had left the temple. In her place was a crowd of people, most of them wealthy and well-dressed, some of them women, who had already surrounded the glass coffin and were looking at her with a predatory intent. Among them she recognised blond-haired Sebastian and the elderly man with the sharply cut beard. All of them were grinning at her knowingly, malevolently. As they began to close in, she heard the sound of a strong sea wind howling outside the temple. She looked down again at the white figure of Annabel. Her sister's face was now streaked with crimson tears, the colour of blood, which ran down in thin trails on both sides of her face.

"Annabel! My darling Annabel! I'm lost without you!" sobbed Abi. Then she screamed with horror as a multitude of hands grabbed her defenceless body, dozens of fingers clawing into her flesh from all sides at once...

Abi twisted abruptly and felt her head push up against the arm of her settee. She gasped with shock and woke up, her eyes open wide. She was lying on her side, her legs drawn up tight, knees pressed together. Exhausted after her session with Paula, she had fallen asleep on her settee, still in her underwear. It looked as if the wind had blown up from the street and pushed in the French windows of her lounge, which gave access to her small exterior balcony, and the curtains were swishing and billowing into the room under the pressure. She shut her eyes and fell back, sighing with relief, stretching her limbs to relieve the tension. After a few moments she opened her eyes again. Her glass of wine, on the tiled coffee table by the settee, had fallen over, perhaps toppled by the gusting wind, and a little red wine had spilled over the table. Fortunately there hadn't been much left in the glass.

As she gradually came to, Abi listened to the flapping and knocking of the French windows and suddenly remembered that they had been locked when she'd fallen asleep. Uneasily she got to her feet and went over to the double doors. The metal keep of the lock, which accommodated the bolt, had been yanked away from the timber frame and was hanging at an odd angle, and the two screws which had held it in place had been almost entirely pulled out. Only a powerful force from outside could have caused such damage. The mild summer wind, blowing with only an occasional light gust, was incapable of doing so. Her hands shaking, Abi pushed the screws and the keep back into position. As a temporary measure she inserted the bolt in the keep in order to re-close the doors; then she pushed them shut, knowing that they were completely ineffective in such a damaged condition. She would have to call out a workman to repair the breakage. In the meantime, she felt even more vulnerable, even more at the mercy of the forces closing in on her. She understood now that they were the same forces which had destroyed Annabel. She knew, therefore, that she would stand no chance against them when they finally came for her. No-one could save her.

XI

Wednesday 19th July, early in the evening. The street outside Abigail's flat in Notting Hill, London.

Abi had finished another day's work. She gazed out of the taxi-cab window as it entered the elegant nineteenth-century street where she lived. The weather had turned grey and cloudy and some serious rainfall looked increasingly likely. She was glad to get home before the downpour began. She was dressed in her short pale orange dress, complete with high-heeled rust-coloured sandals. The open back and plunging V-neck of her dress would leave her uncomfortably exposed if the rain did catch her out in the open. She had neglected to bring her umbrella.

The taxi stopped at a convenient spot a few metres from the big house that contained Abi's flat, which was up on the second floor. All the buildings were large, tall, classically ornamented Victorian townhouses, complete with basement flat and a flight of half a dozen granite steps leading up to the rather grand white-painted entrance-porch. To Abi's surprise she saw Lola sitting half-way up the stairwell leading to the entrance of her house. She walked away from the taxi and stopped at the foot of the stairwell, clutching the strap of her leather handbag. Lola had clearly seen her coming, and was insouciantly smoking a cigarette, looking away. She was dressed in her black leather basque and short red-checked skirt, plus heavy black studded boots. Her hair had been dyed a garish red, verging on purple. She wore her silver death's-head pendant.

"Lola!" exclaimed Abi. "Oh my darling, I haven't heard from you for *ages*! Why haven't you returned my calls? And why are you sitting out here?"

Lola looked at Abi and laughed sarcastically. "I see you've been at work today, Mama!"

"You know what I do for a living, Lola."

Lola stared hard at her. "Fucking hell, Abi! You look so sexy even *I'd* pay to fuck you! And I'm broke!"

"You don't need to pay me anything. You can fuck me whenever you want. You know that."

Emphatically Lola shook her head. "No. No, never again!"

"What's the matter, Baby?"

"Don't bullshit me, Abi. You know what's the matter! You've been fucking my favourite college teacher! A woman I admire. A woman whose respect I desperately want. A woman who can help me get an education and find a decent job. Don't you think there's something the matter about that? Or are you going to deny it?"

Abi sighed. "I see. No, I won't deny it. It's true. Miriam and I have started an affair. It wasn't my intention but that's what happened."

Lola, who had retained some hope that Abi *would* deny the affair, and that there was in fact no affair, became enraged. She threw her cigarette down the steps, narrowly missing Abi. "You fucking old whore! Is there anyone you *wouldn't* shag?"

"Yes, plenty of people. But I'm afraid Miriam isn't one of them."

"Who started it, then? Who seduced who? Whose idea was it to make me look like a total fucking idiot? Jesus, it was *me* who introduced you to each other!"

"We're equally responsible for what's happened. We're both grown-ups."

Lola put her head in her hands.

"I didn't want you to know," said Abi softly. "I didn't want to hurt you, Baby. You must know that."

Lola's head, still in her hands, shook from side to side. The first spots of rain began to fall.

"Who told you?" asked Abi.

"Does it matter? If it's all true?" sniffed Lola.

"No, I suppose not."

"Why did you do it?" demanded Lola.

"Because... Miriam's given me something that nobody else ever has. Something I badly need right now. It's hard to explain, but..."

Lola looked directly at her. "Do you love her more than me?"

Abi shook her head. "No, Baby, I don't. Not at all. Nobody can replace you – nobody, ever." She took her handbag off her shoulder and moved up to join Lola on the steps. She sat down close beside her. Gently she put her arm around the girl's shoulders.

"I'm so sorry, Lola. Truly I am. Please try to forgive me."

Lola eased nearer to Abi. Then she shook her head, forcefully, and pulled away. "No, I'm *not* going to be seduced by you. Not anymore!" She pushed Abi away and got to her feet. She took a couple of steps down and stood over Abi. Her face was contorted with rage. She clenched her little white fist.

"I'd like to smash your face in, you bitch! For totally humiliating me!" The rain started to fall harder, spotting Abi's light dress and her exposed legs.

"All right," said Abi calmly. "Hit me if you want to. I won't try to stop you."

Lola leaned down and moved her fist to within an inch of Abi's head. Abi looked up at her, still and unflinching, sadness all over her face. Clearly she was prepared to take whatever punishment Lola wanted to give her.

"Oh *Jesus!*" exclaimed Lola. "How can I hit you when I love you?" Briefly she sobbed. "But I *hate* you as well, you fucking tart!" Abruptly she grabbed a sizeable chunk of Abi's dark hair and wrenched it to one side, then downwards.

"Ow!" cried Abi. "Ooh!" Under the pressure of Lola's frenzied grasp, she half-rolled and half-slid down three steps, ending up on her side, in an unseemly heap, at the foot of the stairwell. As she hit the pavement, the side of her head bumped against the lowest step, momentarily stunning her. Instinctively she drew up her legs, exposing most of her yellow silk panties in a gross and ludicrous manner. Lola moved closer to her and raised her heavy boot. She thought for a moment of kicking Abi's backside, but couldn't bring herself to do it. Instead she contemptuously pushed her boot down on the panties, leaving a grimy print over one buttock. Abi squirmed under the pressure, then curled up and began to cry, her arms around her face. One of her shoulder straps had slipped off, as had one of her sandals. The contents of her handbag had spilled out over the lower steps. The rain began to fall in earnest, soon drenching her flimsy clothing.

"We're finished, you old whore!" snarled Lola. "Forever! Bye-bye, *Mama!*" She turned and walked away up the street, oblivious of the rain, sobbing, angry, aware only of how much she loved Abi and how much she hated her at the same time.

An elderly woman with an umbrella walked up to Abi, who lay sprawled on the pavement. "Oh my goodness! What *terrible* behaviour! Are you all right, my dear?" Still sobbing, Abi turned her body and sat up. Her hair was soaked and one of her breasts was fully exposed, wobbling as she moved, on the side where her shoulder strap had come off. The silver-haired woman leaned down and put her umbrella over Abi, as if to protect her not only from the rain but also from the gaze of the half dozen passers-by who had stopped to witness her humiliation. Abi tried to compose herself. She sat up on the bottom step and pulled up her shoulder strap, to cover her breast.

"My goodness, you're absolutely *drenched!*" continued the woman. "And you seem to have a cut on the side of your head."

"I'll be all right," said Abi, sniffling. Another passer-by had crouched down to retrieve the sandal and the contents of her handbag. He returned these items to Abi.

"Thank you," said Abi, putting her sandal back on. "Thank you so much." The woman and the man each took hold of one of Abi's bare wet arms and slowly, awkwardly helped her to her feet. She was now shaking from the wet and the cold and the shock of Lola's assault.

"Did she try to rob you?" asked the woman, still holding her umbrella over Abi's head. "Do you want us to call the police? Or an ambulance?"

"No. It's not necessary," replied Abi. The rain eased off momentarily, and the spectators began to move away. The drama was over.

The woman squeezed Abi's arm. "Are you sure you'll be all right, dear?"

Abi mustered a weak smile and nodded. The woman walked off, shaking her head. Abi took a deep breath and let out a long sigh. She felt slightly dizzy, and the side of her head throbbed. Uneasily she sat down again on the steps, now puddled with rainwater, and absent-mindedly checked the soggy contents of her handbag, which rested on her lap. After a few moments she stopped. She leaned forward and dropped her forehead onto the bag.

"Oh darling," she sobbed. "My darling girl! I've lost you again!"

XII

Wednesday 19ᵗʰ July, shortly before midnight. Abigail's flat in Notting Hill, London.

Abi lay naked on her bed, face down, in a profound sleep. Her rain-soaked clothes, shoes and handbag were strewn over the carpet. She had taken a strong painkiller to subdue her headache and dizziness. Then, grieving over Lola, she had cried herself to sleep.

Around midnight she became aware of the sound of pouring rain outside. Slowly she turned her head to one side and opened her eyes. She saw that the bedroom door was ajar and the main light from the lounge ceiling was shining in. The sound of the rain seemed louder than ever before. As she gradually woke up, Abi thought that she could also hear the rain pouring down inside her flat. She listened for a long time, fascinated by the sound. Presently she rose from the bed and stood up. She was in a strangely euphoric state, upright, almost rigid, her arms pressed down at her sides as if she was standing to attention. She couldn't lift them. In fact she couldn't move anything of her own volition. Even her eyes stared ahead, unblinking. It was as if someone else had taken control of her body, even though she was fully conscious of what was happening and could acutely feel every physical sensation. Then she sensed Annabel's presence, somewhere in the flat, and realised that it was her sister who had taken over her body and was now guiding her, trying to make contact with her. But Annabel was trapped somewhere, prevented from coming to Abi. So *she* had to go to Annabel. As soon as she acknowledged this, Abi felt herself walking forward, slowly, methodically, one heavy step at a time, with the deliberate measured tread of a robot. She moved into the lounge and paused by the coffee table. She saw that her hallway door and beyond it the entrance door of her flat were wide open, and that the light in the communal lobby was also on. She sensed that there were people outside, waiting in the lobby to enter her flat… perhaps waiting to see what she was going to do. But none of this disturbed her. She heard the sound of the teeming rain, now louder than before, and finally realised that it was coming from her bathroom. The door was open and the room was also brightly lit. She walked into it. The sound of rain was in fact the water from her shower unit, in the far corner of the rectangular bathroom, pouring down at full pelt from the large shower head in the ceiling, blasting down into the open glass cubicle. The drainage grill could barely cope with the volume of water. Even from a distance of several metres, she could feel the freezing air assailing her skin. The temperature control had been moved all the way over to the blue mark, which meant that the water was set at maximum coldness.

Abi looked up at the ceiling. It had disappeared, revealing a clear night sky filled with a magnificent ocean of stars. She knew that Annabel was up there, trapped somewhere beyond the stars, somewhere cold and harsh and barren, unable to return to this world. So she was summoning Abi to her. The only way to reach her was through the ice-cold waterfall in the shower. She realised that the cascade of freezing rushing water was a portal, a gateway to the realm where her sister was waiting for her. Perhaps she *was* in Hell. But Abi knew she had no choice but to join her. Her body still rigidly upright, her eyes still unblinking, she took a few steps forward and paused at the edge of the shower cubicle. The cold was so intense that it made goose-pimples stand up all over her body and made her nipples erect. The noise was deafening. Abi knew that she would suffer unbearable agony as soon as she entered the gateway. But it was the only way she could meet Annabel… and meet her own destiny. Everything had led up to this point. There was no turning back. It was time to cross the threshold. She took a deep breath and stepped into the shower.

*   *   *   *   *   *   *

XIII

Tuesday 1ˢᵗ August, at midday. The office of hypnotherapist
Dr Paula Masters.

PAULA SAT AT HER DESK, attired as usual. Facing her sat a slim, bearded, slightly balding middle-aged man in a black leather jacket and denim jeans. His hair and his beard were dyed jet black.

"All right, Geoff," said Paula. "What have you got for me?"

Geoff passed a manila folder to her across the desk. "I've typed up my notes and given you prints and negatives of all the pictures I've taken. There's quite a lot of them."

"Good. Give me a quick summary, then." Paula pulled a cigarette case out of her desk.

"Well, let me see… in the last ten days she's been to Oxford twice. Visiting the town centre, the colleges, the Medical School – although she didn't actually go in anywhere. She's been looking around the residential streets in North Oxford, though she didn't seem sure of where she was going."

This seemed to perturb Paula. "So much time in Oxford? Did she drive there?"

"Yes. She drove there on her own, both times. I think she was using a friend's car. An old Jag – quite a nice motor. She picked it up and dropped it off in Camden Town."

Paula looked puzzled. "I thought she wasn't able to drive anymore… after her crash. How strange. Did she go anywhere else?" She opened the case and offered it to Geoff.

"Ah, Turkish fags. I rather like those." He took one of the cigarettes.

"Yes," resumed Geoff, "she's been around a lot of places here in London. Earls Court, Soho, Covent Garden. Three different hospitals – I've listed them in the notes. And she's been walking around Whitechapel, Brick Lane, Primrose Hill…"

"Primrose Hill? You mean just round the corner from here?"

"That's right."

"Did she walk past this building?"

"No. Not that I ever saw. She just stayed in the park, sitting down and staring at the zoo. Then she went back towards Chalk Farm, then down to Camden Market."

"How intriguing. Was she with anyone? Did she speak to anybody?" She flicked her lighter and held it up as he leaned forward with the cigarette.

"No, not that I could see. Thanks…"

"Anything unusual in the way she behaved, or looked?"

"Well, unusual…" He drew on the cigarette and then exhaled the smoke before replying. "I have to say she wandered around pretty slowly, and looked a bit… you know, tranced out. A bit vacant. She didn't seem to have any clear direction, or any sense of where she was going. You know, walking back to the same place a few times… sort of going round in circles. And then she'd return home."

Paula's brow furrowed. "I see. How was she dressed? Anything out of the ordinary?" She lit a cigarette for herself.

"Out of the ordinary? Yes, I suppose so… in the sense that she always wore the same gear when she was out wandering."

"Oh? What sort of gear?"

"Let me think… light blue blouse, short-sleeved, open-necked… grey skirt, maybe three inches above the knee… knee-high white socks… black shoes. She carried a small black handbag and looked quite smart, quite professional. But I thought the white socks were a bit peculiar. They made her look a bit like a schoolgirl, I suppose…"

Paula's hand froze in mid-air as it held the cigarette. Quickly she put it in the ash-tray and opened the manila folder. She ignored the typed notes and inspected the photographic prints. After looking at about a dozen, she put them down and picked up her cigarette. There was now a heavy frown on her face. She looked over at the window, deep in thought.

"Anything interesting?" asked Geoff.

"Yes. Very interesting. She's definitely wearing a school uniform. Or rather, some clothes she's bought which resemble a school uniform."

"Oh? Any particular school?"

"Oh yes. A very particular school."

"You recognise it?"

Paula nodded.

"How come?"

"Because I went there myself."

"Ah. I see." He pulled on his cigarette.

At this point Paula decided to end the conversation. "Okay, Geoff. Thanks for doing such a thorough job." She drew a brown envelope from a desk drawer and handed it to him. "It's the amount we agreed. And I've added a few grams of Charlie as a bonus."

"Why, thank you kindly," said Geoff, getting to his feet. "Let me know whenever you want more surveillance done."

"Will do. Can you see yourself out?" Geoff nodded and left.

Alone, Paula inspected the photos in more detail. The clothes were clearly recent acquisitions by Abi, intended to recreate the mind-set of her time at St Margaret's School. Or was it something more? As Paula examined Geoff's close-up zoom-lens images she noted that Abi had trimmed her hair and removed the chestnut highlights, restoring the original dark brown colour. Then she spotted a slender gold crucifix on Abi's chest. She shut her eyes. It was worse than she had thought. She now realised that Abi was using the semi-schoolgirl apparel and the change of hair to channel the spirit or the presence of Annabel, and was being directed in her wanderings by her departed sister. It was Annabel, through Abi, who had driven the car to Oxford, and then walked around the town. Paula's aversion therapy had failed to exorcise her. And Abi had failed to return for more treatment, no doubt under her sister's instruction. It was a serious setback.

She stubbed out her cigarette and picked up the phone. It was time to talk to the Boss.

"Hello? Frannie?"

"*Why, Doctor Masters. Such a pleasure to hear from you.*"

"Can you get Bernie for me, darling? It's quite urgent."

"*Hang on…*"

After a few moments Bernie came to the phone. "*Paulie? How you doing?*"

"I've felt better, Bernie. I've just spoken to Geoff. He's been tailing Abigail for the past couple of weeks and he's reported back to me, with lots of notes and pictures."

"*Uh-huh. What's the score then?*"

"It looks to me like we have a problem. She's behaving oddly. She's revisiting Annabel's old stamping grounds. I think she's still obsessed by her, even being guided by her. I tried to scare her off Annabel the last time she was here, but it hasn't worked."

"*Have you tried again? Have her in for a few more sessions.*"

"I'd love to. But she hasn't made another appointment, and she's failed to answer my calls. Someone or something has got to her."

"*You mean that fucking dike photographer?*"

"I think it's more than that. Miriam's been away in New York for the last couple of weeks. Abi's been on her own. Lola has walked out on her, after I told her about Abi's affair with Miriam."

"*Was that a good idea – telling Lola?*"

"I thought it would help. I hoped Lola would put emotional pressure on Abi to leave Miriam. But it seems to have backfired. Lola's in a more volatile state than I thought."

There was a heavy sigh on the line.

"Sounds like things are going a bit pear-shaped, Paulie. Your Lola needs to watch her step. A bent copper called Marcus, who's one of Seb's suppliers, is getting all paranoid about her. Seems she let on she knew he was a copper, while he was giving her a seeing-to a couple of weeks ago. Now he's out looking for her. Lucky for her her college has closed down for the summer. I suggest you hide her somewhere for a while, or send her away on a long holiday."

"All right. I'll take care of her. As for Abi, it's possible she's just gone off the rails. Cracked up mentally. It was always a risk, given her condition."

"You were supposed to be straightening her out, Paulie. You've had months to work on her, since she had her... accident. I thought it was all done and dusted by now. You telling me she's flipped her wig?"

"It looks like it."

"Then your Resurrection Project has come off the rails. Mr El Hashem isn't going to pay us a fortune for damaged goods, or for someone who's flaky and won't do what she's told. He's been very patient so far. He could easily buy someone else. Someone a lot younger."

"Yes, but he knows he won't get anyone with Abigail's looks and class. That's why he wants her so badly. She's the ultimate trophy. A beautiful English rose he can display in his vase, to impress his rich and powerful friends. Who's interested in some poor little Third World slave-girl? They're ten a penny."

There was another pause.

"Paulie, if this thing does go pear-shaped, don't forget about my expenses. I invested a lot of money in this project. I'm a businessman.

I hate losing money."

"Don't worry about that, Bernie. I have an idea about how we can recoup your money, and even make a profit."

"Okay, Paulie. I hope you know what you're doing. You realise we have a problem on our hands if the project flops? You understand what I'm saying... what we do with Abigail..."

"I understand. You can leave her to me."

XIV

Tuesday 1ˢᵗ August, late in the afternoon. A hotel in Greenwich Village, New York.

Miriam closed the door behind her and strolled into the light airy hotel room. Merrily she lobbed her slim briefcase onto the cosy white bed. It had been a successful afternoon's work. She had finally agreed terms for her Divine Woman exhibition with the Gallery, after some tricky days of one-to-one negotiation, and now, this afternoon, a meeting of the full Gallery Board had finally accepted her conditions. Artistic control was always the important thing. She had also dispelled concerns about the potential reaction to her Crucifixion photographs, persuading the Board that she was not motivated by anti-Christian sentiments but rather was attempting to redefine the Christian religion for the New Millennium, attempting to integrate it with feminist perspectives in order to preserve it, to make it relevant for the present and the future. She was looking forward to celebrating with her agent and a friendly journalist in the rooftop bar later on. But first she needed a rest and a shower.

She kicked off her shoes and unzipped her navy-blue dress, before throwing it over the bed. She moved to the mirror above the desk to view herself and patted down her short grey hair. She was reasonably happy with what she saw. As she unhooked and removed her beige bra, she noticed the pink envelope on the desk. It was the only item in her morning post, which had arrived after she'd set out for the day. She surmised at once that it was Abi's bold tidy handwriting on the envelope. She felt relieved. Abi hadn't rung her since the end of her first week in New York, and hadn't returned her calls during the last few days. Pink was a friendly colour. Miriam picked up the envelope and felt a sudden rush of delight. A handwritten letter from Abi! She tossed her bra onto the bed. Smiling, she opened the envelope and began to read.

27th July 2000

Dear Miriam
Forgive me for contacting you in this manner, but I have no alternative. I can't contact you directly, but only through Abi, who is willing to allow me to use her in the physical world that she inhabits and I do not. Forgive me if what I say is not clear or doesn't make sense, but my presence is this world is not as strong as I would wish it to be.

Miriam paused and her brow furrowed. For a moment she thought this was some sort of bizarre satire, or a silly practical joke. But that kind of humour wasn't at all Abi's style. She continued to read.

Abi and I are ultimately one and the same person. We are more than just sisters – we are twin beings, our souls are entwined, and we shall in the end be as one, forever united. She is the lesser part of me and I am the greater part of her. She sees only fragments of my existence, for a limited time, and I see all of hers all of the time. Please believe that when Abi had her accident last year, I was the part of her that died, and I am the part that desperately needs to return to Abi, to save her from the evil forces that now seek to destroy her in this world. Abi is in complete agreement with my wishes, and is doing everything she can to allow me to come through and become one with her. She is now alone, and no longer in contact with anyone else, no longer doing the abusive and self-destructive work that she was tricked into doing several months ago, after her accident, so she is now more and more open to my influence. She is willing to suffer great physical and mental pain to contact me, just as I suffered great pain when I died last year. I've been opening up her memory by taking her to many of the places in your world that I used to inhabit, and she is remembering more and more of my past existence, which is also her past existence. But she is prone to forget things and become easily distracted. Sadly her mind has been damaged. Our two worlds, our two pasts, have been broken asunder since the accident last year, which was in truth not an accident but a great crime committed against us by a woman whose soul is steeped in wickedness beyond your understanding. She is truly a limb of the Devil. She must be stopped before it's too late. If she isn't, Abi and I will fall back into the Eternal Abyss, and our souls will be forever frozen in time, forever at the mercy of the Evil One.

Miriam felt hot flushes running over her face and neck. She could feel fresh perspiration under her breasts. Her heart was pounding. She sat down on the edge of the bed and took a deep breath. She went on with the letter.

Therefore we need your help, Miriam. You've already done so much for us, by opening up a gateway for me when you made love to Abi in your studio, when you elevated her soul to a level which at last allowed me to enter her. Please believe that she did allow me to do this, willingly, because she trusts and loves me, as she has always done. But she needs you now, urgently, so that you can help her to complete the connection between us and repair the terrible damage that has been done to us.

Please help us. We need your love and your understanding, and cannot survive without you.

Annabel

Shaken to the core, Miriam put her hand over her mouth and gazed out at the Empire State Building, glittering in the late afternoon sun. She struggled to interpret the letter in a way that made sense, but couldn't. She looked at it again. It was obviously written with the utmost seriousness and sincerity, and was clearly in Abi's own hand. She recalled Abi mentioning her long-deceased older sister Annabel once or twice, but never at great length. Then Miriam had an attack of anguished guilt. The allusion to the opening of a gateway in her studio was an obvious reference to the gold pill that she had given to Abi before the photo-shoot. Miriam recalled the effect it had had on her at the time. Now it was all too obvious. The drug had broken down some inhibition or barrier in Abi's unconscious mind that she, Miriam, had had no idea existed. And now something insane or at best profoundly irrational had come pouring out and overwhelmed Abi's reason. Very likely she *was* on her own, all alone in her flat at Notting Hill, suffering the most appalling delusions and fantasies as her mind unravelled. And it was all *her* fault... for pushing Abi too far, too soon.

Miriam dropped the letter and rushed to the bedside telephone. In a few moments she managed to reach her agent's mobile.

"Sophie, it's me... Yes, I'm fine, darling, but I've just received some bad news from London. A dear friend of mine is sick and needs me to be with her as soon as possible. I'm sorry, but I'm going to have to cancel my talk at the Photographic Institute on Thursday, so I can fly home tomorrow... Yes, I know they'll be disappointed... I know... well, you can let them have the text of the lecture, and send them my profound apologies, but do stress that this is an emergency... a personal matter... Yes, thank you Sophie. I do appreciate it."

Then she rang the hotel reception desk. "This is Miriam Hirst, Room 609. Can you let me have details of the first available flight to London Heathrow? As soon as possible, please. Yes, it *is* an emergency. Thank you."

XV

Thursday 3rd August, in the middle of the evening. Miriam's house in Camden Town, London.

Abi and Miriam sat in the latter's commodious lounge, crowded with books, magazines, vinyl records, photographic prints, pot plants and a big old piano. They reclined on her blue velvet Art Deco sofa, which had reputedly belonged to Greta Garbo in the 1930s, while opera music played softly on the record player. Maria Callas, *La Divina*, was Miriam's favourite singer.

"Abi, I'm so relieved," she said, putting her arm around Abi's shoulder. "I thought I'd return to find you rolling on the floor, chewing the edge of the carpet, or at the very least foaming at the mouth." She ran her finger over the shoulder strap of Abi's pink summer frock.

Abi laughed. "Oh God! I can well believe the letter gave you that impression. But it's not quite like that. As I've discovered, possession is a slow, dreamy process, leaving you in a kind of trance. It's like being hypnotised. You know what's happening, and you know you're following someone else's commands, but you can't do anything about it. Your body no longer belongs to you. It's as if you've turned into a kind of robot, programmed by someone else. You just go along with it." She leaned further in towards Miriam and drew up her legs until her bare feet rested on the thick sofa.

"It still sounds rather creepy, Abi. Someone else taking control of your mind… I wish you'd told me all about this earlier. It's really come as quite a shock."

Abi put a hand on Miriam's thigh and squeezed her brown leather trousers. "I'm sorry, Miriam. I didn't want you to think I was crazy. So I kept a lot of my problems hidden from you. I thought that maybe, in time, they'd pass. Instead they've got worse."

"Was this sparked off by the photo-shoot in my studio? When I gave you that pill?"

"That's probably what triggered the recent episode. But it didn't really start up until you'd left for New York. I had a little… set-to with Lola, who pushed me down the steps in front of my flat, out in the street. I got a bang on the head. Nothing much, but enough to send me into a confused mental state. I fell asleep, then got up a few hours later, around midnight, and found all the lights on, all the doors open and the shower full on, freezing cold. Annabel was telling me what to do. I couldn't resist her. She was always stronger than me, and I was always happy to do what she wanted. But this time she told me to go straight into the cold shower. If I did, I'd join her... in her world."

"So you did as she said?"

"Yes. I trusted her."

"What happened?"

"The cold shower was excruciating, as I knew it would be. But I wanted to show Annabel how brave I was. The pain was intense. But as much as it hurt, I couldn't withdraw. Annabel made me stay there and take the pain until I passed out."

"You poor thing – how awful! What happened next?"

"Eventually I came to, in a cold snowy desert, under the night sky. It was full of stars. Maybe that's what they call the 'astral world'. It was like being lost at the North Pole. Annabel was waiting there for me. She was naked and cold, just like me. She was also completely shaved, without any hair, even on her head. She looked so strange – like an alien from a science-fiction film. But we held each other close and cried. To meet again, after so many years..."

"I can imagine. It must have been very emotional. What did she say to you?"

"More or less what she wrote in the letter. It didn't make much sense to me, and still doesn't. But I had no choice but to send it to you, as she instructed. I'm sorry you had to cut short your trip."

"It doesn't matter," replied Miriam. "I got what I wanted from the visit. My Divine Woman exhibition is now ready to launch in New York, in time for Christmas."

"I'm so pleased for you. When does it open here in London?"

"Next week. You must come along to the opening day at the Black Sun Gallery."

"I'll be there, I promise."

The two women kissed for a few moments. The voice of Callas

rose to a sharp crescendo, then fell back, melancholy and tragic. They listened for a while.

"This is such a beautiful song," sighed Abi. "So sad. So heartfelt. What is it?"

"It's called 'Vissi d'arte'," replied Miriam. "One of my favourite pieces. *Vissi d'arte, vissi d'amore.* It means 'I lived for art'…"

"And 'I lived for love'," interjected Abi.

"That's right! Do you know 'Tosca'?"

"No, but I know Italian," smiled Abi.

"Of course you do!" laughed Miriam. "I'd forgotten that."

They carried on listening, holding hands, until the aria came to an end. There was a lengthy pause before Miriam continued.

"Tell me, darling," she said. "How often have you made contact with Annabel since the first time? By going into the cold shower, I mean."

"About half a dozen more times. And each time was painful and traumatic."

"Six more times? In two weeks? My God!" Miriam shook her head. "So how does it start? The contact with Annabel?"

Abi sighed. "I get the urge to start masturbating… and then, when I've played with myself for a while, I visualise Annabel – in my mind's eye – and pretty soon I can feel her Presence approaching."

"Like a ghost, you mean?"

"No, from inside me. From the deep pool of darkness inside me."

"I see. Do you masturbate about anything in particular?"

Abi looked down at the thick rug at their feet. It was difficult for her to answer the question. But she knew she had to be honest with Miriam. She had cut short her business trip just to come home for her. She deserved to know the truth. Abi took a deep breath.

"I imagine I'm in the morgue… looking at Annabel's dead body, with all her injuries and that horrific expression on her face… and I get excited. I get turned on by her lifeless body, lying there so helpless and so twisted... and I get turned on by the fact that she's been killed by some terrible monster, at the bottom of the sea... that she actually *wanted* to get killed by that monster, or dragon, or whatever it was."

"Oh my goodness!" said Miriam, taken aback. "That sounds so..."

"Sick?" Abi looked up at her.

"I was going to say 'extreme'. Does anything else happen in your fantasy?"

Abi paused and swallowed. "I start kissing her, with the utmost love and tenderness... as if I worship her. That's the point – I always did worship her, as if she was my hero, my very own Wonder Woman. And now she's lying there dead, helpless, right in front of me... and I love her so much!"

"You want to become one with her? By making love to her dead body? By *entering* her body?"

"Yes. If I can enter her body, I can be dead like her."

Miriam raised her eyebrows. "And that's what you want? To be dead?"

Abi nodded, a little shamefully, and looked down at the rug again. Miriam let out a long exhalation. "Do you eventually reach orgasm with this fantasy?" she asked.

"No... I stop just short. When I finally open my eyes and wake up, I can feel Annabel's Presence. It's like she's there beside me... or behind me..."

"Is she upset by your fantasy? By you masturbating over her dead body?"

"No. That's the weird thing. *She's* the one who's encouraged the masturbation, and the fantasy that comes with it. She *wants* me to do it. To become aroused by her. To get close to her."

"How intriguing. So what takes place when you've woken up, and feel Annabel's Presence nearby?"

"While I'm still sexually excited, I stand up and find myself under Annabel's control. That's when she guides me into the shower. Because I'm so aroused, I actually *want* to go in. I actually *want* the pain and trauma of the freezing cold shower. It's the ultimate liberation. That's how I unite with Annabel. By re-enacting her agony, I align myself with her. It's like a demonic ritual. It takes me through the gateway to…"

"To death?"

"Yes, it leads to death, for sure."

"And then your soul goes to Purgatory?"

"No, straight to Hell. If you're one of the damned, there's no point in going to Purgatory first. Hell is the cold dark wasteland where Annabel is trapped. So I go to Hell to be with her, which is where I belong. Hell is being *trapped*, spiritually. Being stuck in the same place, the same state of being, with no chance of escape. That's one thing I've learned from all this."

They paused for a few moments. Miriam, somewhat shaken, decided to change tack.

"Tell me – how does the shower come on, before you get to the bathroom?"

"I'm not sure. Either someone else puts it on, or I do it beforehand and go back to bed. The same with opening the doors. Maybe I'm under Annabel's influence before I realise it, like a sleepwalker, and I prepare everything in advance the way she wants it. Then I wake up later."

"I think the sleepwalking explanation is much the more likely," said Miriam. "And what happens afterwards, when Annabel leaves you?"

"I gradually come round, lying on the bathroom floor, shivering like mad. And then I more or less return to normal. Although… since my first full contact with Annabel, in the snowy desert… up there in the astral world... I've had a nagging pain in my abdomen, just below the navel. It's a gnawing pain that comes and goes. I've never had anything like that before."

"It's probably stress. A psychosomatic reaction to all this trauma. It must have been horribly difficult for you, darling, over these last couple of weeks. Have you really been all on your own, as it says in your... in Annabel's letter?"

"Yes. I've not been seeing any clients for the last couple of weeks. And I've finished with Lola. Or rather, she's finished with me."

"I'm sorry about Lola," replied Miriam. "I'm sorry that someone told her about us. But maybe, in the long run, you're better off without her. A heroin addict is only going to end up dragging you down with her."

Abi slowly nodded.

"I wonder if we'll see her again next term, at the college," went on Miriam. "You just never know."

"I wonder if *I'll* ever see her again," sighed Abi. She looked dejected. The opera music came to an end and the record player switched off. There was a pause before Miriam continued.

"Abi, did you stop taking the medication that Paula's been prescribing for you?"

"Yes. I stopped on the evening I broke up with Lola. Actually, I'd been taking fewer and fewer of the pills during the previous week. I think it was Annabel's influence. She was trying to stop me."

Miriam looked pensive. "I don't agree with everything that your Doctor Masters does," she said. "You know I'm sceptical about psychiatrists, or therapists, or mind-healers, or whatever they call themselves. But unfortunately they are necessary. If Paula was trying to keep Annabel away from you, I think she was acting in your best interest. Especially after what you've just told me. If you carry on fantasising about your sister – if you continue to be possessed by her – you'll end up being sectioned. That would be such a tragedy. For me as well as for you." She stroked Abi's arm.

Abi nodded.

"My darling, you'll have to keep on taking Paula's medication, even if it has side effects that you don't like. It's the lesser of the two evils."

"But it doesn't feel evil when I contact Annabel," protested Abi. "When I'm finally face to face with her, holding her, she's like a dazzling angel, pouring out love and kindness, even though she's suffering so much herself. I've never felt so close to anyone, or wanted to *be* so close to anyone."

"That's because Annabel is part of you, Abi. Literally, she *is* you."

"Yes… I suppose she must be. We're one and the same soul." But Abi didn't sound entirely convinced by Miriam's conclusion.

"In that case I'll have to love Annabel as well as you!" smiled Miriam. Abi leaned into her embrace again. Tenderly Miriam stroked her lover's rich dark hair and kissed the side of her head. After another pause, she went on. "My darling, you wouldn't believe how much I missed you in New York. I thought of you all the time, wishing you were there with me."

"Oh Miriam, I missed you too. You can see just how much I need you here with me."

"Abi, let's not be apart anymore. Not for such a long time. When I go to San Francisco in September, for the whole of the month, will you come with me? As my partner?"

Abi's face lit up. She looked Miriam in the eye. "Oh God, *yes*! I'd love to go with you to San Francisco. And anywhere else you want to take me!"

"I want to show you off, Abi, as my partner. My beautiful lover. I want everyone to see you at my side, holding my hand. Is that something you could do?"

Abi nodded, and held Miriam's hand. "I'd *love* to do that!"

"It would also get you away from London, where you seem to be susceptible to Annabel's… visitations. If you can get away from her old haunts, you can probably get away from *her*. You'd be free! Then you'd quickly get better. You may not even have to see Paula any more. I'm sure she doesn't treat you free of charge."

"No, she doesn't. But I can easily afford what she charges."

"Do you have enough money put aside? Can you stop working for a while?"

"Yes. I've saved quite a lot of my immoral earnings. I don't spend very much."

"Then you can afford to drop everything and come to San Francisco with me!"

"Yes! It sounds wonderful. I'm your girl, Miriam!" They kissed affectionately, then with intense passion. Suddenly they were both aroused. Miriam put her hand on Abi's warm thigh.

"My darling, I have a little gift for you," she said in a low voice. "From New York."

Abi smiled. "Oh? Where is it?"

"It's under that cushion, in the corner of the sofa. Right by your bottom. Take a look."

Abi lifted the cushion. Lying beneath it was a six inch vibrator, gleaming with a bright golden sheen.

"Oh my goodness!" exclaimed Abi. "Is it made of gold?"

"No, I'm afraid not. A solid gold vibrator is rather beyond my means. Maybe a Hollywood movie star could afford one. In fact I've heard rumours of one or two actresses who *do* have such extravagant items. But this one has a shiny metallic finish that *looks* like gold. Lovely and smooth for a comfortable ride…"

Now animated, Abi picked up the vibrator and ran it along her arm. "Oh yes… it *is* a lovely smooth finish. Can I give it a try?" She sat up straight.

"I was hoping you'd ask, darling. If you look at the base, there are three speeds."

"No… I want *you* to work it for me." Abi passed the vibrator to Miriam. "Hold it up between your knees."

As Miriam complied, holding the device between the clenched knees of her brown-leathered legs, Abi stood up, turned and faced her. Looking hard at Miriam she rucked up the light pink frock with both hands and then swept it over her head in a single flowing movement. She dropped the garment on the carpet.

"Oh my!" exclaimed Miriam. "What charming undies!" Abi wore a pair of skimpy white cotton briefs spotted with little red hearts. Otherwise she was naked.

"I put these on especially for you," said Abi, twanging the elastic side strap. "I want to give them to you, as a little present from me." She performed a complete turn to show them off.

"Oh, thank you," sighed Miriam. "They're so *cute*! I want them!"

With a mischievous smile Abi wiggled her hips and slowly slid the briefs down, all the way to her bare feet. She bent down to scoop them up and handed them to Miriam.

"I've had them on all day," said Abi, her smile broadening. "I walked around Camden Market for a few hours before I met you at the restaurant."

Miriam brought the briefs up to her face, directly under her nose. She closed her eyes and inhaled deeply. Then she kissed the white cotton, with genuine passion. "The very Nectar of Venus! Oh Abi, these are absolutely divine… just like the woman who's been wearing them."

Abi blew her a kiss.

"I'm pleased to see that your hair is growing back, down below," said Miriam.

"I'm going *au naturel*, all over my privates," replied Abi. "Take a closer look." She opened her legs wide and planted her feet on either side of Miriam's boots. Miriam dropped the briefs onto the sofa and lovingly stroked Abi's pussy, inserting her finger for a few moments until it was thoroughly wet. She could smell the musky odour of Abi's arousal.

"I think I'm ready now," sighed Abi. "For your present…"

Miriam switched on the vibrator between her knees. It began to hum with a smooth fast monotone. She gripped it tight with one hand as Abi came closer. Abi spread her knees as wide as possible, then bent them to ease herself down over the vibrator. She paused to draw apart her labia with the middle finger of each hand and rubbed herself on the humming gold shaft, moving her hips backwards and forwards to test it.

"Oh it's *cold*!" she gasped, laughing.

"I know. They always are," replied Miriam, mesmerised by the boldness and audacity of her lover.

"It's all right," responded Abi. "I'll soon warm it up!" She took a deep breath and slowly sank down onto the device. The sound of the humming was quickly muted as the vibrator was enveloped by her vagina. She gasped again, loudly. She closed her eyes and arched her back, wriggling from side to side to find the most pleasurable angle. To steady herself, she placed her hands on the outside of her thighs, close to her buttocks. She moved her hips up and down, then round and round, her heavy breasts jiggling and swaying. Enthralled, Miriam caressed them with her spare hand.

After a minute or so Abi paused. She leaned forward and placed her knees very wide on the sofa seat, on either side of Miriam's thighs, and raised her backside. Miriam adjusted the angle of the vibrator as Abi brought her face down to Miriam's and gave her a long lecherous kiss, pushing her tongue deep into her mouth as she unbuttoned her blouse with both hands. They carried on kissing and tonguing as Abi squeezed Miriam's exposed breasts and moved up and down on the vibrator in earnest, her vagina making little sucking sounds as her hips accelerated. Her knees ground into the old sofa, which creaked under the pressure. Miriam moved up the control dial of the machine by one notch. The humming sound sped up, its pitch rising to match Abi's growing excitement.

Gently Miriam touched Abi's cheek. "Oh Abigail," she sighed, looking straight into the bright tawny eyes. "My sweet darling... I love you *so* much!" As soon as Miriam said this, Abi felt a light delicate touch on her hips, as the long hands of her sister slowly ran up her sides, up over her ribs, then over her back... and she felt Annabel flowing into her again, like a wave of shining golden light. Abi's heart surged with joy, and her entire body began to oscillate. Every nerve-end tingled with pleasure as she felt herself again becoming one with Annabel. Her limbs, her spine, her head, her face were filled with Annabel... until every part of her *was* Annabel... In a few moments Abi had departed... and there was only Annabel.

As Abi approached orgasm, Miriam saw that her eyes had become glassy, vacant, aware of nothing beyond her own ecstasy, staring far into the distance. As if suddenly possessed of an extra burst of energy, Abi went down even faster on the vibrator and her vaginal muscles went into a series of frenzied convulsions, almost dragging the device out of Miriam's hand. She gasped over and over again, and seemed to lose all sense of where she was or who she was. Her face was so close it was virtually touching Miriam's. Her eyes bulged, gaping into nowhere, no longer perceiving her partner. Her rapture was almost demonic. Miriam gripped the vibrator with both hands and desperately clung on to it as Abi came with a long noisy cry, her mouth open wide and her eyes rolling up into her head, right in front of Miriam's eyes. Then she let everything go and collapsed helplessly over Miriam like a dead person… like someone who had willingly, eagerly given up the ghost. Miriam sighed with relief and held the quivering body with tenderness but also with apprehension. She knew now that Abi was heading towards a terrible precipice and there was nothing she could do to stop her going over the edge.

XVI

Monday 7ᵗʰ August, early in the evening. Abigail's flat in Notting Hill, London.

Abi leaned back on her settee and closed her eyes. Following Miriam's advice, she had started taking Paula's pills again but the strange vivid dreams hadn't stopped. She had had another largely sleepless night. But no more visitations from Annabel. Maybe things would get better. She had spent another enjoyable weekend with Miriam, who had taken her to Stratford-upon-Avon to tour the town and watch a play at the Royal Shakespeare Theatre, where one of her former students was a star actress. Abi had spent much of the time wondering when to visit Paula again for more therapy before, ironically, finding that Paula had left her a telephone message, asking to see her as a matter of urgency, at her flat in Notting Hill. Paula had stressed that the matter was personal, and nothing to do with Abi's treatment. She sounded unusually agitated. Abi had returned the call on Monday morning and was now waiting for Paula to arrive.

Trying to be as relaxed and casual as possible, Abi wore only a T-shirt and gym shorts. To her annoyance, the sporadic gnawing pain in her abdomen had returned during the day. She leaned forward and poured herself a glass of red wine. A bottle and a second glass stood on the tiled coffee table. Just as she started sipping the wine, the intercom buzzer rang. It was exactly seven o'clock, the agreed time.

After a brief pause, Abi walked up to the intercom. "Yes?"

"Hello, Abi. It's me."

"All right, Paula. Come on up." Abi pressed the entrance button. She returned to the settee. She had drawn up a separate armchair for the occasion.

There was time for one more gulp of wine before the front door-bell rang. Paula had obviously climbed the communal stairwell with great alacrity. As Abi opened the flat door, she stood there looking breathless and agitated, but mustered a broad smile.

"Oh Abi, thank you so much for seeing me at such short notice!"

"Come in, Paula. It's good to see you again." Abi ushered her visitor through the hall and into the lounge. Paula wore her customary professional outfit, a white blouse and pencil-thin green check skirt. Her red hair was as usual immaculately shaped into a short bob. She held a carrier bag.

"Oh, what a fine flat you have!" said Paula, looking around. "But I expected nothing less. It's very tidy. I did imagine that you'd have more on your bookshelves."

"I find it hard to read for any length of time these days," replied Abi. "Since the accident."

"Ah yes, of course. *I* should know that better than anyone! Forgive my tactlessness."

"That's all right. Won't you sit down?" Abi gestured towards the settee.

Paula did as requested while Abi sat on the armchair, slightly to the side of her guest.

"Would you like a glass of wine?" asked Abi. "Or anything else? I have brandy, gin, vodka."

Paula shook her head. "No, thank you, it's much too early for me." She took a deep breath. "If only I could have come to visit you under happier circumstances, Abi."

Abi crossed her legs and picked up her wine glass. "What's the problem, Paula? You sounded quite concerned on the phone."

Paula took another, deeper breath and momentarily shut her eyes. "It's Lola," she sighed. "She's in trouble. Big trouble. And I don't know who to turn to."

"What sort of trouble?"

"She recently fell out with the people in that awful squat in Hackney, so I took her in for a while at my own place in Kilburn. She'd been taking far too many drugs, so staying with me probably did her some good."

"I'm sure it did. Is she still keeping away from Sebastian?"

"Yes, as far as I know. In fact she's told me a lot about her recent… adventures. Not just with Sebastian. She's been having sex with a lot of people. With many of the art-college students, both boys and girls. And with older women as well…"

Abi braced herself.

"Which older women?"

Paula looked hard at her. "One woman in particular, Abi. I have to tell you… Lola confessed to me that she's been carrying on an affair with you over the last six months. Until she broke it off a week or two ago. Is that true? Or is she making it up?"

Abi looked down at her bare feet. "No, she's not making it up. It's true. I'm sorry, but…"

To her surprise, Paula held up her hand. "It's quite all right. Lola is now an adult, albeit an immature and mixed-up one, and she's entitled to make her own choices in life. I know how wildly over-sexed she is. From what she's told me, you've helped a great deal in keeping her from going completely off the rails. You've done her a lot of good. As well as helping her out with money! So don't feel bad about whatever has happened. But as her mother – and as your therapist, Abi – I'm rather … well, not upset, but disappointed that you didn't mention it to me. That you carried on with her behind my back."

Abi shook her head. She felt abjectly ashamed. "I feel terrible about doing all this behind your back. But how could I tell you, Paula? When I was relying on you to recover from what happened to me last year? To keep my mind from falling apart? Surely you'd have thrown me out if you'd known about my relationship with Lola."

Again to Abi's surprise, Paula nodded. "I appreciate your position, Abi. And because you clearly did Lola some good, I'm prepared to overlook what happened, and let bygones be bygones. There's no point in making an issue of it at this late stage."

"You're very understanding," said Abi, much relieved.

"In any case, it's all history now. Now that Lola has disappeared. Now that I need your help."

"Why? Where has Lola disappeared to? She isn't here, I can promise you."

Paula smiled, grimly. "I know she isn't here. I can give you *some* idea of where she is… perhaps I'd better just show you." She put on her round glasses, then reached into her carrier bag and withdrew an envelope. "Over the last year Lola has built up a large drug debt. With various people. Bad people. Drug dealers and gangsters." Paula handed the envelope over to Abi, who put down her drink to open it.

As soon as she saw the photographs, Abi gasped and put her hand over her mouth. There were three photos, all showing Lola in the same posture, stark naked, kneeling on the hard stony floor of what looked like a harshly-lit brick-walled cellar, her hands cuffed behind her back. The first showed her facing front, a black ball-gag stuffed in her mouth. A gloved hand held a long sharp knife to one of her small nipples. On the floor between her knees was a glass bowl full of what appeared to be urine. Abi could see that the picture had been taken recently, as Lola's hair, though wet and dishevelled, was dyed purple-red. Tears fell profusely from both of her eyes, which looked swollen and blood-shot, and her face was a picture of terror and despair. The second photo showed her kneeling sideways on, the knife pressed against one of her breasts; and the third showed her kneeling from behind, the gloved hand lewdly squeezing one of her buttocks as her pee streamed down into the glass bowl. Her pale body bore a number of angry red welts, obviously the aftermath of repeated whipping, and was covered with grime and sweat.

Paula leaned forward and watched intently as Abi picked up the typed message which accompanied the photos.

"Hey, Mumsie! Hope you like these pics of your cute junkie brat Lola. She's been a real bad girl and is going to pay the price big-time if her debts aren't cleared up by next weekend. We'll start by slicing off her little-girlie nipples, then her ears, then her dainty fingers and toes, one by one. She'll die very slow and very painful, I promise you, unless you pay us the money in time to set her free. Shame to get rid of her, either way. She's a fantastic lovely fuck and when she cums she screams like a fox being torn apart by a pack of hounds. Lucky no-one can hear her yelling while she's down here. Poor kid, she's so scared she can't stop

pissing herself! If you want to see her alive, don't even think of talking to the cops. Remember, Mumsie – the full amount in used notes by Friday midnight or we start slicing her up. We'll even take photos and send them to you! Bye now!"

Aghast, Abi looked up. Paula's head was in her hands as her elbows rested on her white knees. She had taken off her glasses and put them on the coffee table.

"It's *terrible!*" exclaimed Abi. "How could anyone do this to her?"

Paula began to sob into her hands. "These people can do anything they want, and get away with it. The police couldn't care less about kids like Lola. Lots of them are in cahoots with the drug dealers anyway. I don't know what to do, Abi!"

"How much does she owe them?"

Paula looked up. Tears ran from her eyes. "The amount they want is on the back of the note. And a phone number for me to contact."

Abi turned over the paper. On it was scrawled a mobile phone number and a large five-figure amount in pounds. She raised her eyebrows. "Does Lola really owe them this much money?"

"Probably not." Paula dabbed her eyes with a tissue. "Probably only half that amount. But they're going to screw as much money out of me as they can. For their trouble…"

"Can you find the money?"

Paula shook her head. "No. That's the problem. I couldn't begin to find that amount. I'm in the process of selling my flat in Kilburn, to make some capital, as my therapy business isn't bringing in enough money. I'm in debt myself, Abi! If I can sell my place and live somewhere cheaper, further away from central London, I might just about be able to pay these bastards. But it'll be weeks, maybe months before the sale completes. There just isn't time!" She blew her nose loudly into the tissue. Then she looked away and began to cry.

Abi got up and sat down beside Paula on the settee. She put a comforting arm around her. Paula dropped her head and blubbered into her handkerchief.

"It's all right, Paula. *I* can find the money you need. I have a fair amount saved up and put away for… a rainy day. You can pay me back when you sell your flat in Kilburn."

Paula looked at her with big blue watery eyes. "Oh Abi! That would be *so* good of you! You're absolutely *wonderful*! A true star! I can't believe anyone would be that kind!" She leaned into Abi's arms and put a hand on one of her smooth brown thighs.

"I like the idea of putting my immoral earnings to a moral use," smiled Abi.

"There's nothing immoral about you, Abi. Nothing at all!" replied Paula.

"When do you need the money by?"

"As the note says – by Friday midnight at the latest. Can you get it in time?"

"Yes. I should be able to draw it out of my account by the end of business on Wednesday. Certainly by Thursday."

"Thank God!" Paula stroked Abi's thigh.

"What happens then?" asked Abi. "Will you give them the money?"

Paula sat up. She looked apprehensive. "I don't know. I'm too scared to deliver it myself. During the last few months I've had some vicious quarrels with Sebastian, over the way he's been treating Lola, and he's threatened to… well, I'd better not repeat what he said. He's threatened to do to me what he's been doing to Lola, but ten times worse. He's sure to be one of the people involved in her abduction. Probably getting his revenge on her for leaving him."

There was a lengthy pause. "All right," said Abi. "I'll deliver the money myself, if you let me have the address. I don't think any of these people know me."

"Oh Abi! Would you really? I can't thank you enough for everything you're doing for us!"

"After all that's happened, I owe it to Lola, and to you, to rescue her. Especially after deceiving you for all these months. I couldn't possibly stand by and let her be tortured and killed by those thugs. It's obvious they've already abused her terribly."

Paula held Abi's hand. She cleared her throat. "Abi, I have to be frank with you. I can't guarantee *your* safety, if you make the delivery. I think the money is what they're after, but… these people are real villains, totally ruthless and degenerate. You know what I'm saying, darling. I couldn't bear it if you came to harm as well. My number one patient!" Her cold hand returned to Abi's thigh.

Abi took a deep breath. She thought about Annabel, and what *she* would do if she found herself in similar circumstances. She knew that Wonder Woman wouldn't hesitate to put her life on the line for someone she loved…

"I'm willing to take that risk, Paula, if it means we can save Lola. There's no other chance for her."

"We'll both be so grateful, Abi. For all time! Maybe Lola will see sense and go back to you. I wouldn't mind at all, if the two of you got back together again, honestly I wouldn't. You'd be so *good* for her!"

Abi shook her head. "I don't think it would work out, Paula. I adore Lola but she's a real wild-child, way beyond my control. In any case, I'm now in a serious relationship with Miriam. So serious that I've quit my sex-work. At least for the time being."

Paula withdrew her hand from Abi's leg. "I'm so pleased, Abi. If it makes you feel better about yourself." She blew her nose again.

"I can assure you it does," smiled Abi. "I've now realised how badly

I was abusing myself… opening myself up for every man with a wad of cash in his hand. I won't do it any longer."

"That shows great resolve, darling. A real sense of identity. I'm so encouraged to hear you say it." Paula sniffed and dabbed away the last of her tears. "Tell me, Abi, have you been taking all the medication I gave you? It's so long since I last saw you in my office."

"There was a period when I stopped taking them, when I was most under the influence of Annabel. But I'm back on your pills now. On Miriam's advice. I must admit my supply is starting to run out. I was about to contact you for another appointment, but… your message beat me to it!"

"That's quite all right, darling." Paula reached into her bag and extracted another packet, this time with a different colour. "A colleague has recommended these to me. They're notably more effective than what I was giving you before, without so many side-effects. Can I suggest you try them? Same dose – take one twice a day, starting tonight."

"Can I continue to drink while I take them?"

"Yes. Alcohol shouldn't be a problem. As long as you don't drink too much."

Abi took the packet and examined it. She nodded. "All right. I'll start tonight, as soon as you've left."

"Good girl! Just one last thing… I would suggest that you don't mention any of this to Miriam. I'm sure she's still jealous of Lola and will try to dissuade you from helping her. In which case – my little girl is done for!"

"I understand," replied Abi. "I won't say anything to Miriam. I won't be seeing her anyway until Friday, when her exhibition opens at the Black Sun Gallery. She'll be incredibly busy until then, getting everything ready."

Paula nodded. "Thank you, Abi. Perhaps I'll go along and take a look at Miriam's exhibition myself. If I'm in the right frame of mind by then."

"Why not? I'm sure she'll be happy to see you."

Paula returned the photos and the typed note to her bag. "You must excuse me, darling, but I have another client to see tonight. It's been hard for me to concentrate on anything, with Lola in such a terrible fix, but now maybe I can relax a bit. Thanks to you!"

"Thank me when Lola is safe and sound. But I'm glad to be able to relieve your anxiety. It makes something of a change. You've been relieving mine for the last ten months!"

Paula grinned and got to her feet. "Then you've paid me back, with interest. I'll never forget this, Abi!" As Abi stood up beside her, Paula leaned over to touch her shoulder and kissed her firmly on the cheek. Then she turned and made for the door, Abi following her. As she passed the wall-mounted shelf above the hi-fi stack, Paula caught sight of the bronze statuette of the winged Greek dragon at the top.

"I'm pleased to see you've held on to my little bronze Drako," said Paula, smiling. "It's a rare antique."

"To be honest, I sometimes find it a bit disturbing," replied Abi. "I think it's the staring eyes. They're so ferocious. Sometimes I gaze at them for ages and find it hard to look away. But I can't get rid of it, since you gave it to me as a present. It *is* kind of fascinating, I must admit."

Paula turned to her, just by the hallway door. "You know, the dragon is an ancient symbol of strength, courage and determination. All the qualities you've just demonstrated to me, Abi. Keep it as a souvenir of the difficult time you've been through. Because pretty soon you'll be clear of this phase of your life, and will move on to better things. Believe me – I know you will!"

"I appreciate your confidence in me."

Paula took Abi's left hand in hers and carefully, deliberately squeezed it while fixing her eyes on Abi's. "See you soon, Abi. Make sure you stay in touch… make sure…"

"Yes," said Abi slowly, returning the gaze, her expression becoming slightly vacant. "I'll make sure… I'll stay in touch."

"Brava!"

Paula left without another word and Abi closed the entrance door behind her, now slightly disorientated. She returned to the coffee table and poured herself another glass of wine. Then she moved over to the French windows to look down at the street. After a few moments she saw Paula walking away, heading towards the nearest tube station, striding along the pavement with an air of great aplomb, smiling happily as she spoke into her mobile phone.

Abi returned to the settee and took out a sheet of the tablets Paula had just given her. They were an odd green colour and larger than the previous type. She pushed one out of the blister packaging and swallowed it, washing it down with her wine. Then she closed her eyes and lay back, pleased to have done something worthwhile for Lola. Something to save her life… to prove to her darling Baby that she truly loved her. Abi suddenly realised how much she still needed Lola. She would do *anything* to rescue her girl from danger, whatever price she had to pay. Perhaps, perhaps… one day they *could* get together again… this time with Paula's blessing. Lola would surely forgive her for the affair with Miriam. She knew that her relationship with Lola was much stronger, much deeper than anything else she had experienced. Except for Dolly, her beautiful long-lost daughter. Oh *when* would she see Dolly again? If only she knew where to even start looking for her.

Abi felt a wave of fatigue come rolling over her and decided to lie down for a while. She walked uneasily into the darkened bedroom, now feeling dizzy and exhausted. The only light was from the lounge, shining in through the open door of the bedroom. She threw off her T-shirt and her gym shorts and fell naked onto the bed. She rolled over onto her back and spread out her limbs. Her head sank back into the pillow. In a few brief moments she was asleep...

She opened her eyes and looked up at the bright light in the ceiling, shining down on her mercilessly. She couldn't shut her eyes. She couldn't move anything... not one muscle of her body. She surmised that she was lying on the grey marble slab in the ugly morgue in Greece, after her naked corpse had been recovered from the sea, following her death at the hands of something too monstrous, too terrifying for her even to recall. Her broken body lay contorted in a strange unnatural posture. She moved her attention over each part of her physique, one area after another, to check her condition. Her body was covered with cuts and scars and slivers of seaweed. Her arms and legs were smashed up. Her backbone and spine had been snapped... her ribs were nearly all broken... her right arm was yanked out of its socket, and trailed at an odd angle under her back... her neck was broken, twisted to one side as she stared up at the ceiling... and her mouth was wide open in a grotesque rictus, as if she had been screaming hysterically at the moment of death. All she knew was that her life had been taken and she was now nothing but a lump of cold meat lying on a slab. The object of her consciousness was solely her own extinction, her cessation in the everlasting present moment... the awareness of eternal sleep, the taste of death without end...

Suddenly someone entered the morgue and approached her.

"Oh Abi! My poor Abi!"

It was Lola. Her darling Lola... dressed in a yellow bikini. Her hair was now its natural gingery red, long and parted in the centre, and she wore no make-up. Tears ran down her freckled cheeks as she inspected Abi's corpse. Sobbing intensely, Lola began to touch her, running her small delicate hands over the cold flesh.

"You died for me, my love. You gave up everything you had for *me*! Oh Abi, I adore you! I love you more than I can say!"

Lola climbed onto the table and propped herself up on her elbows and knees as she leaned over Abi. She was crying. Gently she began to kiss the body, starting with the breasts, the neck, the arms, the upturned palms… but she avoided the face. Her lips moved down to the belly, the hips, the thighs, the calves… then she kissed Abi's feet, even her toes. Wherever Lola touched her, Abi felt her flesh grow warm, as if the loving attention from Lola's mouth was bringing some sort of life back to her body. But she was still paralysed, unable to move a single muscle. Then Lola moved up to her vulva and started to kiss her there, with the utmost care and tenderness. Abi felt a wonderful glowing heat between her legs, which soon spread to her buttocks and thighs. Finally Lola licked her vagina, easing it open with her thumbs before pushing her tongue into Abi's cleft. The long tongue seemed to reach up all the way to her womb, flickering and lunging like an eager little snake, faster and deeper, until suddenly something exploded like a fireball between her legs…

"Ohhh!"

Abi woke in a state of rapture and gripped her crutch with both hands as she climaxed, twisting her hips and rolling over on her side as her body repeatedly jack-knifed. Then she gasped and opened her eyes, relieved to see the light shining in from the lounge. As she relaxed and slowly regained her senses, she felt a warm dampness under her buttock. The orgasm had been so intense that she had ejaculated and left a big wet patch on the bedsheet.

After a couple of minutes Abi got up and walked awkwardly into the lounge, still slightly shaky. She was relieved to see that everything was in its usual place; the doors were all closed and there was no sound of rushing water from the bathroom. There was no hint at all of Annabel's presence. Her mind was tranquil and clear and steady, despite the abrupt climax of her dream. She went to the bathroom to dry herself with a towel. As she wiped between her legs and looked at the dry silent shower unit, she reflected that there was no longer any need for Annabel to visit her. She had now *become* Annabel.

XVII

Thursday 10th August, in the late afternoon. The streets of Soho,
central London.

Abi was of course familiar with Soho. Many of her wealthy and (in a few cases) famous clients frequented the prestigious social clubs dotted around the area, and she would often meet them here before moving off elsewhere to spend the night with them. It was an easy and congenial way of earning a huge amount of money. Today, *she* was the one giving away a huge amount of money. Tens of thousands of pounds in large banknotes were stuffed in a brown envelope in her carefully zipped-up leather handbag, and she was acutely conscious of her precious cargo as she turned off Old Compton Street and made her way up Dean Street. Not only her savings but also Lola's life depended on the safe delivery of that envelope. Her mind was calm and clear: she was completely focused on her task and paid no heed to the colourful shops and restaurants that lined the Soho streets. She saw herself as a special agent carrying out a mission for which she'd been carefully trained and prepared. The only thing that mattered was the success of that mission.

To minimise any unwanted attention, Abi was dressed modestly but smartly in a crisp white blouse and a high-waisted black skirt that reached almost to her knees, with black knee-high socks and sensible matching shoes. Her hair was smartly combed back and held in place by a metal clip, and she wore only basic make-up. Nonetheless she drew several appreciative glances from passers-by.

She paused by a restaurant and took out her mobile phone to dial the number she'd been given by Paula. A young man's voice answered.

"*Yes?*"

"It's Abigail."

"*Do you have the paperwork with you?*"

"Yes."

"*And you're alone?*"

"Yes."

"*Good. It's Flat 7, top floor. Come on up.*"

"All right. See you in a few minutes." Abi returned her phone to her bag and crossed the road to the narrow side street where her destination lay. For moment she thought a man in a leather jacket deliberately crossed the road immediately after her, as if he were following her, but she quickly dismissed the thought. The people in the flat knew she was coming anyway, so there was little sense in anyone tailing her. As she reached the other side of the street, she felt a throbbing pain in her abdomen, an inch or two below her navel. The recent affliction was continuing to plague her. She was also afflicted by the hot humid weather, typical of August in central London, when the air is barely breathable and the baked tarmac smells of irredeemable filth.

The side street was virtually an alleyway, with scarcely enough width for a vehicle to pass through. The tall elegant buildings on both sides were distinguished eighteenth-century townhouses, all three storeys high, and had been refurbished some years ago. The immaculate sash-windows and white portico entrances looked original, a sign that their upgrades had been particularly expensive. At roof level each property had a new penthouse, discreetly set back from the roof-edge. Abi found the required building and pressed the button for Flat 7 on the intercom board. The name typed on the label was "B Kakourgos". The young man's voice answered.

"*Yes?*"

"Abigail."

"*Fine. Come on up. Top floor. Please use the lift in the lobby.*"

The buzzer sounded and Abi pushed her way through the tall heavy entrance door. As she closed it behind her she saw the same man in the leather jacket, passing by on the other side of the road, looking at his mobile phone. Again, probably coincidence. Immediately ahead of her she saw the old-fashioned lift, all made of black iron, with grilles protecting the ornate lift-car, which happened to be on the ground floor as if waiting for her. She slid the folding gate to one side and entered the car, which was surprisingly small and confined. She closed the door, which made a noisy emphatic clang, and pressed the button on the control panel for Flat 7. The car jolted, then whirred and squealed a little as it slowly carried her up, all the way to the top floor. When she got out, she found herself in a small lobby directly outside Flat 7 – there was nowhere else to go on the top floor, apart from the emergency stairs. As she approached the heavy dark mahogany entrance door, it opened and she was confronted by a slim pale red-haired young man, probably in his twenties, who wore a T-shirt and denim jeans. He had an easy-going affable air and smiled at her.

"Abigail?"

She nodded.

"Please – come on in!" He gestured, welcomingly.

She passed through a large hallway, containing coat hangers and a full-length mirror, into the main lounge. It was the most impressively spacious living-room she had ever seen, with massive windows all around, the one at the far end offering a panoramic rooftop view of Soho and beyond. In the middle of the room were two long semi-circular sofas, facing one another, both boasting garish leopard-skin covers. Two men sat on one of the sofas: Sebastian, immediately recognisable by his blond hair and smart suit, and an overweight and rather ugly middle-aged man wearing a Hawaiian shirt and knee length shorts. On the other sofa sat the elderly man with wiry grey hair whom she had so often encountered in her nightmares. As she looked at his hard narrow eyes, sharply cut beard and sly grin, Abi's heart sank and her bowels churned. He was casually attired in a short-sleeved shirt and checked trousers, but was recognisably the same well-dressed old man who had repeatedly attempted to abuse her while she lay paralysed in the brightly-lit gallery of her dreams. Any thought of fleeing was pointless. The young man who had let her in stood behind her, obviously to block any exit. He gently pushed her in the back to guide her forward so that she stood between the curved sofas, in the dead centre of the room.

The elderly man rose to his feet, still grinning. "Hello, my dear Abigail. How *lovely* to make your acquaintance. I expect you won't remember me, but we *have* met before. Quite a few months ago. You don't remember?"

Abi shook her head. "No, I'm afraid not." Her voice had suddenly become hoarse.

"Well, not to worry. I'm Bernie, and this handsome fellow is Sebastian… and next to him is an old friend of mine, Marcus. I don't think you've met him before." They both smiled at her, with more than a touch of irony. Bernie spoke with an odd east London accent, part English and part something foreign, vaguely Mediterranean.

"Nice to meet you," said Abi. She started to feel hot and sticky, and slightly giddy.

"First, to business," said Bernie. "Do you have what we want?"

Abi nodded. She took out the brown envelope and handed it to him. Bernie's smile broadened. "Wonderful! I knew you wouldn't let us down. Or let your sweet friend Lola down." He threw the envelope to Sebastian. "Seb, can you count it for me old buddy?" Bernie then took off Abi's handbag and tossed it onto the snow-white pile carpet. He put his hairy arm around her shoulders. "You won't be needing your bag for a while, my dear." His grin broadened, displaying a set of expensively implanted teeth.

Abi stood rigid, not daring to move, as Sebastian opened the envelope and extracted the money, which had been parcelled up into thousand-pound batches. He started counting, with the expertise of a man accustomed to handling large sums of cash. Abi breathed deeply and stared out of the window at the Soho rooftops. In front of the window, at the far end of the lounge, stood a luxurious glass coffee table with a plastic bag full of fluffy white powder, next to several rolled-up banknotes. She also noticed a camera with a big zoom lens, and realised that the forthcoming session was going to be recorded for posterity. Like a predator gloating over his prey, Bernie continued to grin at her, his arm around her back, playfully squeezing her shoulder. His hand was thickly veined and there was a heavy gold ring on his middle finger. Finally Sebastian finished counting the money.

"Yeah, it's all here, Boss," he said. "All present and correct."

"Used notes?" asked Bernie, looking over.

Sebastian flicked through the notes again. "Yeah, all used."

"Marvellous!" said Bernie. "I think we should celebrate our good fortune by having a nice party. I *love* impromptu parties! You will of course join us, Abi, won't you?" He reached down and squeezed her backside. Abi nodded, realising that her best hope of surviving this ordeal was to co-operate. She knew exactly what was coming. She had had hundreds of sexual encounters in her career, but always, at her insistence, with solo partners, who were invariably men. When some of them had turned aggressive and threatened violence, she had always managed to find a way of defusing the situation. Now she was going to face a very different challenge. She had to trust her survival instinct to see her through.

Bernie turned to the young man behind her. "Bob, can you do the curtains and the lights please? And the sounds."

"Sure Boss," replied Bob. He already had a remote control in his hand and pressed a button. The dark emerald velvet curtains all around the room began to slide shut. Another button switched on the bright spotlights above them. Abi blinked under their harshness. Bob moved to the hi-fi and started up the music, a throbbing bump-and-grind soundtrack, as Bernie affectionately stroked Abi's bottom. Sebastian took off his jacket while Marcus grinned malevolently at her. He started to rub his crutch with one of his thick hairy hands. His eyes gleamed.

"Thanks, Bob," said Bernie. "Now... give Terry a bell and ask him to bring his two lads. I want this to be a *real* party! With as many people as possible!"

"Sure Boss." Bob began to tap his mobile phone. Sebastian, also grinning, got up and stood immediately behind Abi. Marcus rose to his feet and stood to one side of her, very close. She could smell his bad breath. She could hear the breathing of all three men. The proximity of their bodies made her sweat. Her heart raced.

"Okay, boys," said Bernie. "Let's begin the party!" He unbuttoned Abi's blouse as Sebastian carefully unzipped the rear of her skirt.

"How sensible of you to co-operate, Abi," said Bernie, as he undid the last button. "No need for any aggravation, my dear. We're proper gentlemen. We know how to treat a lady!" The black skirt dropped to the floor as Bernie slipped the blouse off Abi's shoulders, exposing the starchy white bra.

"Fuck!" said Marcus. "Just *look* at those tits!"

Sebastian began to caress her buttocks, easing his fingers under the elastic of the black cotton knickers. Then he changed his mind and knelt down and removed the skirt and the shoes from around her feet, before carefully pulling down and tossing away one long black sock after another. Marcus put his hand up to squeeze Abi's breasts, over the bra. "I want to take this off, Bernie!" he panted.

"What a wonderful idea!" laughed Bernie. "Be my guest! Hey, Bob, come and join us over here! Are Terry and his boys coming?"

"Sure Boss, they'll be here in a few minutes," replied Bob. His phone call finished, he threw his mobile onto the nearest sofa and came over to join them. He stood on the opposite side of Abi to Marcus, just as close to her. His eyes widened as Marcus unhooked the white bra and yanked it off. Abi's naked breasts hung down freely.

Marcus groaned and grabbed one of the breasts as Abi closed her eyes. Bob held the other one, hissing with lust as he squeezed it. His finger touched the mangled nipple. "Ooh – someone's given her a rough time here!" he exclaimed.

"Yes," said Bernie, staring right into Abi's eyes. "And we know who did that to her, don't we?" He put his hand down between her legs and pressed his fingers on the black cotton gusset. "But *you* don't remember, do you dear?"

Abi shook her head, almost apologetically.

"Amazing!" laughed Bernie, his teeth flashing. "She really *can't* remember! Hah!" The two men on either side of Abi ignored his comment and continued to fondle her breasts, both of them moaning with lust and muttering to themselves.

"Okay Seb," said Bernie. "Do the last bit for us, buddy!"

Abi felt her knickers being pulled down, almost gently. Sebastian, still crouching, deftly removed them and dropped them to one side with her other clothes. Then he stood up. Abi was now naked. Bernie put his hand back into her crutch, this time brushing her pubic hair before easing his finger up into her vagina. At the same moment she felt Sebastian's finger running down the warm hair-fuzzed valley between her buttocks. She began to feel dizzy.

"Fuck!" said Bernie, triumphantly, his narrow eyes twinkling. "Her pussy's wet!"

"A right fucking whore!" sneered Marcus. "She really wants it!"

"And she's gonna get it!" growled Sebastian, the tip of his middle finger twisting dexterously into Abi's anus. Instinctively her buttocks clenched in self-protection, but as his finger probed further up inside her, she gave in and relaxed, ignoring the sharp spasms of rectal pain. Resistance was worse than futile. It would only make things more painful. She felt the fingers of the two men rubbing against one another inside her, and realised that they had performed this fore-play double-act many times before. She closed her eyes and tried to listen to the deep throbbing music.

"Okay," said Bernie. "Time to get the party swinging!"

"You mean – time for the nurse?" laughed Sebastian.

"You bet, buddy." Bernie turned his head round. He gave a shrill short whistle. "Hey, nurse! We need you, baby!"

Abi opened her eyes and watched in horror as Francine emerged from the kitchen, dressed in her customary short white nurse's tunic, complete with lacy hat. She was smiling broadly and held a syringe in her hand.

"Oh no!" groaned Abi. "Not you as well!"

As Francine approached, Bernie removed his finger from between Abi's legs and stood away, as did the two men at her side, simultaneously releasing their grip on her breasts. She winced as Sebastian abruptly withdrew his finger from her bottom. But even that was a meaningless detail compared to the sour burn of betrayal that she felt now.

Francine came up close, a sardonic smirk on her heavily rouged lips. "Yes Abi, it's me. Your caring nurse! On duty as always!"

Abi felt close to tears. Slowly she shook her head. Francine raised the syringe, which was full of murky yellow-brown fluid, and popped off the needle cover, all the time looking at Abi. "Come on darling," she smiled. "You must have known this was going to happen one day."

Abi continued to shake her head, weakly.

"No? Well, *I* knew, and I've been waiting for this moment for months, sweetie-pie. To see you get the five-star fucking you deserve!"

Marcus moved his face towards Abi's ear. "We're going to fuck your arse off, you filthy whore!" he snarled.

"Now, now, Marcus," said Bernie. "No need to be rude to our guest. She's behaved like a proper lady." He held up one of Abi's arms and nodded at Francine. She looked Abi directly in the eye and smiled happily as she pushed the hypodermic needle into a vein in the crook of her elbow. Abi felt a sharp prick, and Francine pressed the syringe piston all the way down.

Almost at once Abi felt a delicious wave of numbness flow over her body, everywhere at once, dispelling all anxiety and discomfort. It was pointless to worry about anything, she thought, as her legs gave way under her and she felt herself falling backwards in slow motion…

falling back slowly into Sebastian's strong arms. As she floated down to the thick pile carpet she heard Bernie calling for something, but could no longer comprehend what it was... she lay back and closed her eyes, as the light above her was so very bright. Then everything disappeared...

When Abi opened her eyes again, a little while later, she found herself lying on the deck of a pristine white boat, like a large yacht, apparently anchored in the circular bay formed of steep sloping hills covered with trees and bushes where she had gone swimming with Annabel on that fateful day her sister had died... the boat was surrounded by the same still silent clear water, dazzled by the midday sun in the spotless azure sky. She lay on the bleached white timber deck, on her back, alone and naked, unable to move. From a long way behind her, somewhere on the shore, came the sound of an incessant drumbeat, heavy and primitive.

Suddenly there was a movement, and a lithe naked man – she surmised he was some kind of pirate – climbed over the side of the boat and leaned over her helpless body. He was baring his teeth in a frightful grin. His penis was erect. Another naked man, black-skinned and muscular, with blond hair, climbed over the other side, again with an erect penis. Abi was sure they had emerged from the jungle of swirling weeds that covered the sea-bed under the boat, like wild submariners who from time to time invaded the land to seize and abduct hapless victims, or attacked vessels like hers, anchored in the bay. A third pirate, fatter and hairier, with a malevolent grin, also climbed on board and approached her. Then a second dark-skinned pirate followed, then another one, pale-skinned, then an elderly pirate with grey hair and a sharply cut beard, then even more of them until she couldn't keep track any longer. They began groping and grabbing her flesh, all of them at once, a multitude of hands clawing and scratching, pulling and squeezing... numerous mouths biting parts of her at the same moment, her neck, her breasts, her belly, her thighs, her arms, her back, her buttocks, her calves, her feet, her toes, all being grabbed and nibbled as she surrendered, unable to resist, and gave herself up to be devoured... her earlobes, her pubic hair, her vaginal lips, all being tugged and pulled and yanked as she stared into space... more and more pirates came over the side of the boat and joined in, until she was being groped and pulled and opened up by a whole gang of panting assailants... her legs were held wide open by numerous hands as the first hard cock entered her, thrusting into her in a frenzy of lust, ruthless, merciless... her legs were drawn up and back until her knees were almost at the side of her head, her feet pointing to the sky... She was fucked like this for some time, her body rocking back and forth, her breasts jiggling, until she was turned over on her side and her buttocks were drawn apart... her anus was hungrily licked, then probed with an oily finger... and then a hard cock thrust straight into her rectum, so indecently deep inside her... yet strangely she felt no pain or trauma... just an impudent invasion of her bowels, which she relaxed to allow the pirate to penetrate her painlessly. Then her hair was dragged upwards and her cheeks squeezed in to force open her mouth... she closed her eyes as a long musky black cock eased into her mouth... she sucked on the insistent member as it pushed all the way down to her throat, almost choking her... and another cock pushed into her pussy, to join the one in her arse, as they made alternating thrusts, rubbing against each other, one pushing in as the other withdrew, then the other way round, over and over again... Her body was sandwiched between theirs, almost crushed. She was being squeezed and pressed and probed everywhere, and she was covered in saliva and sweat, her own sweat and her body fluids and the fluids of others mingling into one hot sticky swamp... from time to time she felt bolts of warm semen spurting over her genitals, over her breasts, over her face and her hair, into the palm of her hand, into her armpit, even over her toes… and all the time her flesh was being nibbled and pinched, clawed and scratched, by those pirates who weren't actually invading her… it seemed as if all her fingers and toes were being eaten… her nipples and her earlobes were being sucked and bitten… she felt tongues pushing into her ears, soaking them with saliva… fingers were pulling away the lips of her mouth and even probing up inside her nostril to feel the inside of her gold stud… there was no part of her that wasn't being invaded or devoured… everything she possessed was being taken. From time to time the cocks changed, so that another pirate would have his chance to invade her, and she would be turned over the other way, or turned over on her belly so that her arse or her pussy was open to a fresh invasion from behind… each successive thrust easier and faster as her orifices relaxed and dilated… then there was one pirate on top of her to complement the one underneath her as again and again both her intimate vessels were invaded and plundered, robbed of whatever lay inside them, of whatever was hers… until finally she could no longer distinguish her body from the bodies of the others… she was no longer a single creature but one big heaving writhing mass of hot sweating flesh, the centre of an orgiastic pandemonium of squirming, wriggling, thrashing bodies… a hydra-headed Beast with countless twisting torsos and limbs knotted together, writhing wildly and ecstatically in the lowest darkest pit of Hell… she was an entire universe of surging pumping churning flesh… the savage mother allowing herself to be eaten by her savage offspring, like a giant insect queen, until she was no longer present, her body and her mind replaced by the feral creatures who had feasted on her, taking *her* life so that *they* could live…

After what seemed like hours of relentless heaving motion the pandemonium of flesh slowly began to disintegrate, to disentangle itself, as one part after another fell away from the centre, moved away... and her centre of being, her separate existence, was slowly, slowly restored as she lay alone on the white pile carpet... her self-awareness gradually returned. Although largely numb, she sensed how badly her body had been mauled, but she couldn't observe herself, and had no desire to do so...

Suddenly she felt herself rising up, supine, limbs spread-eagled, held aloft by a dozen big masculine hands. She opened her eyes and saw that she had been lifted almost to the ceiling of the lounge, held up by a group of panting chattering laughing men as if she was a trophy kill they had bagged on a hunting expedition and were now triumphantly showing off... The men whooped and began to chant in unison, in a strange exotic tongue, until their words rose to a crescendo and finished in an exultant climax which ended with repeated shouts of the name "Typhon". She lay serenely on her back, still unable to move, grateful for the cessation of the assault on her body... she gladly allowed the strong hands to hold her aloft by her arms and her legs, her back, her buttocks and her neck as she remained suspended up in the air, close to the bright spotlights in the ceiling that glared down at her. She was vaguely aware of sporadic flashes from below her, and realised that one of the gang was taking photographs of the event, and had indeed been doing so from the beginning, moving rapidly from one position to another as the action unfolded.

Then there was a shout – "Nurse!" – followed by sardonic laughter. Abi slowly turned her head to one side. Francine, now naked apart from her faux nurse's hat, her huge breasts wobbling, was approaching with another syringe in her hand. The men lowered Abi to the level of their waists, to give the nurse the access that she required. Grinning, she pushed the needle into Abi's wide open groin, at the very top of her brown thigh. Francine was jubilant as she looked at her victim's exhausted face and battered soaking body. "Goodbye Abi!" she said, in a strangely distant voice. "It was nice knowing you, darling!" She pushed the syringe all the way in.

As the narcotic surged into her, Abi gasped and her head fell back. There was a roar of triumph from the men, who once again hoisted her body all the way up to the ceiling. Her arms and her legs flopped about helplessly. There were more camera flashes. She closed her eyes and let out a long sigh, as if to acknowledge her demise. Relieved that it was all over, she let herself slip away into a vast lake of darkness and disappeared into its measureless depths.

XVIII

Thursday 10th August, in the mid-evening. Paula's office overlooking Regent's Park.

Paula sat waiting at her desk in the semi-darkness, and picked up the phone as soon as it rang.

"Yes?"

"Hi, Paula."

"Hi, Bob. Did everything go according to plan?"

"Oh yes, it sure did! It was just amazing!"

"Good. Is the Boss happy now?"

"Haven't seen him so happy since I've known him!"

"And the money?"

"All present and correct."

"Excellent. Is the Boss willing to handle the transportation?"

"Yes, he'll see to it. What's the date of the ceremony?"

"Tuesday. That's the date of the Full Moon. The weather conditions should be just right in the late afternoon."

"Okay. That gives us plenty of time."

"What will the Boss do with her till then?"

"He's going to keep her here for a few days, on ice, for himself and some of the lads to play with. I think they're going to have one hell of a time with her."

"I'm sure they are. All right, Bob. Give my regards to the boys. And to my nurse!"

"Will do. Bye, Paula."

Paula put down the phone and took a deep breath. She looked over at Lola, who was kneeling naked and motionless on the black leather pillow, in the centre of the room. Her pale skin still showed signs of the countless whip marks that she, Paula, had given her the previous week, but they were now starting to fade into a faint pink. Lola's body was illuminated by Paula's desk lamp and, behind her, by two black candles in brass holders on a makeshift altar, the aluminium patient's chair, the seat of which had been covered with a black velvet cloth. Between the candles sat the bronze statuette of the winged dragon, Typhon.

Paula took her hand-mirror from a drawer in the desk and examined herself. She adjusted the long dark-brown centre-parted wig until it looked just right. Then she stood up and brushed down the St Margaret's School regulation grey skirt, which was of course too short for her – it was six inches above her knee, twice as high as it had been for its original owner. She undid the top button of the light blue short-sleeved St Margaret's blouse, which was likewise too short for her, but just about tucked into the waistband of the skirt. The white bra underneath the blouse was much too loose for her chest, although she loved the feel of the elastic straps over her shoulders and her back. She checked that the white socks were up, or almost up, to her knees. The flat black shoes still pinched her feet, but she ignored the discomfort. Most importantly, she straightened the big gold crucifix that hung around her neck, and lovingly stroked the figure of Christ that was so finely carved on it. Then she was ready for the ritual.

She walked over to Lola and stood immediately in front of her, looking down at the girl with a mixture of pity and disdain.

Lola looked up at her, with some trepidation. "So what's the news?"

Paula smiled. "As you no doubt heard, everything went to plan. Your debt has now been paid off, sweetheart. You're free again!"

"And Abi? Did they…?"

"Yes, they certainly did. Abi got her brains well and truly fucked out. And you got your revenge on her, for Miriam. Are you happy now?"

Mournfully, Lola shook her head. She looked close to tears. Paula grabbed hold of the garish purple hair at the top of her head. "You *should* be happy, Lola, or at least pretty damn grateful. I could have fed *you* to those wolves, rather than Abi, or let you walk the streets until Marcus caught up with you and cut your throat. You've been a very foolish girl."

"I know, Paula. Thank you for saving my arse."

Paula yanked her head to and fro. "No, *wrong* name! Get it right! Who am I?"

Lola swallowed. "Annabel. Thank you, Annabel, for saving my arse!"

"That's better." Paula let go of the hair. "Now… you know what to do, you little sorry-arsed bitch."

Lola nodded. Paula opened her legs wide, so that the shoes were a metre apart. She closed her eyes and leaned her head back, listening to the brutish, sometimes grotesque sounds of the zoo animals through the slightly opened window. She took a deep breath and smiled as Lola bent down and began to kiss the black shoes. Soon she made her way up along the white cotton socks, then kissed the bony knees. Despite everything, Lola started to get excited – due not only to her many years of submission to Paula, but also to the top-grade cocaine that her Mistress had given her a short while ago. She lifted the grey skirt and, beneath it, the half-slip petticoat with the finely embroidered hem. She reached for the top of the tan-coloured nylon tights and carefully drew them down – they were already laddered in several places – until they reached Paula's knees and became stretched too wide to be taken down any further. Paula picked up the skirt and the half-slip and held them up around her waist, to give Lola access to her crutch. Lola moved her mouth up to Paula's long hard white thighs, licking them then kissing them with a studied devotion. Paula moaned, and kept her eyes shut. Finally Lola reached the white knickers, which were somewhat loose on Paula's slim body and in danger of falling down, and planted a long kiss on the gusset. As always, she could smell Paula's excitement beneath the cotton fabric. Her eyes still shut, Paula moaned again, this time louder as Lola's mouth made contact with her hot crutch. Lola knew it was time to speak.

"Oh Annabel," she said, "you're so beautiful…"

Paula's smile broadened. Lola continued.

"You're the most perfect, the most divine creature I've ever seen…"

"Yes," sighed Paula. "Oh *yes*…"

"I can't resist you," said Lola. "I want you, Annabel, more than anything else in the world…" She pulled at the waistband of the knickers and they slipped off with the greatest of ease, exposing Paula's smoothly shaved pussy. Lola slowly tugged them down until they were also at knee-level, the elastic stretched to the maximum. The amber streak was wet again, reflecting Paula's arousal, but the gusset was now like a vaginal palimpsest, with layer after layer of fluid having been secreted over it during the past year. The smell of it made Lola go moist between the legs. She looked up and saw that Paula had opened the labia of her pussy. The smell from *that* was even more pungent. Lola prepared herself.

"Go on, you slut. Do it – *now!*" growled Paula. "Lick the divine vessel!"

Lola obeyed, embracing her customary surrender to her Mistress, and thrust her tongue straight into Paula's cleft; then she flicked and twisted it around deep inside her soaking vagina with the expertise that comes only with long practice. With one hand Lola reached behind Paula's hips and eased her middle finger into the crevice between her buttocks. The anus had already been carefully oiled. As the finger touched it, Paula started to tremble. She was coming already, thinking about what Bernie's gang had just done to Abi.

"Yes!" shouted Paula, twisting and pushing her groin into Lola's face. Her eyes were still shut. "Now! Do it *now!*"

Lola rammed her finger into Paula's sphincter with a vengeance, as she always did, as if to get her own back for all the intimidation and punishment she had suffered at the hands of her Mistress. Paula's eyes opened wide and her mouth broke into a manic-triumphant grin as she climaxed into Lola's face with a guttural shout, almost like a man's, squeezing the girl's head between her leanly muscled thighs with each convulsion. Lola groaned as her mouth and her face were flooded with Paula's acidic come-fluid. As the spasms gradually slowed, she withdrew her finger from Paula's backside, as per the rules. Paula, in ecstasy, clenched her buttocks, straightened her long legs and lifted her crutch from Lola's head as her orgasm took her entire body upwards, upwards all the way to Heaven...

"Annabel!" groaned Paula, her face a picture of utter bliss. "Oh

Anna…*bel*!" She closed her eyes again and pressed both of her hands hard over her vagina. "Anna… ohh!"

A gust of wind suddenly blew into the room, from the open window, and extinguished one of the black candles.

Paula opened her eyes wide in astonishment. Her hands continued to clutch her genitals as her climax abruptly died away. Lola, still on her knees, twisted round to look at the candle. Then she turned back to Paula.

"What was that?" she asked.

Paula let out a long slow breath. She was shaking from her orgasm but nonetheless managed to respond. "It was Annabel!" she gasped.

"Annabel?" said Lola, incredulous.

Paula nodded, swallowing hard and closing her eyes for a moment. "She answered my call. She's still here, trying to save herself. Even though Abi is no longer in any fit state to be contacted by her."

Lola wiped her mouth with the back of her hand and looked up at her Mistress. "You mean it isn't over yet?"

Paula shook her head. She released the grey skirt and half-slip, which didn't drop far enough to conceal the tangle of underwear around her knees. Still breathing heavily, she looked down at Lola. "No, sweetheart… It isn't over yet. There's one more job still to be done – to remove the last vestige of Annabel from this world, so only *one* of us remains in it! And I need you for that job as well."

"Why?"

"Because the job has to be done properly. By following the correct procedure. According to ancient tradition."

Lola nodded, and smiled slyly. "All right, Mummy. Whatever you say. I owe you one!"

"You do," grinned Paula, baring her teeth. "And it's going to be a really *big* one. This time, sweetheart, you'll have to give me everything you've got!"

Lola suddenly felt uneasy. Not for the first time, she wondered whether Paula had lost her mind. But she knew she had no choice but to do what she was told. And if she stayed in the game, there was some chance, however remote, of saving Abi's life. Nothing else seemed to matter much anymore.

"Now," said Paula. "Be a good girl and pull up your Mummy's knickers!"

XIX

Friday 11ᵗʰ August, in the late afternoon. The Black Sun Gallery, off Brick Lane, east-central London.

The taxi-cab turned off Commercial Street by the old Hawksmoor church, opposite the entrance to Spitalfields Market, heading towards Brick Lane. Another turn, into a narrow side street, took the cab to the short alleyway that led to the Black Sun Gallery. Paula directed the driver to pull over. She paid the fare and exited the cab with Lola.

"It's just a few yards up here," said Lola. She pointed to a sign on the wall.

"You lead the way, sweetheart," replied Paula. She crooked her arm and Lola, like a dutiful daughter, linked hers in it. Paula had put on her customary short bobbed wig and looked every inch the respectable mother, dressed in a silky pale green blouse and checked pencil skirt, while Lola wore a short black leather dress, conspicuously zipped up at the front, with garish red fishnet tights that matched her hair, plus the usual boots. She carried a black latex handbag with rows of little white skulls imprinted over the outside.

After they had strolled some dozen yards down the high-walled alleyway they came to a black-painted double-door entrance, with a sign above it showing a spinning black vortex on a white background. The foyer within was brightly lit, with a teenage girl behind the desk and a burly middle-aged security guard by her side. He wore a dark uniform.

The girl's face lit up when she saw Lola. "Lolly! How *lovely* to see you again!"

"Hi, Donna," replied Lola. She was relieved to see another student from the college.

Donna leaned over the desk and the girls kissed each other firmly on the lips.

"You been on holiday?" said Donna.

"Sort of," replied Lola. "This is my mum, Paula."

Paula and Donna exchanged brief greetings.

"Where's that yummy sister of yours?" asked Donna.

"Sister?" replied Lola. "Oh, you mean Abigail?"

"Yeah. The dark-haired angel in the long white dress. Everyone was talking about her after the college party. Wondering whether she got off with Miriam!"

"She's away at the moment," said Lola, somewhat curtly. "On holiday."

"Oh. What a shame. I hope she can come and see the exhibition. She's a big part of it!"

Paula had wandered over to a poster on the wall advertising the exhibition. Under the title "Divine Woman" was a monochrome portrait of a pretty young girl with swept-back blond hair wearing a black crown of thorns, which had scratched her head and caused several trails of vivid red blood to run down over her face. Her bare shoulders suggested that she was naked.

"I like the poster," said Paula. "Is the model one of Miriam's students as well?"

"Yes," replied Donna cheerily. "It's Alex. Doesn't she look great?"

The poster had a label stuck over it at the top declaring "Opening Day".

"Excuse me, ladies," said the security man to Paula and Lola. "As you can see, today is the Opening Day. Entrance by invitation only. Do you both have an invite?"

"It's okay, George," said Donna. "They're both with the college. Miriam said to let them straight in."

A little reluctantly, George nodded. He turned away and sat down on a chair.

"We've hired a number of security men, for the whole of the exhibition," explained Donna.

"Why?" asked Lola.

"Because we've had some threats from religious extremists. Ultra-Catholics, as Miriam calls them. They think the exhibition is blasphemous and have threatened to protest against it, or even disrupt it. So we have to be careful who we let in. Especially today."

"I'm sure any controversy will attract lots of people," smiled Paula. "There's no such thing as bad publicity if you're an artist."

"I suppose not," laughed Donna. "Anyway, feel free to go in. Enjoy the show!" She handed them each an introductory leaflet.

Paula and Lola linked arms again and proceeded into the main gallery, which was as brightly lit as the foyer. Dozens of photographs, many of them very large, lined every wall. There were a few people milling about, but not too many to spoil the occasion.

"Remember, sweetheart," said Paula. "Let me do the talking. Especially when we're with Miriam."

"All right," replied Lola, glumly.

"Now," said Paula. "Where's the picture with you in it?"

"Over there," said Lola, pointing to a nearby exhibit. They strode over to the large photo, positioned in landscape orientation, which had been expanded to some four feet in length and three feet in height. Like all the others in the gallery it had an explanatory text by its side, with an appropriate quotation from the Bible to provide a scriptural context. Paula, whose interest in the scriptures was limited, ignored the text and gazed at the image. It showed Lola on her knees, naked, struggling under the weight of the long black cross she was carrying. Her body was coloured in a very pale yet luminous orange, which suited her ginger hair, while the crowd of people in the background were all in monochrome, mainly various shades of grey, and were smartly dressed in modern clothing. Many of the men wore suits, the women evening dress. They were sneering and laughing at the Christ while she groaned, almost crying, under her burden. She wore a black crown of thorns.

"What do you think?" asked Lola.

Paula smiled. "Why, she's captured you *perfectly*, sweetheart! It's the essence of Lola!"

"It's the story of my life," sighed Lola.

"A self-imposed burden, you mean?"

This annoyed Lola. "No. A burden other people have imposed on *me*. Going right back to my natural parents."

"You *poor* little thing!" Paula changed the subject. "Was that cross actually heavy to carry? It looks as if it was."

"It was made of light wood, but because it was so big it was quite heavy. Miriam wanted to get an authentic expression of pain on my face, so she made me struggle for real under the weight."

"She sounds like a very astute woman," replied Paula. "I must get a copy of this photo, at the front desk."

"I'm sure you'll enjoy viewing it back at home," said Lola sarcastically. "Maybe you can stick it up on the wall and show it to your devil-worshipping chums."

"What a good idea!" replied Paula, sharply pinching Lola's arm.

"Ow! That hurt!"

"Now let's look at some of the others, shall we?" They moved up along the side wall, Lola ruefully rubbing her upper arm. The pictures were all depictions of the female Christ's Journey to the Cross, each station featuring a nude young girl. Paula nodded approvingly.

"I take it these are all Miriam's students?"

"Yes."

"She obviously has a very close relationship with them."

"She's very charismatic," replied Lola. "She can talk you into doing anything."

"So it seems. I can't wait to meet her."

"Well, now's your chance," said Lola. "She's over there, in the middle of the gallery."

Paula turned and saw Miriam, dressed in a long white gown, talking to a large rotund middle-aged man with a heavy beard. By her side stood a twenty-something girl with long black hair down to her waist, clothed in a white mini-dress, designed to resemble an ancient Greek toga. The group stood in the centre of a black circle painted on the white floor, which sent big black sunrays spreading out to the walls of the gallery in every direction.

"Who is Miriam talking to?" asked Paula.

"It's Rickie Squires, an art journalist," replied Lola. "He hangs around the college a lot, trying to find things to write about. And trying to get off with the girls. Yuck!"

"And the young lady?"

"I think that's Naomi, Miriam's assistant. She also works here at the gallery. I met her once. She's quite sexy."

"She certainly is…"

At this point Miriam turned and spotted them. She waved cheerily to Lola, who waved back somewhat less cheerily. His conversation over, Rickie walked away to look at the exhibits. Paula took Lola by the arm and in a few moments they were at the centre of the gallery.

Miriam held Lola by the shoulders and affectionately kissed her on both cheeks, even though she saw that the girl was feeling resentful, and knew the reason why. Then she extended her hand to Paula.

"You must be Paula! I'm so pleased to meet you at last. I've heard *such* a lot about you!"

Paula responded with her most charming smile and shook the hand warmly. "Not as much as I've heard about *you*, Miriam! And it's all merited, from what I've seen here."

"Thank you. You like the pictures?"

"Oh yes, they're very powerful. Whoever thought that Christianity could be so sexy?"

Miriam grinned. "I've tried to make it sexy. By giving it a distinctively female quality. Why shouldn't Divine Love and sex be one and the same?"

"Indeed. Why not?" replied Paula, still smiling. She was favourably impressed by Miriam: by her severe grey hair, her dark eyes, and her full-length white chiffon Greek goddess gown, which showed off a daring amount of cleavage – enhanced, Paula surmised, by an artfully concealed strapless bra. Just above the plump cleavage hung a large gleaming gold crucifix. Matching gold Venus-shaped ear-rings dangled down at either side of her neck.

"That's a sexy way of drawing attention to your crucifix," said Paula, pointing at Miriam's chest. "Is it part of the exhibition?"

Miriam, who was always excited by provocative remarks, laughed. "Yes, it certainly is! I'm glad people are noticing it. But it's actually a genuine crucifix. I've had this for many years – since I was at convent school in Ireland."

"I had one as well, many years ago. I was at convent school too."

Miriam raised her black-painted eyebrows. "Really? How very interesting." Her expression became rather less cheerful. She turned to her assistant. "Naomi, darling, would you be kind enough to show Lola around, while Paula and I have a little chat?"

"Come on, Lola," said Naomi, taking the younger girl's arm. "Let me give you a little tour." Lola nodded and happily walked away with her, grateful to escape from Paula for a while.

Now not cheerful at all, Miriam turned to Paula. "Thank you for phoning me to let me know about Abi," she said. "Have you heard from her again?"

Paula shook her head. "No, I'm afraid not. The last I heard was that she rushed down to the West Country, to visit a distant relative she has there. Somewhere in Devon, I believe. Apparently the relative has made contact with Abi's long-lost daughter, Dolores. So you can imagine how desperate Abi was to go down and see her."

"Yes, of course," replied Miriam. "Still, I don't understand why she couldn't have rung me, however briefly, just to let me know. I do hope she can return in time to see the exhibition." She gestured towards an unoccupied corner of the gallery, where they could talk without being overheard, and they slowly made their way towards it.

"Abi doesn't always behave rationally, as you've already found out," went on Paula. "I think I know what's in her mind better than anyone, and even I can't believe everything she tells me."

Miriam sighed. "Yes, the poor thing is very confused."

Paula rolled up the exhibition leaflet in her hands. She looked deeply reflective. "I appreciate everything you've done to help her, Miriam. But you must understand that... Abi is prone to some very serious delusions."

Miriam feigned ignorance. "Delusions? What sort of delusions?"

They reached the quiet corner of the gallery and Paula turned to face Miriam.

"For example – Abi is convinced that she was caned by her headmistress at St Margaret's School, when she found out about her affair with her art teacher."

"Did the affair really happen?"

"Oh yes, the affair really happened. And someone informed the headmistress about it. But Abi wasn't caned. She was expelled from the school. Hot on the heels of her art teacher, who was immediately sacked."

Miriam was puzzled. "But she's always been so insistent about being caned – by Sister Helena. She's told me about it in such detail."

"Yes, she's told me about it as well – in intimate detail. But it wasn't true. By the time Abi went to St Margaret's, schoolgirls weren't being caned anymore, at least in this country. Not legally, anyway. And Sister Helena scrupulously abided by the law."

"So it's all in Abi's imagination?"

"Yes. I've tried to persuade her that she wasn't flogged, but she won't let go of her fantasy."

"How do you know about all this? How can you be so sure that Abi is... fantasising?"

Paula took a deep breath. "Because... *I* was at St Margaret's School as well. And I was in the same class as Abi."

Miriam was astonished. "Goodness! Abi never mentioned that to me. Not once!"

"That's because she's forgotten me. A result of her impaired memory, no doubt. That's why I've been happy to treat her, for a very modest fee."

"Well, you're very kind, Paula. Trying to help someone who's forgotten all about you!"

"It's more than just kindness," said Paula. "There's another reason."

"Oh?"

Paula looked down at the floor. She breathed deeply again. "*I* was the one who overheard Abi having sex with her teacher, when I went to the art studio, after lessons. *I* was the one who betrayed her to the headmistress. I took some damning evidence that was lying there, in the art studio, and went straight to Sister Helena and showed her. She believed me and summoned Abi to her study. Abi confessed and was duly expelled."

"Oh my God!" Miriam was shocked. "Why did you do it? Why did you betray her?"

"Why? Because I was madly in love with her. As were many of the other girls. Miriam, you should have seen Abi at sixteen. She was the most beautiful, most perfect creature you could imagine – like something that had come down from Heaven. One look at her face was enough to make you melt away. Of course, she didn't like me and did her best to ignore me. So what better way of getting my own back than destroying her when she fell from grace?"

Miriam turned and looked back across the gallery, as if to recover her bearings. "Yes, I suppose so. Unrequited love can be a bitter experience... as we all know."

"I'm not proud of what I did to her. In fact, as time went by I grew more and more ashamed of myself. So when a colleague told me about Abi, after her crash last year, I thought I might repay her by helping her to recover. The fact that she couldn't remember me any more actually made it much easier to treat her."

"What about her daughter? Dolores – or Dolly, as she calls her. Is she a fantasy as well?"

Paula shrugged. "I don't know. Abi may well have given birth to a daughter, nine months after she left the school. There's every likelihood that her art teacher was the father."

Miriam was relieved. "So she may have rushed off to the West Country for a good reason."

"Yes, she may well have done. I hope she did. But there's an even more serious delusion that you need to know about."

"Which is?"

"Her older sister, Annabel, never existed. There was no such person in the year ahead of us at St Margaret's School. Annabel is a complete fantasy."

Miriam put her hand over her mouth. She was now visibly shaken. "So why…?"

"Why invent her? I'm not sure. It's probably the result of her accident last year. In my opinion Annabel is Abi's lost self, the stronger self that she used to be but was separated from by her accident. The self that she'd like to become again but, sadly, can't find anymore."

Miriam's bosom heaved as she momentarily closed her eyes and took a deep breath. "Paula, thank you so much for explaining all this to me. A lot of things make much more sense now. And I feel sorrier than ever for poor Abi. Oh goodness. She's gone through so much."

"Yes. She really needs all our love and support. I know you'll do your best for her, Miriam. As I will, too."

"You think she'll be back by Monday?"

"Well, that's what she told me. Let's hope her trip is successful and she finds what she's been looking for. A reunion with Dolly would mean *ever* so much to her."

"Yes, let's hope she finds her," said Miriam. She touched Paula's arm.

"You know, Paula, *I* owe a lot to Abi as well. Without her, I wouldn't have the main item of this exhibition. The centrepiece of the show."

"Oh?"

"Let me show you, my dear." Still touching Paula by the arm, Miriam led her towards a side room. By the entrance there was a sign on a stand with an arrow pointing to the room, which read: "Future Perfect".

"Is that the name of the exhibit?" asked Paula. "'Future Perfect'?"

"Yes. It's an ironic title, as you'll see. The picture is on show all by itself in the Chapel."

"The Chapel?"

"That's what we've called the side room."

As they paused at the entrance, Paula raised her eyebrows in surprise. The room was dimly lit and had been filled with half a dozen church pews, which looked well-worn and authentic. A few spectators sat on them, gazing at the far wall. There were two young nuns kneeling on cushions at the front row of pews.

"You actually have nuns in here?" asked Paula.

Miriam put her finger to her lips. "Please keep your voice down in the Chapel!" she whispered. "No, they aren't real nuns. They're two of my students who've dressed up as nuns, to create the atmosphere we want. And the pews are genuine leftovers that we bought from a local church when it closed down. Can you smell the frankincense?"

Paula coughed. "I can hardly avoid smelling it. But what a great idea!" In the gloom she spotted Lola, in the second row, staring up at the wall, looking stunned. Paula entered the Chapel, ahead of Miriam, and stood behind one of the pews in the middle of the room. Miriam joined her.

All the ceiling lights were trained on the far wall, like rays of sunlight shining down from Heaven. The picture, vividly illuminated without reflecting back any light, covered the whole of the wall, and for the most part featured a charred post-nuclear landscape, with bits of rubble, shards of metal, human remains, domestic furniture, children's toys, car parts, empty food cans, bits of cardboard and many other commonplace items scattered far and wide, all depicted in grim shades of monochrome. It was the debris of an entire civilisation. In the foreground, nailed to a vertical jet-black cross, was a life-sized crucified nude woman. She was completely shorn of hair and her strong beautiful body was rendered in what looked like perfect unalloyed gold, shining with a magnificent divine radiance. There was a crown of black thorns on her bald head. Her crying face was turned up to the louring sky with an expression of profound, unutterable despair, transcending the physical pain of the big black nails which had been hammered into the palms of her hands and her twisted feet. Her right nipple was wrenched and disfigured, and a trail of bright red blood snaked down from it to her navel, then down again over her lower belly to the cleft of her shaved genitals, into which it disappeared. Despite the graphic explicitness of the image, its posture and its expression conveyed something noble and majestic, as if the martyrdom of the subject had brought forth the true divinity of her nature. By crucifying her, it seemed that mankind had destroyed divinity itself. And thus destroyed its own future.

"Oh my God!" gasped Paula, taken aback. "It's Abi!"

Miriam nodded, carefully observing her reaction.

Paula gulped. Then she shook her head. "No, it's *not* Abi. It's Annabel!"

"Annabel?" whispered Miriam. "But I thought you said…"

Paula turned round to Miriam and looked her directly in the eye. "You know what I mean," she said in a sharp whisper. "You've photographed *Annabel*. That's why she's made of gold!" There was a strange ironic smile on her lips. Her large blue eyes were wide, almost bulging. Then she looked over at Lola, who was sobbing uncontrollably as she stared at the picture. Tears streamed down her cheeks and her flooded eyes reflected the light from the ceiling. Her goth-girl make-up was smudged all over her face. She sniffled noisily. One of the faux nuns, who knew Lola well, had turned round and was watching her with some concern.

Miriam followed Paula's gaze. "Oh goodness," she whispered. "Lola seems very upset."

"Yes," replied Paula, recovering some of her composure. "She was very close to Abi."

"It's only to be expected, I suppose. It's all my fault."

"No, Miriam. It's not your fault," said Paula.

This reply puzzled Miriam. But Paula offered no further explanation. "You must excuse me," she said. "I have to take Lola out of here. It's all too much for her."

"Of course…"

Paula's cold hand touched Miriam's arm in farewell and she quietly moved over to a position just behind Lola. She held her by her shoulders and leaned forward. "Come on, sweetheart," she whispered. "We need some fresh air." She attempted to lift Lola from her seat. At first the girl resisted, and angrily twisted away from her, still sobbing. Most of the spectators were now looking over at them, much to Paula's annoyance. Then Lola glanced up at the picture for one last time before abruptly turning away and bolting out of the Chapel. Paula picked up Lola's handbag, which had been abandoned on the seat of the pew, and moved hastily after her, giving Miriam a little wave as she departed. Miriam, nonplussed, waved back, now much concerned about Lola. Clearly it was the right thing to take her out of the Chapel, but there was something about what she'd seen and heard that deeply disturbed her. As if the revelations about Abi hadn't already shaken her enough…

By the time Paula had gone out into the oppressively bright main gallery, Lola was already running towards the foyer and the exit, again attracting attention from some of the spectators. Paula strode briskly after her, the heels of her shoes loudly tapping the black sunrays on the floor. By the time she reached the foyer, Lola had already left the building.

"Is everything okay?" asked Donna from behind the reception desk. She looked bewildered. "Lola just left…"

"It's all right, she'll be fine," said Paula, now panting for breath. "Thanks for everything. It was a great show!"

As Paula exited via the double doors, she saw Lola up ahead in the alleyway. The girl had fallen to her knees, having almost reached the opening of the alley onto the street. Finally Paula caught up with her, puffing heavily and holding onto her bobbed wig.

"For God's sake, Lola! Try to control yourself!"

Lola looked up at Paula. Her eyes were still flooded with tears. A long strand of purple hair hung down over her smeared face. "You saw that picture! *We're* the ones who've crucified Abi! *We* did that to her! And Miriam's seen right through us. You can tell from her picture. She knows what we've done to Abi!"

"Don't be ridiculous. She doesn't know anything. She's just a photographer."

"I want to see Abi! I want to know she's all right! I don't want her last memory of me to be my boot stamping down on her and me abusing her! I can't bear it, the thought of her remembering me that way!"

"You're being hysterical, Lola. You need to calm down. You've been doing too much Charlie again."

"I can't take any more of this crap. All this pretence and deception... it's disgusting, it's cruel, it's wicked. It's totally wrong, what we've done to her all these months!"

"It's too late now to worry about right and wrong," replied Paula disdainfully. "You knew the score, sweetheart, from the start of the game."

Lola got to her feet, rather unsteadily, as if preparing to walk away. She snatched her handbag from Paula's grasp.

"It's not too late for *me*. I'm going to find Abi, wherever she is. Right now. And I'm going to ask her to forgive me. And if you don't like it, you can go fuck yourself, you evil bitch!"

Paula abruptly slapped Lola's face, so hard that the girl fell back against the nearby brick wall and slithered down to the granite pavement. Then she fell on her side and drew up her legs, once again crying helplessly. Paula squatted down to talk to her.

"Like I said, darling, it's too late now. Don't give me any of that moralistic nonsense. I'll tell you what you are, Lola. You're a mangy little alley cat who's used up all its lives. The only reason you're still breathing is because *I've* protected you from the wolves. Don't forget that!"

Lola carried on sobbing miserably, her eyes closed. Still squatting, Paula turned and looked back along the alleyway, towards the art gallery. She had to admit that she'd been deeply impressed by Miriam's crucifixion picture. It had genuinely shaken her. And now she had just thought of the perfect way of returning the compliment.

XX

Monday 14th August, at ten o'clock in the morning. Miriam's studio in Bethnal Green.

With a smile of satisfaction Miriam closed the newspaper on her desk, where she sat in the reception area at the front of her studio-workshop. Another good review in the weekend press, with more no doubt to follow in the art journals. The gallery directors and the publishers in New York and San Francisco would be delighted to see her "Divine Woman" receive such a positive response. So far hostility from religious quarters had been muted, with only a single Catholic bishop, in a remote diocese of the country, voicing any criticism of the exhibition. Perhaps the twenty-first century would after all usher in a more tolerant and diverse cultural outlook, an era of peace and harmony. But somehow, she doubted it.

There was a ring on the bell at the front entrance door. Through the reinforced window panel she could see one of her regular postal delivery men, with a special parcel for her. She rose from the desk. As per usual when in her studio, she was dressed casually, today in checked shirt and denim jeans. She opened the door, exchanged greetings, signed for the delivered item, and took it over to her desk. It was a thick board-backed A4 manila envelope. She opened it with her paper knife and pulled out a yellow wallet folder. On the front of this was written the title "Past Perfect" in large, black, almost minatory capital letters.

Suddenly feeling uneasy, Miriam opened the folder. It contained some twenty oversized photographic prints. Nothing could have prepared her for the contents. Each print, rendered in full colour, featured a naked young woman hanging lifelessly in a large walk-in shower enclosure, which had been constructed of two black marble side panels, set about two metres apart. It looked as if the water had just been turned off. The woman hung from two thick metal rings, about five feet high, to which she had been shackled by handcuffs. Her head was slumped on her chest. Both legs were bent sharply at the knee: one because a toe had got stuck in the drain grill, the other because the thigh extended sideways at a wide angle, as if the knee had been trying to reach the marble panel. The woman's body and hair were completely soaked; but much more striking were the injuries to her body, a multitude of scratches and bites and scars that covered her flesh, in many cases bringing spots or lines of blood to the surface of the olive skin. The most severe was the injury to her right nipple, which had been cruelly twisted and pierced. Both of the large splayed breasts had been extensively scratched and bitten. Bizarrely a heavy gold crucifix hung down between them, featuring a carved figure of Christ. As Miriam examined each print with mounting horror, she realised that the lifeless body was Abi's. Each successive picture moved in closer towards the hanging body; after the first half dozen, the head was raised up by a length of rope under the chin, as if lifted to pose for the camera; and Miriam could see without doubt that it *was* Abi, although her face was grotesquely distorted, her mouth wide open and her eyes crossed and rolled upwards. Miriam's heart began to pound; the blood whistled in her ears. It felt as if a huge ice-cold hand had gripped her from behind the chair. The final pictures were almost pornographic, giving detailed close-ups of the face – the gaping mouth, with the tongue and the white teeth plainly visible, and the upturned tawny eyes – as well as intimate close-ups of the swollen genitals and the multiple wounds, dwelling in particular on the brutal laceration to the nipple. It soon dawned on Miriam that these photographs were not recent. Abi's nasal stud was absent, with no sign of any removal scar; the wound to the nipple was obviously fresh; and the hair, hanging in a mess of ragged strands, appeared to be somewhat shorter than Abi's. But the woman in these pictures looked unquestionably dead. Blotches of blood had gathered in several places under her skin. Miriam had seen corpses before, notably those of her parents, and as a photographer and an artist she knew very well what a dead body looked like. Then she remembered something that Paula had said in the Chapel in the Black Sun Gallery, while staring at her crucifixion picture, and she repeated the phrase out loud...

"No, it's *not* Abi. It's Annabel!"

With shaking hands, she pulled out the final item from the folder. It was a Tarot card: The Hanged Man. In this case, there was little doubt that it meant the Hanged Woman. Miriam knew enough about the Tarot to recall the meaning of the card: suspension in a state of uncertainty... sacrifice... and of course, crucifixion.

In a state of near panic, Miriam reached for her phone and rang Abi's landline. Now she couldn't even obtain Abi's voice message, as she had done a few days ago, but only a shrill engaged tone. She rang Abi's mobile number and got the same voice message, to which she didn't bother to reply, having already left numerous return messages. She had found no way of contacting Paula, and had no idea where Lola was. She drummed her fingers on the desk. As she glanced at the back of the big manila envelope, she noted the name of the mailing office stamped on it: Notting Hill. Had the package been sent from Abi's address? It was inconceivable. But it was a possible lead. Miriam hurriedly pushed the photos and the Tarot card back into the folder, put this into the envelope, and tucked it under her arm. She grabbed her car keys, her mobile phone and her address book. Hastily she exited the building and got into her old Jaguar sports car, parked directly outside. She started up the throaty engine. Miriam had never visited

Abi's flat, preferring instead to have her lover come to stay at the house in Camden Town, an arrangement that suited both women; but now, to her consternation, she realised it might be her only chance of finding Abi. She put her foot down hard and the Jaguar roared away.

In less than half an hour Miriam arrived at Notting Hill and parked the car near to the front of Abi's residence. She checked the address in her book before dashing up the stairwell to the intercom panel in the white-painted entrance porch. To compound her dread, she saw that the name label next to the button for Abi's flat, which was on the second floor, had been removed. The slot was empty. Miriam pressed the button and the buzzer responded, but predictably there was no answer. After several fruitless attempts, she gave up and sat down at the top of the entrance stairwell. She waited on the granite step for what seemed an eternity, her head in her hands, her heart pounding, hoping against hope that Abi would suddenly appear walking along the street, returning home, and all would be well. She breathed deeply, trying to quell her rising terror. The images of the lifeless body hanging in the shower kept flashing before her eyes whenever she shut them.

Finally someone opened the entrance door behind her. It was a long-haired young man in a T-shirt and jeans, on his way out to walk his dog.

"Thank goodness!" said Miriam. "Would you please let me in to call at Flat 6? It's on the second floor. I think my friend who lives there may be unwell, and may need help. Her name is Abigail."

"Abigail?" replied the young man. "I'm on the second floor but I don't know anyone called Abigail. There *was* a lady in Flat 6 called Maria – a dark-haired lady. I think she was Italian. She moved out last week. The flat's empty at the moment."

"Yes, yes, Maria – I think that's her middle name!"

Seeing her obvious distress, the young man relented. "Well, I guess there's no harm in you checking, if you want to go up and have a look for yourself." He held open the door for her.

"Thank you so much!" exclaimed Miriam. She darted past him and once inside turned to race up the carpeted communal stairs. When she reached the first floor she had to pause for a moment as she felt a stab of pain in her arthritic knee. She proceeded up to the second floor more carefully, though still hurrying, until she arrived breathless at the front door of Abi's flat. She rang the bell. Something about the way it sounded immediately told her that the flat was empty. After a couple of rings, she pushed against the heavy door and twisted the handle, but it was firmly locked. She knelt down on the doormat, took off her glasses and opened the flap of the big letter-box to peer in, ignoring the throbbing pain in her knee. She saw at once that that not only the hall lobby but also the lounge beyond, its door wide open, were deserted. There wasn't a stick of furniture in sight. Even the carpets had been pulled up, exposing the bare timber floorboards.

"Abi!" she called through the letterbox. "Are you there? Abi darling – speak to me! Please!" Her despairing voice echoed back from the hollow emptiness of the flat.

"Abi!" she shouted once again. Once again, nothing but an echo. It was as if Abi had never lived here. As if she had never existed.

Miriam's bad knee finally gave way and slowly she sank over to one side, her hip sliding down towards the rough doormat as her hand remained forlornly grasping the letterbox. She pressed her face against the lower panel of the timber door and began to weep, realising at last that Abi had been taken from her, taken for some dark insane reason she couldn't fathom. Her worst fears had been confirmed. She thought again of the words of the ancient poet, which had so preoccupied her in recent years: What is life once the page of love has turned? The page of love had now indeed turned, and there was no way of retrieving it. She wept bitterly for all the wasted chances of her life, for all the connections broken, the avenues unexplored, the words unspoken, the hopes unfulfilled, the people left behind, rejected, ignored, forgotten... and she wept above all for her one last chance of love, the Golden One whose surpassing beauty and gracious heart would have redeemed all that had been lost, and would have made what remained of her life a heavenly procession. Now the Redeemer was gone, and there was nothing left for her to do but limp her way through an unending vale of tears.

XXI

Tuesday 15ᵗʰ August, in the late afternoon. The day of the Full Moon. A dark desolate wood to the west of St Margaret the Martyr School, North Devon.

Abi no longer knew whether she was in a dream, a dream within a dream, or had departed the real world and been resurrected in some murky hellish afterlife. Bereft of all clothing, a ball-gag stuffed into her mouth, she staggered forward with her hands cuffed behind her back and a collar around her neck attached to a long chain. Pulling her forward with the chain was Sebastian, dressed in a full length black ceremonial robe. The hood was down and his dyed blond hair was in full view, some three metres ahead of her. Behind her followed another black-robed figure, the pale red-haired young man who had let her into the Soho flat a week ago, many days ago... or perhaps it was as much as a month ago. It felt like a long time, during which she had lain drugged and helpless, tied down to a large bed while one man after another had taken possession of her body in every conceivable way. Some of the time she'd been awake, some of the time drowsy and half-conscious, some of the time completely unconscious. Afterwards she vaguely recalled being carried to the rear of a large van in the middle of the night, naked, chained and gagged, before being driven away on a long journey. She guessed she was by now a great distance from London, but had no idea where she'd been taken. Perhaps she was already dead. If not, she knew that her death was close at hand.

As she walked on, barefoot, she repeatedly stumbled and fell to the ground, scraping and cutting her knees, occasionally falling all the way over onto her side or even her front. Every time she fell, Sebastian and the other man lifted her up, again and again, with great care and patience, as if to preserve her for what lay ahead. Her feet were already lacerated, after walking for some distance on the twigs and stones of the forest floor. Her body was covered in scratches and cuts, most of which had been administered with needles and razor-blades while she'd been held captive in the Soho flat. Fortunately she was too numb from repeated drugging to feel the pain too acutely. Her hair hung down in dishevelled clumps, and occasionally flopped over her face. Splotches of mud and fragments of leaf and even small pieces of grit and stone had gradually attached themselves to her wet sticky skin.

She surmised it was late in the afternoon, as there was some light in the sky, above the layer of cloud, although the weather was damp and chilly, and an occasional cold breeze swept over her body. It felt as if rain was on the way. She was constantly shivering, and felt weak and exhausted after many days without food. The forest of slender trees ahead of her seemed to reach up out of the muddy ground like a multitude of dark frozen tentacles, meeting far above her head in triumphant unison as they greeted her approach. Occasionally their branches swayed in the breeze. There was no sound of any living creature. The middle distance faded into a gloomy grey-green haze. It was as if all life in the wood had been paralysed, placed on hold for her arrival. Sebastian continued to lead her up a gradual incline, along a winding muddy path which had for many years been used by ramblers to reach the top of the woods. Despite the numbing effect of the drugs, her feet hurt terribly.

Finally they left the thickest part of the wood as the crooked path joined a straighter, broader track, on higher ground. This was easier on Abi's feet. The light here was still good, and she could see the way ahead slightly better. After another couple of minutes they arrived at an old stone bridge, probably built in the eighteenth century, straddling a deep narrow gorge in which a river ran some twenty feet below them. There were high steep banks on both sides, full of trees and bushes. On the bridge, over which the footpath ran, stood three more figures dressed in full-length black robes, complete with tall hoods which concealed their faces. They were all waiting there for her... waiting to perform the final act.

Sebastian drew Abi to the centre of the bridge. To her great relief, he released the rubber ball-gag from her aching mouth. It was soaked with saliva. Then he removed the chain and undid the collar, freeing her neck. Finally he removed the handcuffs. Abi was now surrounded by the black-robed figures; there was nowhere for her to escape, and in any case she lacked the strength or the will even to try. She held her hands down by her sides, standing obediently to attention as the figures moved closer to view her naked body. They turned her round, from side to side, this way and that, examining her wounds in minute detail. Gently they lifted her breasts and handled her buttocks and her legs, as if inspecting a slave being auctioned for purchase. But none of them spoke. As they examined her, she looked downriver and saw that on her right there was an embankment of worn granite, which followed the river for some distance before giving way to the natural steep bank of vegetation. A long time ago it had probably been used for mooring boats. It looked as if it had recently been cleared of undergrowth, to bring it back into some kind of use. Vegetation had likewise been cleared from the slender pathway and the stone steps that led down from the bridge footpath to the embankment. As Abi gazed downriver, a faint memory of this scene slowly came back to her. She recalled that she had been here before, more than once, presumably in her dreams. And she recalled that it had always been a place of foreboding and dread. Behind her, in the distance, she heard a rumble of thunder.

Presently all the black-robed figures except one withdrew a little. The foremost figure slowly dropped her hood. She was completely bald, even denuded of her eyebrows, but Abi recognised her at once. It was Paula.

"Are you surprised to see me here, Abi?"

Abi slowly shook her head. "No. Deep down, I always suspected… right from the start."

Paula's blue eyes widened. She looked genuinely surprised. "Really? And you did nothing?"

"What could I have done to resist you?"

Paula came closer and tenderly touched the side of Abi's face. "My poor darling, there was nothing you could have done. You were in my power all the time!"

Abi smiled, helplessly, and nodded. "I knew it was you, yet I wasn't able to recognise it clearly in my mind, or say it to myself… It's strange."

"No darling, it's not strange. It's hypnosis." Paula moved her hand down to gently squeeze Abi's breast. She fingered the deformed nipple, which was now surrounded by fresh wounds. Abi offered no resistance. "You were doomed from the start, Abi. From the moment you had your accident last year. You knew that as well, didn't you?"

Abi nodded again.

"We had very different plans for you, darling," went on Paula. "Much bigger plans. Which would have made us a huge amount of money. But it wasn't to be. It all went wrong, as soon as Annabel came back from the dead. She ruined everything. So now we have to bring this game to an end – much sooner than we'd planned."

Abi nodded once more. She was ready for the end, and prayed that it would bring her the peace of oblivion rather than the torments of Hell. Paula smiled and unclasped her robe. It fell to the footpath around her feet. Abi gazed in astonishment at her long white naked body, and at the enormous tattoo on her front. It depicted a winged black dragon, which stretched from her shaved pubic bone up to her chest, culminating between the small tight breasts. Each of her nipples was pierced with a zig-zag silver lightning bolt; and, incongruously, from her neck hung a hefty gold crucifix with a carved figure of Christ, looking as if it were about to be devoured by the open mouth of the tattooed dragon immediately below it.

"You recognise this tattoo?" asked Paula.

"Yes. I've seen it before... somewhere."

"You have indeed. It's the full-sized version of the tattoo on your back, which I arranged to have done several months ago – as a reminder that you belong to me."

There was another rumble of thunder. Paula moved close up to Abi and put her arms around her. She dropped her hands to caress Abi's scratched and bruised buttocks and proceeded to kiss her, affection-ately, passionately, like an ardent lover. Abi responded, keeping her arms down by her side as their tongues met. She felt the gold crucifix dangling and pressing against her breasts. After several tender kisses, Paula drew back slightly.

"Do you object to me kissing you, darling? Making love to you?"

Abi shook her head.

"I thought not. Because it's happened to you many, many times since you've been treated by me. But not at my consulting-room. It's happened in your flat, in your own hot sweaty bed… I've been there a hundred times over the last few months, Abi, fucking you regularly, making love to you non-stop, for hours at a time! Do you remember anything of what I did?"

Abi shook her head again. Her eyes were dull and glazed.

"Good! You know the best thing of all, my darling? You enjoyed it! Every time I fucked you! You surrendered to me on every occasion. That's been the biggest thrill of all!" Joyfully she squeezed Abi's buttocks.

"You're insane," replied Abi. "I would never have let that happen, for such a long time."

"You did, Abi, believe me. Until Annabel arrived on the scene – and you stopped taking my pills. At that point I had to withdraw, or she would have detected me. But when I did visit you again, last week, with your conscious consent, she was no longer there. I knew that her Presence had receded. And you were taking the pills again."

"And the cold shower running in my flat?"

Paula shook her head. "Non est mea culpa! That was Annabel, trying to get closer to you – trying to return to this world through you. The shower was her gateway. Why would I resort to such a trick, if I could have you anyway, any time I wanted? You shouldn't underestimate Annabel's strength of will, Abi. She's not the type to give up without a fight. But she *will* give up in the end – when she knows she's beaten. Then she'll surrender magnificently!"

Abi smiled forlornly. "What does any of it matter now?"

"It matters to *me*, darling, more than you could possibly imagine. But you're right. It's no longer of any consequence to *you*. All good things have to come to an end. Even you, Abi!"

"I don't care about my end. I can't even remember my beginning," replied Abi mournfully.

"Don't blame yourself," said Paula. "Your beginning, like your end, has nothing to do with you. *I* began you, Abi! From the very start you've been *my* creation, my pet, my toy – my masterpiece! You're a narrative I've constructed, a story I've written, a performance I've scripted. A performance which has now run its time and come to an end."

"Why now?" asked Abi. "You could have finished me at any time. Brought the story to an end whenever you wanted."

Paula nodded. "Yes. I could. But I had to finish you in the way I wanted – with *your* co-operation. That's why I sent you to the address in Soho – to give away all your money and deliver yourself up to Bernie and his gang. In doing that, you proved to me who and what you truly are – by willingly sacrificing yourself and everything you owned. At my behest! Surely you knew what would happen to you when you went to that address?"

Abi nodded. "Yes. I knew exactly what was going to happen to me. But I couldn't help doing what you asked me to do. I was compelled to do it… because it was my duty. It was my fate."

At this, Paula sighed with ecstasy and hugged her victim in triumph. This admission by Abi was the ultimate demonstration of her power. There was another rumble of thunder, this time closer and louder. A gust of cold wind blew over the bridge.

"Isn't it time to start?" asked Sebastian, looking up at the sky. A big black cloud was approaching above the line of the trees.

"Yes," replied Paula. "It is." She put her finger under Abi's chin. "I'm afraid it's time, darling. Time for you to go."

"Go where?"

"Into Eternity. Let me assure you, Abi, the universe is infinite and everlasting. It's made up of an endless number of realms, all connected. Sometimes the contents of one realm can spill over into the adjoining one, as you've recently discovered. But a person – a soul, if you will – exists in many of these realms at the same time, like a string that links up several beads on a rosary. The aim of Black Magic is to control the string. Then you control what happens in all the beads, in all the realms. The person's soul, the string, runs through them all, forever. And the rosary, the sum total of the soul's existence, is there for all eternity. From now on, your string will be forever in my hands. And the circle will finally be closed!"

Uncomprehending, Abi shook her head.

"There's no need for you to understand, darling," said Paula. "All you need to know is that your entire rosary now belongs to me. Or rather, to Typhon-Set. The Great Dragon. The Devourer of Souls!"

"You mean the Devil…"

"Yes, if you want to use the traditional term. But it's *so* out of date!"

"And Annabel?"

Paula nodded. "Annabel will belong to the Dragon too. When this day is over…"

The wind now began to whistle through the air, heralding the approach of the storm, followed by a crack of thunder. The first drops of rain began to blow in the air.

"All right," said Paula. "Time to get her up!"

Sebastian and another figure, still hooded, each took one of Abi's arms. They led her to the parapet wall near the middle of the bridge, facing downriver towards the embankment, and slowly lifted her up, each putting a strong hand under her thigh while carefully holding her by the wrist. Abi's feet momentarily slipped on the rough stone, but the men steadied her and held her up by her thighs and calves.

Abi looked down at the swirling water below the bridge and gasped in horror. The petite nude body of a teenage girl lay on the riverbed, right below the parapet, her head a couple of feet beneath the surface of the water. It was clear that she had been lying there for some time. Her limbs were spread-eagled and held down by ropes attached to metal tent-pegs, which had been hammered deep into the rocky riverbed. Her head and her vulva had been completely shaved, giving her the appearance of a smoothly sculpted doll. Her lifeless green eyes stared up into infinity and her mouth hung half-open, as if she'd been astonished by what had just happened to her. For a moment Abi thought that this was her long-lost daughter, Dolores. But as the pale body waved and bobbled helplessly with the flow of the current, she spotted the tiny gold stud in the girl's left nostril and realised that it was Lola.

"Oh no, *no*!" cried Abi. She felt the grief rise and burn in her chest like scalding water, and as it reached her face she burst into tears. She could take any amount of punishment, but *this* was more than she could bear. She shook her head in disbelief. "My Baby! My poor Baby!" She shut her eyes and cried like a child, her chest and her shoulders shuddering under the pressure of her sobs. The men held her tight as she shook.

Abi opened her eyes to look down again. Lola's body was still there. She turned and looked back over her shoulder at Paula, who was observing her intently.

"Why? Why did you do it? She was your daughter!" cried Abi.

Paula shook her head. "No, Abi, she wasn't my daughter. She was just a girl I made use of. A stray cat who finally ran out of lives."

"But why kill her? She was so young!" Tears flowed freely down Abi's cheeks.

"She was going to die anyway, before long. Let's just say she over-dosed sooner rather than later – at a time that suited us."

"You evil witch!" shouted Abi. "You killed her! You're totally out of your mind!"

"We'll see who's out of her mind, Abi. Very soon!" Paula smiled and moved closer to Abi as the men continued to hold her fast on the parapet. Slowly she held and kissed each of the scarred bruised buttocks, which were precisely at her head height. Then she turned to her collaborators and reached out her hand. One of the robed figures passed her a wand, made of a greyish-white human thigh-bone, approximately eighteen inches long, tipped with a large crystal shaped like an arrow-head. She raised the bone-wand with both arms and pressed the sharp tip of the crystal against the small tattoo high on Abi's back. She held it there for several seconds, pushing hard between Abi's shoulder-blades while she muttered a barbaric impre-cation ending in "Typhon-Set". Abi, still in despair, continued to cry.

Still holding the wand, still naked and barefoot, Paula strode away to the nearest end of the bridge. She made her way quickly down the stone steps and in a few moments reached the granite embankment. The rain now started to fall in earnest, swishing down on everyone, spattering over Abi's bloodied skin and flattening her dark, already bedraggled hair, instantly washing away her tears. Still sobbing, she looked down at the embankment, where Paula had taken up a position a few metres along the granite structure, not far from where Lola's body lay. A short way further down the river, a couple of metres beyond Lola, was a squat irregular knoll, covered in exotic dark green weeds that undulated as the river ran over them, which it did now with increasing speed and urgency as the storm neared. The rain came down harder and faster. Abi saw the first flash of lightning, coming from somewhere behind her, followed moments later by a big heavy crack of thunder.

Paula undid the large gold crucifix around her neck and with her left hand raised it above her head. It dangled from its chain.

"To Megalo Drako!" she shouted. "Typhon, take her soul!" She whirled the crucifix round and round above herself a few times and then flung it high into the rain-swept air. The wind blew it downstream and it plunged into the rushing water, vanishing instantly.

Then Paula crouched down on the edge of the embankment and eased herself into the river. As she made her way towards Lola, wading through the knee-high rushing water, she held the bone-wand aloft and looked up intently at Abi. In a few seconds she had reached the knoll. Carefully she placed a foot on either side of it and opened wide her long slender legs, well over a metre apart, so that she straddled the mound of wildly billowing weeds. On the riverbed right in front of her lay Lola's swaying, heaving corpse, its hairless head bobbing about in all directions. Paula was now at some risk of being swept away by the seething current, which flowed by above the level of her knees, but she ignored the danger and held the wand above her head with both hands. The rain lashed down on her body, splashing her bald head, showering down over the long dragon tattoo and streaming down between her widespread legs, but it had no perceptible effect on her. She stared up at Abi with her crazed, bulging eyes and grinned. She nodded at her brethren, who promptly raised Abi's arms aloft so that her body formed a star shape, legs wide apart and arms held straight out to the side. Abi wobbled slightly on the loose stones beneath her feet, but Sebastian and his companion gripped her thighs securely.

With both hands Paula pointed her wand straight at Abi and shouted, her voice rising above the whistling wind and the hissing rain. "To Megalo Drako!"

The four robed figures on the bridge, who had now crowded around Abi, shouted back the same phrase in unison, all looking up and raising their left arms to the darkening sky. The black cloud was now almost directly above the bridge. Barely a second after their shout, a jagged fork of lightning zipped down and hissed into the shrubbery on the embankment, its ultraviolet flash vividly illuminating the entire granite construction for a terrifying moment. A huge roar of thunder followed instantly.

Paula continued, her bone-wand still pointing up at Abi, her eyes still bulging. The rain now teemed down all over and around her, making the river chop and swirl and surge. She was undeterred. "O mighty Typhon, Lord of Lust and King of Death, I offer you the flesh of this Whore! Take her now, O Typhon!"

"Take her, Typhon!" shouted the men on the bridge. Another lightning bolt, even closer, even brighter, struck a large old tree by the embankment. With a sickening crack, a branch broke away and dangled for a moment from the tree trunk before slowly twisting and crashing down to the granite embankment. Immediately there was a gigantic clap of thunder, exploding right above them, which seemed to shake the stone bridge to its ancient foundations.

Paula repeated her shout, even louder. "Take her Typhon! Take the Whore!" Then she called out in a deep, throaty, growling voice: "ZAZAS, ZAZAS, NASATANADA ZAZAS!"

Abi looked down at the river swirling below her. She knew what was coming. But she no longer cared. She no longer wanted to live. All she wanted now was to join Lola, to embrace her in death.

"ZAZAS, ZAZAS, NASATANADA ZAZAS!" roared the four men, hastily stepping away from Abi and pointing their left arms at her back.

She took a deep breath and gazed down at her beloved girl for the last time. A moment later there was an eruption of blinding ultraviolet light all around her, as if she was at the epicentre of an exploding bomb, and what felt like a long dazzling silver spear tore through her upper body, entering precisely between her shoulder blades with a monstrous hissing flash, making every part of her body convulse before bursting out through her crutch and down between her outspread legs, striking the stone parapet in a splash of glaring white light between her feet. In an instant Abi ceased to exist, dissolved and dispersed by an electrical force a thousand times more powerful than her. The last sensation that registered in her mind was the buckling of her knees, the breaking away of the stones beneath her feet, and her twitching burning body falling forwards and hurtling down towards the river, down to the surging water, down towards Lola, down and out of the world forever... falling, falling into an abyss of nothingness, endlessly falling, collapsing into a bottomless void without awareness of anything... nothing but the sensation of falling, forever falling into eternity... forever falling into nothing forever nothing

*   *   *   *   *   *   *

0

What is this face, less clear and clearer
The pulse in the arm, less strong and stronger –
Given or lent? More distant than stars and
nearer than the eye

WHAT WOKE ANNABEL WAS the touch of a cold hand on her bare back, midway between her shoulder blades. Slowly she opened her eyes. When she saw bright daylight she sighed with relief. She felt as if she had come through a long sequence of nightmares in which she'd been assailed by a succession of villains, harlots and gangsters... all of them, it seemed, connected in some inexplicable way to the person whose icy hand now touched her.

As she came to, Annabel gradually got her bearings. She was lying face down on the granite embankment, naked, being stroked and caressed by Pauline, after so recklessly diving from the old stone bridge... diving down into the rushing turbulent water that lay so far below her as she stood terrified on the parapet... She groaned inside as she recalled how she had disgraced herself as she stood there, legs wide apart, arms stretched sideways, pleading for God to come to her aid. Then she had dived in anyway... and she had realised, not for the first time, that courage and recklessness often amounted to the same thing, and were based on a faith that somehow things would work out for the best. She had proved her courage... then she had had to beg for her life while she desperately held on to the crook of the hockey stick that Pauline had dangled down towards her as she struggled to get out of the water. Annabel looked ahead of her and saw the scratched wooden hockey stick now lying on the ground only a couple of feet from her face. Oh God! It had been so humiliating...

a defeat so abject that she felt as if some part of her soul had died. Despite the shivering cold that racked her body, Annabel burned with shame at the recollection of it. She closed her eyes and tried to push the memory out of her mind.

She heard a long sigh from Pauline and turned her head to look up at her. Pauline was down on her knees, which were wide apart, and her eyes were shut in an ecstatic reverie. Her coarse sandy hair hung in untidy curls over her shoulders. Her heavy overcoat was unbuttoned and her right hand was pushed far up her grey skirt, all the way up to her crutch. It was obvious that she had just been pleasuring herself with it while her left hand had been fondling Annabel as she lay on the ground in front of her. Annabel realised that her own legs were splayed out wide and felt that her fanny was wet and sticky inside. She knew what had happened. Pauline had been fingering her most intimate parts while she had lain unconscious and helpless. She recalled her tormentor's touch, as if her body had somehow been imbued with the memory of that cold white hand and was now yielding it up to her conscious recollection...

There was another long sigh from Pauline and slowly she opened her big blue eyes. She looked far into the distance, across the river, as if contemplating infinity. There was a smile of satisfaction on her pimply face. She withdrew her hand from under her skirt. Annabel turned her head forward again, so as to prevent Pauline from knowing that she'd seen her masturbating. She moved her body slightly from side to side, and suddenly winced with pain. She was lying on a mass of long weeds and nettles, which had stung her everywhere, all over her chest and belly and legs, and over much of her arms. This was the spot where Pauline had hauled her out of the river. She was still so close to the edge of the embankment that one of her feet was poised over the water. One knee was slightly bent and her shin pressed against a rusty mooring ring. She lay like this for some time, not daring to move.

Finally Pauline took a deep breath and stood up. She reached for her duffel bag and drew a large towel from it. She crouched down by Annabel and gently began to rub her shoulders. Annabel sobbed with relief at the touch of the warm dry towel.

"It's all right, Jamey," said Pauline soothingly. "Come on, sit up. You must dry yourself now."

Annabel moaned and stirred. Pauline grasped her beneath the shoulders and lifted. Annabel moved her legs and with some effort twisted herself up into a sitting position. Pauline gazed at the front of her body and raised her eyebrows in surprise. Annabel looked down at herself and was horrified to see the multitude of angry red blotches and scratches all over her breasts and stomach, and over the front of her thighs, even over her upper arms. But the wounds were light, superficial only, and would heal in a few days. She clutched at her neck and realised that her slender gold crucifix had gone, torn away by the impact of the water and forever lost in the river.

Pauline rubbed Annabel's back with the towel. "Will you be all right?" she asked.

Annabel looked away from her and nodded. She was far from sure, but as always she wanted to appear hardy and self-sufficient. Pauline turned back to her long duffel bag and from it drew a jumble of clothes – Annabel's school uniform. She tried to lay the garments out on the prickly weeds as tidily as she could, first the heavy items – the mud-coated black shoes (placed to one side), then the navy-blue blazer, the grey woolly jersey, the now-crumpled grey skirt, the sky-blue blouse – followed by the lighter things, the silky half-slip petticoat, the white cotton socks (splattered with mud), the dark opaque tights (now laddered), and finally the white lacy bra and cotton knickers (both flecked with mud). While Pauline did this, Annabel continued to dry herself with the towel, but she was trembling with the cold and was still dazed by the shock of what had happened. She could feel the weight of her wet tangled hair, which hung down over her head and shoulders in a mess of dark rat-tails.

"And I haven't forgotten these either," said Pauline. She drew an exercise book from the pocket of her overcoat and handed it to Annabel. At first she couldn't grasp the significance of this item. Then she saw her name and the title on the front cover: "Annabel James – Biology". She glanced up sharply at Pauline, who smiled back at her.

"Don't worry, his Licence is in the book." She looked proud of herself. "You see, *I* keep my promises too."

Annabel opened the exercise book. In the middle of it lay a driving licence, bearing the name "Dennis Roger Murray". Her Biology teacher. Her lover. The man who had taken her virginity in the Biology Stock Room. Hastily she closed the book, as if she didn't want to acknowledge what was inside, or acknowledge how much distress it had brought her. She put the book down on the granite stone by her buttock and turned away from Pauline. She was still horribly cold and wet, and began to wipe herself faster and more effectively. But the front of her body stung so badly, it felt as if it were on fire.

When she had more or less dried herself, Annabel dropped the towel and awkwardly draped her blazer around her shoulders. She drew her knees up. Suddenly she resented the fact that Pauline could see her naked body.

Pauline reclaimed her towel and put it back into her duffel bag. She did likewise with her hockey stick. Finally she stood up and hauled the bag over her shoulder.

"I'm going now," she said. "You can find your own way back to school."

"Yes," replied Annabel, without looking at her.

Pauline walked away along the embankment, towards the stone steps that led to the bridge. But after a few paces she stopped and turned.

"There's one last thing," she said.

Annabel, hunched in her blazer, looked round.

"What?"

Pauline smiled, as if at some secret joke that she alone could appreciate. "Remember, remember." Her smile broadened into a grin, revealing her yellow teeth. "Just… be perfect!"

Then she turned away and jauntily ascended the steps, as if supremely satisfied with her day's work.

Glad to see her go, and oblivious of the meaning of her final remark, Annabel turned back to look down the river. It was now roaring at full pelt, rising dangerously close to the level of the embankment, and she doubted whether even a strong swimmer like her would survive if she dived in now. She had been lucky to get out alive. She looked down at her abdomen and noticed a vivid red mark a couple of inches below her navel, a little to the left. The skin was slightly raised and swollen. She felt a dull pain there, as if a fist was slowly clenching inside her, and recalled that this was where she had struck something in the water when she had dived in. She looked back upstream but couldn't see anything beneath the turbulent rushing current, rising ever higher and racing ever faster. Then, in the distance, a long way behind the bridge, she heard a rumble of thunder, which instantly filled her with dread. A storm was coming. She had to get back to school before it arrived. There was little more than an hour of daylight left.

Annabel slipped off her blazer and knelt up. In a gesture of defiance, ignoring the cold, she put her hands on her hips and bared her nude body, as if to repudiate the power of the river. She looked downstream and observed the trees on either bank swaying gently in the wind. Their leaves were just coming into bud, speckling the branches with green. It was the first flush of spring. She took a deep breath and suddenly felt a huge wave of relief surge through her body. Yes – she had come through! She had saved herself... and saved Dennis from destruction. That alone made all the pain and humiliation worthwhile. She had sacrificed herself for a worthy cause, something she had always wanted to do. But to sacrifice yourself for someone you loved – what nobler and finer thing could there be? And her future still lay before her! All her plans and dreams were intact; and she was now more determined than ever to realise them. She would sail through her exams in the summer, captain the hockey team to victory, spend two years at sixth-form college, go on to Oxford to study medicine, then become a doctor and work in a big hospital in London, where she would run her very own team, and where she would meet and marry another doctor, a successful and handsome man who would provide her with beautiful children, including a daughter who would grow up to be just like her. It was all going to be... just perfect!

There was another rumble of thunder, now closer. Annabel turned to reach for her clothes. As she leaned over she felt an excruciating pain in her abdomen, so severe that for a moment she thought she was going to die.